*

*The Birth of
a Grandfather*

Books by May Sarton

POETRY

Encounter in April
Inner Landscape
The Lion and the Rose
The Land of Silence
In Time Like Air
Cloud, Stone, Sun, Vine
A Private Mythology
As Does New Hampshire
A Grain of Mustard Seed
A Durable Fire
Collected Poems, 1930–1973
Selected Poems of May Sarton
  (edited by Serena Sue Hilsinger
  and Lois Brynes)
Halfway to Silence
Letters from Maine

NOVELS

The Single Hound
The Bridge of Years
Shadow of a Man
A Shower of Summer Days
Faithful Are The Wounds
The Birth of a Grandfather

The Fur Person
The Small Room
Joanna and Ulysses
Mrs. Stevens Hears
  the Mermaids Singing
Miss Pickthorn and Mr. Hare
The Poet and the Donkey
Kinds of Love
As We Are Now
Crucial Conversations
A Reckoning
Anger
The Magnificent Spinster

NONFICTION

I Knew a Phoenix
Plant Dreaming Deep
Journal of a Solitude
A World of Light
The House by the Sea
Recovering: A Journal
At Seventy: A Journal
Writings on Writing

FOR CHILDREN

Punch's Secret
A Walk through the Woods

*
*
*

The Birth of a Grandfather

*
*
*

BY MAY SARTON

*
*
*
*
*

W· W·NORTON & COMPANY   NEW YORK · LONDON

First published as a Norton paperback 1989

Published simultaneously in Canada by Penguin Books Canada Ltd,
2801 John Street, Markham, Ontario L3R 1B4

LIBRARY OF CONGRESS CATALOG CARD NUMBER: 57-9630

Library of Congress Cataloging-in-Publication Data

Sarton, May, 1912–
The birth of a grandfather.

(A Norton paperback)
I. Title.
PS3537.A832B57   1989   813'.52   88–33036

ISBN 0-393-30591-0

W. W. Norton & Company, Inc.,
500 Fifth Avenue, New York, N.Y. 10110
W. W. Norton & Company, Ltd.,
37 Great Russell Street, WC1B 3NU

1 2 3 4 5 6 7 8 9 0

Contents

PART I

The Island . . . *1*

PART II

Children of the Ice Age . . . *99*

PART III

The Birth of a Grandfather . . . *199*

*

PART ONE

The Island

"Nous arrivons tout nouveaux aux divers âges de la vie."

La Rochefoucauld

*

CHAPTER ONE

WHERE am I? Frances thought, opening her eyes to the faded flowered wallpaper, and then she remembered, smiled, closed her eyes again to let pleasure soak in, the sense of holiday; they were really here on the island, the long summer opening ahead, lazy and timeless. For just a few moments more she would indulge herself (it was only a quarter to seven) and then think about getting breakfast for the family. Far off she could hear chopping—Sprig must be out already. How fast asleep she must have been not to hear him get up! She turned over to contemplate his empty bed, to think how lonely it looked, to wonder if he had stooped over her sleeping face, almost kissed her, then tiptoed out instead, happier to be alone, anxious above all that she should not wake. It's so strange, she was thinking, as she lay there, her arms crossed under her head, staring at the ceiling and the band of sunlight that lay across it, that we are only ourselves alone, separated. Now, for instance, for a few moments she could be herself, fully herself, before she was pulled here and there by a thousand invisible threads; she could gather herself up into a quiet whole and be—what? For who am I? she asked herself, Frances Wyeth, forty-five years old who have somehow

3

come to this place and this time with my husband, my two grown children, to this dear house where Sprig's father and grandfather have come and all the aunts and cousins and friends, for half a century of island-living—the comfort of it, the continuity. There had been world tragedies (two great wars), and there had been private tragedies (the death of Sprig's mother, the strong growing weak with age, the divorces, the fabric torn and made whole again over and over), yet the island had not changed. Here one took a candle to bed and lighted oil lamps to read by in the evening. The house with its faded wallpapers, its cretonne curtains, its old-fashioned bathrooms, its great stone fireplace, had remained intact, a fortress against time and change. The comfort of it, the continuity, she said to herself again. We are part of a great river—we flow down it—why was this depressing?

Because one also wished to be oneself, unique, solitary, quite unattached and free to make one's soul and find one's joy, Sprig with his axe, aboriginal man, remaking the world (if only a grove of pines that needed pruning) in his own image. It was strange to wake up after this night when she and Sprig had slept together at last after a long interval of sleeping apart, to wake to such thoughts, to ask, "Who am I?" Was the answer "Sprig's wife"?

Yet he was less hers than he had ever been. It took a moment of passion to break down the walls of silence between them. Even then, after he had gone back to his own bed and fallen asleep so quickly, so deeply, she had felt the tears running down her cheeks onto her pillow in the middle of the night, tears of relief that the tension between them had been broken at last, tears of childish despair because even when the walls fell down, she and Sprig seemed as distant from each other as two stars. Their union was not the flowing together of two deeply joined selves, but only a desperate moment of possession of each other, which disappointed because something was always withheld.

I wonder if we shall be able to give that, whatever it is, before we die. She had thought that people forty-five were old, had arrived, but now she realized with astonishment that she was still a child, that she was nowhere nearly grown-up, that there was still a long journey inward to be made, and would she ever arrive, whole, free and at peace? Did any one?

Who am I? she asked, jumping out of bed suddenly to go and peer into the rather dim mirror over the dresser. She had on a pair of mens' pajamas and in them, her brown boyish hair tousled, she looked as she always did to herself like a rather unfinished young man. "Dear me," and she chuckled, "how can I look like this and be all I have to be?" From the dresser, the photograph of Sprig's grandfather Wyeth in a small gold standing frame, judged her. She picked it up and stared back. "You made all this, didn't you?" she asked him. He was the founder, the man who had sent his ships to the Indies bearing ice from a New England pond through the tropical oceans, bought this island, built the first house here, left his children and grandchildren rich, and still, across the years, molded them. He had been much too busy about things to ask himself who he was, and so he towered in the background, character personified. He *was*; they merely hoped to be.

Just then Frances heard a groan from the room next door, a groan followed by a roar of pain. Old Mr. Wyeth, this man's son, was awake. He wanted someone to come in and commiserate with his arthritis. "Damn it," she heard him say.

"Are you all right, Gran-Quan?" she called from the hall. "I'll be dressed and in to help you in half a shake of a lamb's tail." She heard her own cheerful managing voice with dismay, as it rang out. She felt the mask of her family self come down and lock over the fluid, hesitating, probing person she had been a few moments before. Now her job was to sustain, to center, to be everyone's security and comfort. But, as she dragged on a pair of blue jeans and a shirt, and tied double knots in the laces of her old sneakers, she felt suddenly happy, and began to sing, "What shall we do with the lazy sailor, early in the morning?"

This voice took possession of the house, floated into every room, unlocking doors into cupboards, flooding the downstairs living room—always rather dark in the daytime because it was entirely surrounded by a vast porch—like sunlight. Hannah, the old beagle who slept in the kitchen, gave two sharp barks and thumped her tail on the floor. Mr. Silence, the immense tiger cat who had been curled into a tight ball in an armchair, yawned, stretched, and jumped down to wait for Frances at the swing door into the kitchen.

"Early in the morning," she sang, as she pushed open Gran-Quan's door.

6

"Go away, you're much too cheerful." He was sitting up in bed reading, lifted his eyes for a moment, raised his bushy gray eyebrows at her, and smiled. "Sprig woke me at dawn with that chopping," he complained. "No respect for the old," he added, enjoying himself now he had her attention. "I thought I was a goner when I woke, couldn't move a muscle, lay there like a log. You have no idea!"

"It's the change of air," she said.

"Best air in the world. A tonic. Nothing wrong with the air. Old age, that's what's wrong."

They all flew to the defense of the island of course. And Frances withdrew, seeing that he was after all in a good mood, complaining in this way being only a form of joy.

"Time to get up, Caleb!" she called down the hall. There was no answer from Caleb, but she could hear the water running in the bathroom.

She went in to Betsy, who lay fast asleep, her face buried in her pillow, the soft reddish hair flung out around her head like a halo. Frances stood a moment at the door, moved by the helplessness of this grown child of hers. Let her sleep, she thought to herself. It was an unusual indulgence, for most of the time Betsy's indolence made her fearfully impatient. But this morning, this holiday morning, let Betsy sleep—her young man would be turning up this evening. Frances turned and ran down the stairs, shutting off the thought of Tom Dorgan as too complicated for the hour, too complicated when scrambled eggs and coffee should be uppermost in her mind.

She paused at the top of the stairs and listened. Great

7

Aunt must be up already—her door was open. And indeed when Frances pushed back the swing door, the two animals were being fed and Aunt Jane was just filling the coffeepot.

"You angel!" Frances said, "you shouldn't!" taking the coffeepot out of the trembling hands and stopping to kiss Aunt Jane's cheek. "This is my job."

"Couldn't sit still another minute," Aunt Jane said. "Too bright a morning altogether. My, doesn't that sun pull one out of bed! I've been up since six," she said. "Is Quincy all right?"

"Giving yelps of pain and enjoying it thoroughly."

The two women exchanged a glance, the immemorial glance of women about the frailty of men.

"I'd better give him a look-in."

"Don't take the stairs again. He's all right."

"Limbers me up, don't you know?" and she turned to go. "I'm stiff in the mornings," she said as if this were unheard of. But she was ninety, ten years older than her brother, Frances thought, as she laid the table, the sun pouring all over her hands like a blessing and getting in her eyes, so she felt quite blinded in glory. The kitchen window looked straight into a tall grove of spruce, well pruned these, by every man on the island since grandfather himself. The patch of brilliant green lawn that surrounded the house made it an island within the island, an island of humanness all surrounded by the sea of great trees, moss of every kind and softness spread out below them, and lichen-covered boulders lying here and there to remind one that this was a

8

granite world, primeval, still wild, to which the deer swam over in the fall to escape the hunters.

"Yes, Hannah, dear," she said to the old dog whose tail was thumping a request to go out. "You shall. Go and find Sprig!" she called. "Tell him to come home for breakfast." But Hannah's nose was fastened to a lane in the grasses and she was off after a vole, giving short excited barks, her tail wagging furiously all the time. No errands for her, not today, not on this holiday.

Mr. Silence sat in a patch of sunlight, washing his face, and for a moment Frances stood still in the middle of the big kitchen, the jar of orange juice in her hands, stood there arrested by the joy of it all, the being here, the summer opening out ahead. It seemed too precious suddenly to go uncelebrated, and she bowed her head in a wordless prayer.

For would it be the last? Aunt Jane wouldn't live forever, Gran-Quan sometimes seemed to be slipping off into a world of his own, full of demons. Would Betsy be married to her Irishman by this time next year? And Caleb gone off somewhere into his lonely life? It's all so perilous, she thought, this brief moment in the sunlight, when we are still all together, safe.

Then she hurried to pour the juice and went to the door to ring the gong Grandfather Wyeth had brought home from China eighty years before.

At half past eleven when she had taken a cup of hot bouillon out to Gran-Quan and Aunt Jane and found them

9

deep in an argument over a point in the New Testament in Greek, and fetched a dictionary and set up a little table for them; and after she had unearthed Betsy who was apparently composing a poem, lying on her stomach on the unmade bed, and told her what to get ready for lunch, Frances filled a small thermos with sherry and stole out by the back door, running when she heard the telephone ring, so she would be safely out of sight. It was a feat to get away, a triumph of speed and organization to have managed it at all. Now the question was, could she find Sprig? She stopped on the path, drew in a deep breath of pine, and listened. There was no sound of chopping. No sound at all except the yank-yank of a nuthatch, then far off a woodpecker hammering. Sunlight came through a gap in the branches and rested on her hand like a caress. After all, this was *it*. This standing alone and taking time to breathe and smell and look was it. Even if she couldn't find Sprig, she would have a half hour now in which to be herself; not hurry; received whatever was coming toward her out of the day. She came past the overgrown flower garden (I must get to weeding tomorrow) and out onto grassy meadows, the one stretch of open field on the island, with a farmhouse at the end out on the point. From here one could see the mainland clearly, a detached scene as in a picture, the smoke coming out of the chimneys and going straight up into the blue air, and someone raising a sail by a pier. The soft uncut grass stroked her ankles. Crickets chirped. She walked very slowly, drinking in the gentle, ample curve of the meadows as they swept down to the shore, the pink and beige rocks and the dark sparkling water, all this lying low under the dazzling sky. So much air and light, she half closed her eyes, felt a little drunk, and on an impulse lay down where she was, wanting to feel hard earth under her, to give up entirely—make no more effort for a moment, even that of looking for Sprig. Here low on the earth, her hands felt for the tiny roughnesses, the wild cranberry which would ripen before they left, reindeer moss, a small stone. Somewhere very near a cricket chirped loudly. She was startled by it and lifted her head—and there she saw Sprig, as if in a dream, walking toward her across the meadow smiling and waving, as he caught her answering smile.

"Well," he said, dropping down beside her, "you look very cosy."

"I was looking for you. I brought some sherry in the thermos." She felt shy. She couldn't move, even to open the sherry, as if she had been caught in some violent gesture of abandon, so strange must it seem to him to find her lying all alone in the grass on such a busy day.

"Good," he said, pouring out two tumblers carefully.

Still she lay there, looking up into the sky, catching in the focus just the line of his chin and shoulder, feeling his presence all through her like the sunlight.

"I cleared out a big patch; amazing how you have to keep at it."

"Yes." She felt she was in a dream. "I married an island," she said out of the dream.

"Rather a nice one, you must admit."

She turned over and leaned on her elbow, looking up at him.

"Strange," she said, "very strange."

He looked down at her for just a second, then looked away, half shutting his eyes as a sailor does before the sea glare. But in the second she knew she disturbed him, and he did not want to be disturbed, or to be reminded of that hour of passion in the night. So she sat up, pulled herself back out of the dream, drank her sherry, and was silent.

A small sail flapped in the distance, struggling to catch the wind, tautened as the boat came about and stood toward them across the channel.

"There he is," Sprig said, watching this maneuver intensely. "There's Caleb."

"Yes," she sighed. The sail in the distance meant responsibility, the thread tightened that held one all around and could never be broken, and so she turned to Sprig and said, "I wish you would have a talk with Caleb. I think really that's what he wants, though he doesn't know it."

"He makes it rather difficult." Sprig was watching the boat as Caleb tacked again, skillfully, and she knew he was thinking, *He learned that from me.*

"Besides," he added, "talk to him about what?"

"He's become an alien," Frances said. "It's too painful. For him. For us."

"He graduates next year."

"What has that got to do with it?"

"He's gone already—off there in the boat. We can watch him."

"But that's all we can do?" Frances asked. It was a beautiful day, why worry at it? Why spoil it by digging down under the surface? She silenced the questions, at least did not say them aloud to Sprig, but only to herself: Your grandfather, who bought this island, would not have let Caleb get away with being so rude at breakfast. He would have commanded and expected to be obeyed. "If Caleb were happy, it would be different," was what she said aloud.

"No one who's any good is happy at that age."

Just then the little boat ran in dangerously near to the rocks. Caleb stood up and waved.

Sprig was on his feet in an instant waving back, making a wide happy gesture with his right arm.

"He's too close to shore, Sprig!" Her voice was sharp with anxiety.

"Nonsense, he knows every rock by heart—look at that!" Sprig cried, exultant, as the little boat came about, barely not grazing an island of seaweed which concealed a reef. "Nice work, boy!"

How free Sprig and Caleb were, separated by a safe quarter of a mile of meadow and rock and sea, yet sharing the moment of skill, recognizing each other, and all their unspoken love expressed in that wave from boat to shore! She knew that it didn't matter a hoot to Sprig, now, that he had been pointedly rebuffed by his son that morning, that Caleb had deliberately refused to accept his responsibility as a workman on the island. It was all forgiven and forgotten, and who was she then to make demands, to say it was not enough? She lay back in the grass and closed her eyes. "Who am I?" The question rose behind her eyelids, the morning's question. And now the answer was, or seemed to be, "I am the child of loving parents." Saying it to herself, like this, in the middle of the meadow with the great arch of sky overhead, she felt diminished, tiny and frail as a beetle in the grass, a piece of nothingness. For the immense warmth of her father's and mother's marriage, the way they walked down the garden together in the evening, the way life flowed between them, unstopped, unstinted, shook her suddenly with intense grief. She turned over on her stomach and pressed her fists into her eyes to hold back the tears.

"Good Lord, it's half past twelve," Sprig said. "Come along, old lady, time for lunch."

Still she lay there, hoping willfully that he would stoop down and give her the reassurance she had needed so badly all morning.

But when she finally lifted her head, she saw that he was walking away, swinging the axe loosely in his right hand, the islander safe on his island, not to be touched.

*

CHAPTER TWO

THEY were gathered in the big living room after dinner, a lobster dinner in honor of Tom Dorgan's first visit to the island, and also to welcome Sprig's sister Hester, who had decided to fly up unexpectedly for a few days and sat right opposite Tom on the plane, it turned out, though they had not met before. Tom liked her at once. She seemed more open, less insulated than the others, and that, he suspected, was because she was head of a school. Her presence had smoothed this crucial arrival for him, for he had entered the strange tribe on their island bearing her bags up from the pier.

Now he and Betsy had found a haven on the window seat where they could hold hands unobserved. Tom looked out into the great cavelike room, firelight throwing shadows on the ceiling, and everything here massive and dark. The Aladdin lamp made a circle of bright light around the old man sitting in an armchair, a book open on his knees. Caleb, curled up on the black fur rug on the hearth, leaned his head against the bear's head, and seemed to be asleep. Mr. Wyeth walked up and down smoking his pipe, as if he were walking the deck of a ship. And Tom was grateful for the dark, for the pause, for the chance to get his bearings, to be the observer, for he had felt terribly exposed, vulnerable at the dinner table where they were always laughing at private jokes or—even worse—on the brink of some private quarrel. They seemed to pay no attention to him, their courtesy being to let him alone, he sensed, but nevertheless he was clearly being immersed in this atmosphere to see how it took. How did an Irishman, an Irishman who had stroked the crew to be sure, but whose father had made his money in cement, fit in with these people softened and civilized by a century of money and power? They never ran for office, got the cushy jobs in banks and paid someone else to do the work; owned entire islands and hired a boatman to run them back and forth to town, spent fortunes in order to be able to chop down a few trees and pick cranberries in peace. "Mind your manners," his mother had said, she who had learned the hard way to substitute salad and risotto for meat and potatoes. But the thing was—he had learned that much at Harvard—not to mind your manners, to take it all as casually as possible. The way these people flung their lobster shells into a big wooden bowl in the middle of the table!

He was suddenly filled with excitement, alive, conscious of his own power, and squeezed Betsy's hand hard. Whatever they might think or do, she was his, flesh of his flesh, whom he would carry off into a life he and she were going to make together, no part of all this. For she was different. Something had never jelled for her; he had felt it strongly at the dinner table. Such a warm, soft creature had no place in their world, the Wyeth world; they didn't know what to make of her. But I'll make you a nest and a soft, safe place, my love, and I'll cherish you, said his hand to hers, and no one will scare you or make you feel inferior ever again. And we'll lie on the moss . . .

"Where are those damned women, anyway?" Gran-Quan growled, lifting his head at a burst of laughter from the kitchen. He murmured,

> "Only the Ass, with motion dull,
> Upon the pivot of his skull
> Turns round his long left ear."

Then he gave a great roar. "Genius, I say! 'Turns round his long left ear,'" he shouted, and looked toward his son, suffused with delighted laughter. But Sprig was not listening; his back was turned. Caleb did not move a muscle, and Tom, who sensed that someone should respond, was silent because he had no idea who had written this poem, nor did he recognize genius in it.

"Frances!" the old man shouted, "we are all waiting!"

Aunt Jane, waving a dish towel, appeared in the doorway to say, "Just a minute, you impatient people!"

"Gran-Quan is going to read Wordsworth," Betsy explained.

"Oh he is, is he?" Aunt Jane smiled at him. "We're almost through, dear. Hold your horses!"

"Young man, do you read Wordsworth at Harvard?" The old man turned half round in his chair and frowned at Tom.

"I was not an English major, Sir."

"Do you hear that, Sprig? They call it a liberal education, and they think they can have a liberal education" (he said the word 'liberal' quite savagely) "and ignore one of the great civilizing minds of the last century."

"But there's so much else, Gran-Quan; that's what you don't realize." Betsy came to Tom's defense.

"Rot. Essentials are essentials. They don't read Greek. What do they read?" He glared around him, and Tom was fascinated by the passion in this old man, the way he never said anything at all without the greatest conviction, seemed in fact to be in a state of perpetual indignation.

"There." Aunt Hester came in and sat down on the sofa with a sigh. "Now for poetry," she said, smiling warmly at her father. Aunt Jane and Frances settled themselves, Aunt Jane beside Hester, and Frances on the floor, cross-legged. The circle in the firelight was complete. Tom looked from one of these faces to the other. He thought he had never seen such a collection of characters in one room. No wonder Betsy was a bit overwhelmed. They were not so much larger than life as singular, each in his way intense beyond the usual, taking things hard. You could see the family resemblance, those clear blue eyes that could look so cold, but had flame back of them, even in the old lady, sitting there now, smiling to herself, and such a gentle person. Gentleness, he thought, and slid an arm round Betsy's waist, transported into regions that had nothing to do with anyone but her. The old man began to read in his fine voice with the trace of theatre—or was it the pulpit? —in its emphasis:

18

The Island

"There was a roaring in the wind all night;
The rain came heavily and fell in floods;"

Tom heard the words but only half listened to the meaning; he was too absorbed in all the sensations of the moment, and this strange new world. He looked up at the ceiling and the enormous window that framed the stairway and just now reflected the fire and Gran-Quan, and off into the shadowy distance. They had brought in branches of fir and spruce and put them in a big jar on the center table so the two ladies on the sofa seemed to be sitting under a fringe of woods. There were piles of books on the table, everything from a book on wild flowers to the latest novels, and all over the house he had noticed sweet-grass baskets and birchbark frames for photographs; bought from an old Indian, Betsy said, dead now.

"I thought of Chatterton, the marvelous Boy,"

A new quality had come into Gran-Quan's voice which forced Tom's attention. For the first time he listened.

"The sleepless Soul that perished in his pride;
Of Him who walked in glory and in joy
Following his plough, along the mountainside;
By our own spirits are we deified:
We Poets in our youth begin in gladness;
But thereof come in the end despondency and madness."

It seemed for a moment as if the old man were about to burst into one of his roars. His fist clenched on the arm of the chair and Tom was astonished to see what looked like tears standing in his eyes, so fiercely bright had they become. There was no sound at all except far off a bird singing its night-song—"a purple finch," Sprig noted aloud—and the put-put of a motor boat out there on the dark water all around them. The silence was full of emotion. But just what it all meant Tom couldn't figure out. He was relieved when the reading went on, Gran-Quan's voice a pitch higher now, as if he were climbing out of some woe of his own, or as if the poem itself were lifting him. Yet the mood of the poem was sombre:

> "My former thoughts returned: the fear that kills;
> And hope that is unwilling to be fed;
> Cold, pain, and labour, and all fleshly ills;
> And mighty Poets in their misery dead.
> —Perplexed, and longing to be comforted,
> My question eagerly did I renew,
> 'How is it that you live, and what is it you do?'"

At the last line, Gran-Quan took off his glasses, threw back his head and laughed aloud. "He is so absurd," he said. "Thank God for that, or it would be quite unbearable, don't you know?"

Tom caught the amused glance exchanged between Hester and her brother. No doubt they had heard their father stop and laugh at that line in the poem for years, since they were children. The whole performance had the quality of something often repeated, one of the rites of this ritualistic household. They are bound together by all they have shared, Tom was thinking, and realized that every object in the room came from somewhere they knew, but he did not know—that stuffed head of an elk over the mantel, for instance (who had shot it?), that Norwegian ash tray, the blue bowl beside Gran-Quan. It was all part of a fabric, so closely woven together they were hardly aware of it themselves, of what they stepped into when they stepped into it.

Every time his own family moved they made a new start. The mahogany bedsteads, of which his mother had been so proud when Tom was a kid, had now been replaced with Hollywood beds; in the Belmont house there wasn't any wallpaper, just flat white walls, though Tom could remember clearly going down to Central Square with his mother and poring over designs of pink roses on gray when they had the old house done over. But the Wyeths had been coming back to the same faded, flowered chintz bedrooms for fifty years, and never bothered to change anything.

Gran-Quan had let the book fall and was staring into the fire.

Caleb sat up. "Aren't you going to finish?" he asked. "It's grand stuff, isn't it. Grand and innocent——"

"Innocent?" The old man turned to the boy as if he were coming back from far away. "It has heartbreak in it."

"Well," Caleb flashed a smile, "that's innocent, Gran-Quan. Only the innocent have hearts to break."

The old man sighed deeply and—Sprig thought—rhetorically. How they had suffered, Hester and he, from their father's indulgence in emotional rhetoric. No wonder we grew up shy of it all, shy of words, of feelings, Sprig thought, locked up in ourselves. Would Caleb break through? Would Caleb make himself free?

The Birth of a Grandfather

"Go on, Quan," Aunt Jane said, rousing the old man from his thoughts, for he was frowning, whispering to himself. He turned back to the page and read on.

Happiness, which had been hovering in the shadows, seemed now to come forward, to settle amongst them, before the dying fire.

Tom's hand, resting in Betsy's, rested there at peace.

The last stanza was just being completed as the telephone rang. Everyone sat up to count four longs one short.

"Darn it," Frances said, running out to the library. "I did want to hear the end."

"That's what you get for having a telephone!" Sprig called after her. It had been installed only three years before when Frances insisted that they must be able to call a doctor in case Aunt Jane or Gran-Quan fell ill, but it had made the island less of an island.

Frances closed the door—long distance no doubt, someone wanting to come and stay. Always they imagined the summer as peaceful and solitary, but it never would be like that. Minutes later, Sprig read in Frances' face as she came back, bad news. . . . Who? Where? He stiffened slightly, and met her glance, and for a second she looked at him in the strangest way as if she were asking some very important question.

"Well?" Sprig asked.

"Lucy in Cambridge. She's upset." Frances ran a hand through her hair. Whatever it was that had upset Lucy had also upset Frances. Lucy was Frances' oldest friend, the person she felt closest to in the world she had often told Sprig, half teasing him, but it was probably true. What could be wrong? "I asked her to come down for a while, Sprig—I hope that's all right," and she went and stood behind his chair and laid a hand on his shoulder. He froze at once. "Yes, yes, of course," he said.

"Dear me—dear me——" Gran-Quan leaned forward, "What's wrong with Lucy?"

Other people's unhappiness, Tom sensed, would seem to the old man like an affront. Frances frowned and shook her head; she was visibly embarrassed, and Tom who, as the only stranger must be the cause of the embarrassment, got up, wondering how he could make a graceful exit. Obviously this was a crisis.

"Come on, Betsy, let's go for a walk." All their eyes turned to him.

"Put on coats, you two, it's chilly," Frances said in her practical voice.

"And don't stay too long!" Sprig called after them.

"Really, Pa," Caleb too, had scrambled to his feet and now stood with his hands in his pockets, glaring. "Leave them alone, can't you?"

"What are you talking about?"

"He's not going to rape her."

"No," Sprig said evenly, "but I dislike the way they carry on in public."

"He seems a very nice boy," Aunt Jane said.

"Never trust the Irish," Gran-Quan growled. "Cold green eyes——"

"Tom has gray eyes and they're not cold," Caleb answered sharply.

"Catholic, I presume?" Gran-Quan was on his mettle.

"Oh, you all make me tired." Caleb slipped off upstairs, shrugging his shoulders. He called down from the landing, "I've asked him to sail with me tomorrow."

"Well, I've asked him to chop wood with me," Sprig called back.

There was no answer.

"Perhaps Betsy has plans," Aunt Jane said gently.

Each in his own way felt irritated, ruffled, warding off the blow for which they waited, now the children were out of the way, for it was clear that Frances was upset, that something had happened. She stood behind Sprig's chair, her hands clasped tightly, lost in thought.

"Can you tell us, dear?" Aunt Jane asked, after a considerable pause.

"Well, I guess so," she turned directly to her aunt. "It's" —she swallowed—"it's that John wants a divorce."

The round, perfect bubble of the island day had burst, Frances thought, and it seemed years ago since she and Sprig had lain in the warm grass and watched their son sail past, years ago since she had brought in the great pewter platter of lobsters and looked around at them all, sitting there, as if they were enclosed in a magic circle, Betsy suddenly beautiful, her face flushed, awake—yes, that was it. Betsy looked awake and Frances realized that she had never looked really awake before. Frances was lying in bed with her arms crossed under her neck, a candle throwing a faltering circle of light on the ceiling; she was waiting for Sprig, stretching her toes down to where she could brace them against the brass bedstead and stretch her back, for she was tired.

Sprig emerged from the bathroom, still rubbing to get the pitch off his hands, businesslike, abstracted. She took one look at his face and blew out the candle. For Sprig was irritated with Betsy, with Lucy too for coming to interrupt the summer peace with her problems, she sensed.

"Where have you put my slippers?" he asked, feeling around on the floor with his hands.

"Under the bed, I expect."

"No," he said irritably, "they're not here." And then, "Light the candle, will you?"

The candlelight laid gaunt shadows on Sprig's cheek as he sat on the floor, lit up only him in this room where Frances felt herself a stranger. And what was the woman like who had been Sprig's mother for such a short time, four or five years in all? Slept here beside a husband who had loved her so much that he threw his life away when she died and would have no more of it?

"What was your mother like, Sprig?" she asked, as he grunted and produced the slippers, not from under the bed, from under the night table. He was not smiling. He sat there on the floor, hair brushed straight up on his head, one slipper poised in his hand and the candle reflected in his eyes, so what Frances saw was two tiny flames. "I think of her always when we come back to this room, each summer—how she has vanished away and we never speak her name, Emily. What was Emily Wyeth like?" she asked those two unwavering flames in Sprig's eyes.

25

"You know," he said thoughtfully, "I've almost forgotten. She smelled of lavender, had a ruffly blouse with a velvet bow, used sometimes to lay a light hand on my head and stroke my hair." But this embarrassed him evidently; he got up and blew out the candle.

"I suppose they were very much in love."

From the next room they could hear Gran-Quan give a hoarse cry in his sleep, then breathe deeply and lapse into regular labored snores. So strange, Frances thought, that he is old and she will never be old. She is always here, a young woman with a curiously intense face, dark eyes, a stubborn rather beautiful mouth. She doesn't know any of us. We don't exist yet.

Sprig had not answered her last remark. She could hear his bed creak as he turned over, face to the wall, away from her.

"Oh please, darling, don't go to sleep right away. I need to talk," she said, sitting right up. "I haven't seen you all day. And besides——"

"I'm upset," he said crossly.

"I know. It's Betsy and Tom. You don't like him?"

"I don't like all this pawing in public," he said.

"That was made rather clear this evening."

"Don't badger me. Caleb is bad enough without you starting on all this." There was a pause then, rather tentatively, "Am I old-fashioned, Fran?"

"Well, they do take all that rather more comfortably than we did." She remembered how Sprig had first taken her hand in his, how he had stood at the door of her parents'

26

house after a dance, and taken her hand and kissed it very gravely. Then at that moment, the pang, the queer pang she would always feel in his presence, shot through her. "And I expect they miss something by being so casual—but——"

"But what? It just seems like dissipation to me. Public dissipation, at that." And perhaps, she thought, he is smiling now.

"But Sprig, by the time they marry they know each other very well in that way; I'm not sure I think that's a bad thing."

He grunted. "I like decorum," he said after thinking this over.

"Other things may be more important."

"What things?"

"Have you looked at Betsy, really seen her, since Tom arrived? It's just as if she had a light inside her, as if she had been nothing but darkness. It's rather wonderful."

"She could look that way, if she does, without holding hands in a corner," he said, with what amounted to violence from Sprig.

"I'll have a talk with her, if you like."

"Good God, no! She's way beyond our ken. They both are. Perfect strangers."

"Yes," and Frances sighed, "they're growing up." In a little while, in a few years, she thought, I shall be alone with Sprig. It is what I have always wanted. But now she was frightened. She reached across and searched for his hand. "Dear love," she said, "how are you?"

"Disgruntled." But he held her hand for a moment and

gave it a friendly squeeze before letting it go. "What's all this about Lucy?"

He said Lucy, though it was John after all who was the trouble, John who insisted on marrying his secretary. Frances had been wanting to talk about it but now she winced for Lucy, felt that she couldn't discuss it at all, that it was too painful.

"It just doesn't seem possible," she said. "Last year, all those evenings we spent together, the warmth. John seemed so loving. I don't understand."

"Sordid. Still," Sprig was thinking aloud, "you can hardly blame him for getting tired of the disorder."

It had been there in Sprig's tone from the beginning, a shade of sympathy for John. And Frances was up in arms, "The disorder is very much alive. It's the most friendly house we ever go to, a house where there's real conversation, and real meeting, and where all ages feel at home—how rare that is, Sprig, you must admit. Lucy is a remarkable person," Frances said passionately.

"She forgets to send his shirts to the laundry."

"Oh Sprig."

"All right, I'm an insensitive brute."

"But they've been married twenty years. How can he break all that, tear up all those roots? I hate it. It upsets me dreadfully." In fact she was close to tears.

"Yes," he granted, "it's upsetting."

"It's an attack, that's why."

"What do you mean?"

"I want to come over into your bed."

"Very well."

When she had scrambled in and was lying with her head against his shoulder, held in the crook of his arm, the tears oozed out and she could not stop them.

"You're making my pajamas all wet," he said tenderly. "Here, here's a handkerchief."

"It is as if everyone, we—were th-thr-threatened. It t-tears into things we felt sure of, somehow—it scares me, Sprig."

"I feel rather cross with John," he conceded.

"Cross? I could kill him."

"Sh—— You'll wake Gran-Quan."

Then they were silent. Sprig held her close and stroked her hair, as he did when he was moved, and did very rarely. She burrowed her nose into his shoulder, and sighed. It was strange that the day should end like this, as she had dreamed all morning that it might, though she had not dreamed that it could happen because of such a cataclysm, that the breaking of her best friend's marriage would bring her and Sprig together in the old way. For the first time in years, she slept against his shoulder, and he did not stir.

It was he who lay awake, listening to the silence of the house as if it were speaking to him, so that old memories he did not know were there, came up and filled his mind. He remembered his father quite suddenly saying to him after he was engaged to Fran, "Cherish her, Sprig. Cherish her." Had he cherished her? It seemed to Sprig as he held this sleeping child in his arms, that he had not known how to cherish her. Thinking of that broken marriage so close to them, he wondered about it all. We have been kind to each other, he thought, always. But is that enough? How strange to live with the woman you love a whole lifetime maybe, and still not come to any final and absolute gift of the self. But if you did, if you could make that gift—and surely his father had done so—then you were no longer safe, separate, you were caught. You might be destroyed.

"Cherish her," his father had said. And at the time it had only seemed to Sprig one more variation on the theme of his grief, on the loss of his own wife, and meant "Cherish her because she may die." But he saw now that it meant "Cherish her that she may live." Was this what Tom was doing for Betsy? Could it be true that she was lit up from inside as Frances said? Fran noticed such things. He never did. And if he had noticed anything today, it was Fran; if he had thought about anything, it was his marriage. Why had it felt upsetting afterwards to have got back to the passionate union after such a long time? Why had it seemed like violence? Violence to himself, to some part of himself he wished more and more to hold in reserve—but in reserve for what?

He was alarmed at the extent of his need to get away, of the way in which dreams of Japan persisted with that nostalgia for the ordered sensual world he had known as a young man, flowing through him like an obsession. For there he had felt free for the only time in his life, had had intimations of what he really might become—and now at fifty felt that he had wasted the years since then, and emerged into maturity impoverished, a kind of cripple.

Had China meant anything of the sort to his grandfather, he wondered. He too had taken a strange world into himself and never quite "belonged" afterwards. But he at least had been fired by ambition, had busily amassed a fortune, had seemed well armed, invulnerable—and, if he had grown fond of China and especially of a few Chinese friends, had been able to absorb it into the whole pattern of his life. While I—Sprig very gently turned over on his side, and Fran sighed and laid her cheek against his back where he could feel her breath breathed in and out like a small delicate bellows—have become a man whose secret life is all a dream. No connection.

He felt tired now. The first bird was waking up. But he could not sleep. It seemed as if there were some knot to untie and as if his roving, exhausted thoughts could not even find it, let alone untie it: I want to get away. I want to get right away from all of them, all responsibilities, marriage.

He was amazed when he woke at seven to find that he must have, after all, at some point fallen asleep. Frances was already downstairs. He could hear her singing in the kitchen, his wife whom he adored, who had slept against his shoulder like a child, and whom he would have liked, all night, to leave.

*

CHAPTER THREE

FOR once Sprig had been definite and unanswerable when he handed Tom a small axe and said, "We're off to the woods," without even a glance in Caleb's direction.

"We'll sail this afternoon," Caleb called out to their backs, and Tom turned to wave and grin. Everyone had gathered on the porch after breakfast, so this departure had the air of a determined expedition to which the assembled family were saying farewell. Hannah made appropriate remarks, barking three times, her head thrown back and her ears flapping, before she trundled along ahead. Caleb and Betsy, sitting on the steps, exchanged a smile. And Gran-Quan gave one of his more expressive sighs, then chuckled, "Sprig looks ten years younger already. Those long legs——" he said. "He always did walk faster than most people can run. On the rampage——" and he chuckled again.

Mr. Silence opened his eyes a slit, walked over to Aunt Jane's chair, wound himself round her legs, and finally jumped up onto her lap.

"Dear me, he is heavy," she said, stroking him. He pummelled her with his kneading and would not settle, but finally he curled his nose into his tail and lay there like a huge velvet pillow.

The morning sun was so bright, the smell of grass and fir so subtly relaxing that after these few remarks it seemed as if they had all gone fast asleep though their eyes were wide open.

Tom had been afraid this was to be a man-to-man talk, but after they had walked about a quarter of a mile through open groves and all Sprig volunteered was a few remarks about the names of mosses, or pointed to a rock where he and Hester had had a fort as children, began to relax and look around him. Tom enjoyed the springy feel of the pine needles under his feet, and the silence, for only when his shoe broke a twig was there any noticeable sound.

What would it feel like to own trees, mosses, great sun-splattered reaches of open woods, to walk here as master and friend, as Sprig Wyeth walked, glancing up at a broken branch or down at a rabbit hole, all his? What did it do to people to have all this and take it for granted? And for a moment Tom wished he could bring his mother here, set her down in a soft place and see the sunlight on her hands. Maybe sometime—if ever he and Betsy could come here quite alone. But now the barrier between them, of all she knew and had, seemed enormous. For the first time Tom was afraid.

Just then Sprig turned and waited for him to catch up. He was not smiling, and Tom felt he was being looked over in a way that became disturbing. I can stare you down, too, he said to himself, meeting Sprig's glance head on.

"Is this where we get to work?" They had come into a rough semicircular place deep in bracken and small growth, but clearly meant to have a shape. At the edge big stones, now entirely covered in velvety moss, had been shifted to make rough seats.

"Well," Sprig glanced around at it. "It used to be a theatre. Always a bit damp, as a matter of fact. But I'd like to cut, at least here and there. Can you handle an axe?"

"I can learn."

"Yes—well—let's have a cigarette first."

They sat at a little distance from each other, Sprig leaning the small of his back against a stone, Tom on a stump. When they had lit their cigarettes, they just sat there for a while. Some kind of small bird was trotting up the trunk of a tree, pausing to peck at insects under the bark, nice little thing, striped black and white with a red mark on its head.

"What's that?" Tom asked, glad to have an excuse to break the silence.

"Downy woodpecker." Sprig frowned, then lifted the axe and balanced it in his hands, as if he were weighing something. It occurred to Tom that it must be excruciatingly difficult for this sort of man to speak at all about anything important.

"About Betsy—" Tom was surprised at the roughness of his own tone.

"What about Betsy?" The axe was very still in Sprig's hands.

"I'm serious."

"So I presumed."

"We would like to get married as soon as possible."

The silence that followed this was rather hard to take. But Tom reminded himself not to lose his temper, whatever happened. He smoked furiously, not bothering to take the cigarette out of his mouth. You won't stop me, he thought; you with all you are can't stop this. He could feel his teeth clenched hard and his throat so tight he felt strangled. Oh, come out with it, he implored silently. But Sprig sat there, apparently lost in thought.

Finally he coughed that embarrassed cough and threw his cigarette away. "You're a Catholic, I suppose?" The shy, wary eyes turned toward him and Tom saw real anxiety there. So that was it. He was so relieved that he felt an impulse to laugh. For this surely was the least of his worries.

"I go to Mass occasionally because of my mother. But I am not a good Catholic, haven't taken communion since I was seventeen, or thereabouts." He hesitated. Anything he might say now was a betrayal of his family, of his mother. "Stand up for your religion," she would say. But it wasn't his religion any longer. Tom stamped out the cigarette. "I wouldn't bring up our children in the Church, if that's what troubles you. It doesn't matter that much to me."

Sprig gave a little grunt. There was no relief visible in his face, in fact he was frowning.

"I don't like it," he said quietly.

"I don't understand."

"It looks a little irresponsible to me. As if you had shed it because it bothered you—but of course," he added quickly, "I don't know what I'm talking about." He looked as if he were going to say more, but instead changed the subject,

"I have no objection to your marrying Betsy, if you're both quite sure. My wife, who is more observant than I am about such matters, believes that Betsy is changed, that you have in fact"—and Sprig smiled a fleeting smile—"waked Sleeping Beauty."

"Betsy is a very wonderful person," Tom said gravely.

"In case I don't know?"

"Excuse me, sir."

"Well——" and Sprig suddenly yawned, as if with relief. "I have no illusions about parents and children. Betsy has always been a mystery to us. You apparently have the key to the mystery: I congratulate you."

Tom was angry; he felt suddenly terribly angry with these peoples' cold way of doing things, the circumspection. He didn't like a father who talked ironically about his own daughter.

"She's just a very loving person, and if you'll forgive my saying so, sir, I think she's been starved for love." Tom stood up. He would have liked to find an excuse to biff Sprig Wyeth in the jaw. He was trembling.

"Yes," Sprig said, getting up too, and apparently completely unaware of the effect he was having. "Well, you may be right."

A man who could take such an insult and just turn it over in his mind as if it were an abstract idea to be reckoned with left Tom helpless. He had to look around for something to use as a weapon and what Sprig had said earlier about not caring about his religion came to mind.

"I'd like to make something else clear," Tom said.

"Yes, let's get it all straight," and Sprig smiled at him in an absolutely friendly way.

Preposterous man, Tom thought, how can you deal with it?

"I don't think losing your religion is a good thing, Sir. But faith is not something you can force. It does happen that people have to leave the church they were born to—from what Betsy has said, I gather something of the sort happened to your father."

Sprig lifted his head, alert. "What was that again?"

"Your father, sir——"

"My father paid a very high price. After all, he had been wholly committed. He was a Unitarian Minister, you know. And he has felt committed ever since to a perfectly fruitless war against God—he's really half mad, I think. But for him it all came out of intolerable grief—the death of my mother, you know. It was that. So you might say he had been wounded and never got over it." The tone was brusque, commanding. "How was it with you?" Sprig asked.

And Tom thought, Queer, he sounds like the old man sometimes.

"I'm not mad," Tom said with the ghost of a smile. "But I expect it always does cost something. Maybe you'll have to give me the benefit of the doubt." The fact was, though he would never admit it, that Tom could never pass a church without a twinge, never meet a priest on the street without lowering his eyes, and found going home such a difficult business because of his mother's feeling about just this. There in the fresh morning light under the trees, he felt suddenly tired, and sat down on his stump, his hands clasped loosely between his knees. The last thing he had expected on this walk was to be quizzed about religion. He realized that nothing at all had been said about whether he could support Betsy, for instance. None of the expected things had been said. Instead, Sprig had gone right in and touched him where he lived. It was disturbing.

"I like the Irish," Sprig said, looking up now at a pine which had sprouted some branches on the side facing the open semicircle, "always have liked them."

"I hate feeling inferior," Tom heard himself saying, and at once wished he had not said it. It came out of the depression which had settled on him in the last five minutes. "Damn fool," he said to himself. "Where's your pride?"

"Yes," Sprig went up to the tree and began to chop with sure, hard strokes at one of the straggly branches. The words came between the strokes. "None of it's easy. I've always felt inferior myself. Know all about it." He hacked away.

You? Tom thought. Inferior? You don't know what the word means.

"Want to start in on that one?" Sprig said, panting a little.

Hacking away at dead branches was just what Tom needed. He went at it furiously, so the axe slipped out of his hands and clattered down.

"That's all right," Sprig said, in the same brusque voice which Tom felt was his real voice, "Don't put so much energy into it. Boomerangs."

Then for some ten minutes there was silence except

for the sharp blows of the axes, an alternate rhythm, the two men unconsciously adjusting their strokes to each other. It was Sprig who broke the rhythm and came over for a moment to watch. "Fine, you've got the hang of it now."

Tom smiled, but went right on, giving a final hard stroke to the thick branch, and then watching it crack off slowly and fall.

Sprig raised his voice slightly to be heard. "I was given a lot and haven't done much with it. My grandfather was the man in this family, great old boy, you know, hard as iron and knew what he wanted." Sprig gave a laugh. "What he wanted was to make a fortune. Easier to be a grandfather than a grandson. Ever think of that? Maybe you're to be a grandfather. Maybe that's the point. Up with the Irish," Sprig said, and his eyes were bright, though he did not smile.

Tom laughed suddenly, felt free to laugh, felt pride swell up in him because he found he could do this outdoor work and enjoy it, because Sprig Wyeth was talking to him this way, teasing him a little, because everything was there ahead and he was young and ready for it.

"Heavens!" Sprig called loudly, "where's Hannah? Bet she's after a porcupine. We've got to find her. Frances will never forgive me." He was charging off into the woods, whistling and calling. He seemed like a young man, and Tom, watching him go, felt like an old one.

*

CHAPTER FOUR

IT was three o'clock in the afternoon. Gran-Quan had been put to bed for a long nap; Aunt Jane, too; and Frances, getting meat loaf for supper ready in the kitchen, looked anxiously at the clock. Sprig had gone to the airport to get Lucy—and there were still a hundred things to do: flowers for Lucy's room, the fire to lay there, but most important of all she must try to quiet down, to subdue the buzz of excitement vibrating still, for the children's engagement had been formally recognized at luncheon and they were all a little tipsy with delight. Frances let her hands fall and stood for a moment, quite still, lost in thought: it's going to be hard on Lucy—and yet one can't stop life flowing in; one can't arrest life even to care for the wounded. It goes on, carrying us all along with it. She paused to stroke Mr. Silence where he lay curled up in the rocker by the window.

She paused while the jumble of emotions and practical things whirled around inside her, the sage for the meat loaf sweeping in beside the sense that life was cruel as well as kind, the question of what to have for tea—it was all arranged that she and Lucy go off with a thermos and Aunt Jane would pour out for Sprig and Gran-Quan on the porch. Caleb was off somewhere, of course, and no one expected to see the engaged couple before supper. I could open that tin of Scotchbread she was thinking—and suddenly she put her hand to her heart—Lucy, darling Lucy—and shortbread a poor kind of comfort when your world breaks in two.

Frances nearly dropped the thermos she was so angry when she thought of John, that charmer, that spoiled child who was willing to throw away wisdom, goodness, all those shared years because wisdom had grown fat, no doubt, because goodness had been taken for granted like an old shoe. Never take anything for granted, she admonished herself angrily, wrapping up cookies in wax paper, and then she went out to the porch to look down the channel and see if the boat was in sight.

"Are you all right, Aunt Jane?" she asked. Lying down as Aunt Jane was now, with a rug over her, she looked such a wisp, it was a little frightening. Then she opened her eyes and smiled.

"I am still intoxicated, I think," she said. "So much wine—and dear Betsy—they've gone to my head."

"Well, you just lie quiet. Gran-Quan's fast asleep. I could hear him snoring."

The old lady gave a sigh and closed her eyes.

"I was thinking about Emily and Quan——"

"So long ago, dear."

"Like yesterday to him——" the old lady murmured as if a world were there alive under her eyelids, a whole world Frances did not know. "Faithfulness is a very beautiful thing," she added, and then rather surprisingly sat up with one of her quick changes of mood, and added drily, "though

41

it ruined Quan. I must admit it would have been far better if he hadn't clung so to the tragedy."

"I wonder——" Frances said, shading her eye against the light, and she was going to add, "Is that faithfulness?" but just then she saw the boat. "There they are! I must run!" And she was off down the side sandy path, flying like a bird, Aunt Jane thought—and so young!

The young did not have to live in this world where the whole past was going on all the time, more vivid even than the present. She felt sometimes she could hardly bear its all staying so vivid. Forgetting would be peace. You woke up out of some meadow where you had been weaving a daisy chain, in a little pink frock and high button boots and there you were with Quan inexplicably old and cross beside you, and your own throat horribly wrinkled like a turkey's—and it seemed so strange and unfair. We've been put into these decaying bodies—whatever for?

She could hear their voices now, coming up the path. And she felt tired, unwilling to have to pull herself together and meet a new face, though God knows she had seen Lucy often enough; still she was not the family. The family was what consoled, sheltered, kept the past and the present flowing together; understood things without being told, remembered names when you forgot them. Dear Sprig, she thought, hearing his voice now, threaded through the women's—he's grown up, such a dear funny face, so shy, even now. The old and the young, meeting and parting, the rising and ebbing tides—she closed her eyes. A moment more of this floating and then she must be ready to give Lucy a proper welcome.

42

They sat, Frances and Lucy, on a high grassy bank, looking out, Frances thought, like birds in a nest, through the branches of a wild cherry to the shimmering dark blue water, could not see across to the shore, so it might have been open sea, going on forever. They had been talking about Aunt Jane. Lucy was shocked, she said, as if Aunt Jane were vanishing before their eyes—still there, but just about to go. Yes, it had been a shock, she said, adding as she so often did, "It's all so strange. One understands nothing. The older one grows the less one knows." But this time it was not said lightly, and in its shadow, the silence fell. They had arrived.

"It's queer," Lucy said, "I thought I wanted to talk. And now"—she bowed her head—"I can't."

"Don't talk," Frances turned to busy herself with the thermos and shortbread. "It's enough that you're here, enough for me," she murmured.

Frances lay back and crossed her arms under her head, and looked up through the leaves at the sky, pockets of blue here and there among all the greenness. When she and Lucy were together, Frances thought aloud, and thought things she would not have come upon otherwise, or admitted if she had. Looking up into the leaves, talking as if to the air, she said, "I feel as if I were on the edge of some transition, as if"—she hesitated—"everything were in peril. Oh Lucy," she turned over now and put a hand on Lucy's knee, rubbing the coarse wool absent-mindedly, "when you called, it was like the end of the world. Gran-Quan had been reading Wordsworth aloud (you know how he loves to); we were sitting by the fire. But when you called it was everything breaking apart. Caleb is leaving us—Betsy—Aunt Jane won't live much longer." She sat up abruptly and lit a cigarette. "It's awful what I am saying—why am I saying it?"

She turned to Lucy, the tears starting in her eyes, looked up and met Lucy's straight honest gaze, so perfectly able to absorb shock.

"I know," she said evenly. "You're saying that every marriage is a compact with society as well as a compact between two partners. A divorce, especially at our age, breaks the delicate net of safety we all walk on. I myself have fallen down the abyss," and she lifted her chin in a gesture of pride, of self-dependence that Frances recognized.

Frances looked at her friend without compassion, with only a kind of recognition and out of this she said, "You'll have a chance to find out who you are."

"Does one find that out by being thrown aside for a pretty young woman?" Lucy's voice was harsh.

"Why does he want to marry her? Can't they go away somewhere and live it out? After all, people do have love affairs——" She added lamely, "The French do."

"Unfortunately John is a New Englander. He can't offer the woman he loves anything less than marriage. And, of course, they're in that state of madness. You might as well try to stop the rising tide. Not that I didn't"—the tone was bitter—"I begged him to wait. You know what he said? That it would be a bad example for the children. That he wasn't going to have them despise their father."

"As if they wouldn't now."

"He thinks he's being heroically honest, you see. Paying

the price, *et cetera*. What can you do against that kind of reasoning?"

"It isn't reasonable, of course."

"And neither, I suppose, am I," Lucy said, then turned to Frances with a troubled look, her hand beside her plucking at the grass absent-mindedly.

"Do the children know?" Frances asked the direct question because she could not wait any longer.

"Of course they do. John's moved out, living at the Brattle Inn."

"It's awful." This actual fact of the separation, the physical separation struck Frances like a blow, took her by surprise.

"Luckily they're grown-up, or nearly. Jack goes around frowning all the time and tries to console me in a doglike way, bewildered, poor darling. Susy is hard as nails and refuses even to see John."

"Oh, why did it happen?" Frances cried out. She leaned her chin on her knees, staring at all she remembered, the clear image of Lucy and John raking leaves in the garden and burning them, of their long lazy talks about everything under the sun (how often she had envied this, the way they talked about and shared everything), the affectionate way John called her 'old lady' and followed her into the kitchen to dry the dishes. "You shared so much."

"That's what I thought a month ago. Now I begin to see how much of that sharing, as you call it, must have been habit, sharing on the simple level of existing side by side in the same house."

"It wasn't existing. It was a whole good life you had made. What about Sandy?" Frances asked, thinking suddenly, too, of the big Irish terrier who had grown old while the children grew up, and who was always coming over to lay his head on John's knee.

Without warning, Lucy laid her head in her arms, and her shoulders shook with the force of the grief.

Frances slid over and put an arm around her and held her close. There was nothing to say.

"It's j-j-just . . ." Lucy brushed the tears off against her arm, and fished around for a handkerchief.

"I know," Frances said, "animals——" the way Sprig talked to Mr. Silence for instance, and said things in a tone of voice he could never never have used to her.

"Sandy lies by John's door every night and cries. He waits at the front door and every time it opens, gets up and wags his tail. He does everything I feel like doing and can't, because of p-pr-pride——" Lucy was sobbing now uncontrollably. "How can John do this to *us?*" she said after a moment, blowing her nose.

"To what you were together," Frances said quickly.

"It was something, wasn't it?" Lucy entreated. "I haven't just dreamed it, Fran? We were something together——"

"That's what I can't understand, how he'll ever do without it. He'll regret this, Lucy—I'm sure he will."

"He may, but that won't change anything."

They sat now, close together, and it seemed to Frances

as if in all the ripe summer stillness, as the light on the water took on its intensest blue just before the sun began to set, they themselves were an ugly gash, troubled, troubling, having no connection with the beauty around them, set apart in their humanness, in their suffering.

Frances looked at her watch. "Oh dear, we must get back, it's after five—they'll all come home ravenous——" She began to close the thermos and pack up the cups and paper napkins, and Lucy watched her—the impatience, the nervousness of her gestures.

As they walked single file along the edge of the shore just where the trees gave way to rock and pebbly beach, Frances stopped, turned back to say, "What Sprig really wants is to leave us all and go back to Japan."

"Everyone has fantasies of escape——"

"But why shouldn't he?" Frances asked passionately, "why shouldn't people do what they want, become what they have to become? What keeps us from being ourselves?"

"Each other, I suppose," Lucy said thoughtfully.

"Do you think I enjoy being something that prevents Sprig from breaking through?"

"It's not you, darling. It's life. You just can't start again at the beginning—even though John thinks so. One might as well imagine flying in the air—we're all held where we are by a million human threads."

"It's terrible," Frances said with a sigh. "I'm so tired, Lucy."

"Yes," Lucy answered, resting her eyes on the shore,

melancholy now with bits of seaweed floating about on the surface and the brilliance gone with the sun, and the dank evening smell rising up, the roots of rotting trees, seaweed, pine needles all mixed together. "We all are. About half-way up the mountain one feels very tired. Have you noticed?"

CHAPTER FIVE

"OH, there you are," Sprig said with some asperity. He was sitting on the porch rail swinging one leg, smoking his pipe.

"Why? Are we late? What's happened?"

"Nothing's happened." Hester spoke from the porch step. "Sprig's anxious because the sailors aren't back."

"Gran-Quan's in a depression. Won't get up for supper." He said it as if this had been brought on by Frances' disappearance for an hour.

"Where's Aunt Jane?"

"Coddling Gran-Quan, I expect."

"Well, darling"—Frances stopped just below and looked up at him with a slightly mocking look—"supper will be ready in forty-five minutes. Everyone's furious from sheer starvation—why don't you mix us a cocktail?"

The hundred threads were drawn tight again and Frances, feeling them tug at her, was amused to find that she was glad. But the children? She went in by the long way round the porch so as to take a look—there were a few sails bearing round the point, but it was hard to distinguish one from another. On how many evenings like this had someone run down the long porch, and peered out to sea, and heard the gulls wailing, and hurried in to light the lamps and cook the dinner, to build walls of shelter and safety against the night?

"Go and have a wash and a rest, Lucy, and come down for a drink when you feel like it." Frances called, "Light the fire, Sprig, will you? Hester will help me lay the table. . . ."

Now she was back, the tide of life was rising again. The house had light in it; the fire crackled; and soon her voice could be heard singing above the sound of running water, the comfortable rattle of pots and pans.

" 'How lovely is thy dwelling place, O Lord of Hosts,' " she sang in her clear soprano while Hester sang a bar or two in her alto, always a little bit off tune.

Upstairs Aunt Jane was sitting by Gran-Quan's bed, stroking his hand.

"A bit too much excitement, that's all that's the matter," she said, perhaps for the fourth time in the last hour.

"I feel dreadfully ill," and he gave a groan as he shifted his legs. "Why am I not ready to die, Jane?" he asked her suddenly, looking out from his cavernous eyes like a suffering animal, she thought.

"I don't expect anyone ever is, not anyone in good health anyway."

"If only Frances would stop caroling that hopeful religious music—'how lovely, how lovely, how lovely,' " he roared suddenly. "Not lovely at all. Blackness. Nothingness——"

The Island

Jane knew this mood well. There was nothing to do but let him blow off steam.

"That seems to me so peaceful," Aunt Jane sighed. She sometimes thought it would be lovely to go to bed and sleep for a week, just rest and have someone bring delicious food on trays. Mary, her old servant, was now almost as old as she; half the time Aunt Jane was waiting on her rather than the other way round. Besides, "being up and around" was a moral obligation to the universe.

"Dear, I think I'd better go down and see how Fran is getting along——"

"Don't go," he pleaded. "Please don't." Then, as if he had exposed himself enough, he added crossly, "You're ninety and it's high time you stopped behaving as if you were Atlas with the entire world on your shoulders. Hester's there, isn't she?"

"Quan?" she asked.

"What?"

"Do you remember that place where we went for a summer when we were quite small, that field where we used to lie in the long grass and make fairy houses, cushions of daisy centers (I can smell that bitter smell now of the daisies)—where was it?" she asked.

"Danged if I know. I don't remember any of that," he said irritably. "All gone, as though it had never been. I feel as if I don't know who I am, what I'm doing here."

"Pa was in China." She pursued her own thoughts. "We must have been staying with cousins somewhere, but where?" It bothered her fearfully not to remember. When

51

the past got displaced like this, it made her feel panicky. One had to keep going back to be sure it was all there. But Quan was paying no attention. He groaned.

"A blundering old man who has made everyone miserable including himself—that's who I am. Oh Jane, I'm so tired of it all."

"Well, I'm not," she said tartly. "I want to see Betsy's first child, for one thing. I get a bit tired," she said, "but I'm still interested."

"Curiosity killed the cat," he muttered crossly.

"It's kept me alive." There were times lately when Aunt Jane's patience seemed rather short. She was surprised at herself, and these gusts of irritation that swept over her. "I'm going now," she said. "You've made me cross and I hate being cross."

"Oh please, Jane," and he leaned toward her, caught hold of her hand and held it very tightly, for he was amazingly strong, she thought. "Who do you think *you* are, for example?"

"I haven't the slightest idea," she answered crisply. "It doesn't seem important."

"Women," he said, leaning back against the pillows with a martyred look, though he was chuckling, "quite impossible to have a conversation with—always evading the issue—go away, Jane," he said, "I want to think."

She stopped halfway down the stairs because it seemed so very noisy. The house was being taken by storm as the children clattered up the back stairs, banged doors, shouted, and Sprig called up, "You'd better hurry. Your mother's been waiting for hours." She felt she was going down into chaos and she was a little bewildered, shaken, as if she might fall. How idiotic. She grasped the banister, and looked up at the ceiling because looking down seemed rather too perilous.

"Walpole," she said aloud. Yes, that was it. That was the place, Walpole. Relief flooded her. Walpole was where we went that summer, of course, at the Greene cousins'. There was a fat little boy who teased me and kept unrolling my curls. We had our nurse with us, the German one whom we hated so. Thank goodness, she murmured, I have remembered. The sense of chaos ebbed away. She had it all firmly in hand again, and she took the dangerous steps carefully but quite in control.

"He shouldn't take these chances," Fran was saying passionately. "It's not fair!"

"Don't be silly, Fran. He knows what he's doing." Sprig turned as Aunt Jane appeared at the foot of the stairs and went to give her his arm, and to pour her a small glass of sherry. She glanced from one to the other and then at Lucy whom she had hardly seen.

"Come and sit beside us," Hester said, making room on the sofa.

"Dear Lucy," said Aunt Jane, giving her arm a pat when she was settled. Then she turned to the others. "What is all this about?"

Frances and Sprig exchanged a look, a rather cross look, and Frances said, "Never mind. It's Caleb, of course."

"But we haven't described the day!" Hester broke in. "I have no idea what's been happening!"

It was the moment in the evening when traditional things must be done, after the long private day, erratic and personal, when all must be gathered together and sorted out.

"What have you been doing, darling?" Frances asked.

"Sleeping, writing letters—nothing I ought to do—pure bliss," Hester said, and indeed her face already looked smoothed out, some of the tension gone. She yawned, just thinking of the lazy day. "I did weed for an hour—" she added, "for conscience sake. The garden is rather a mess."

"I've almost finished clearing out the theatre," Sprig announced, rocking on his heels in a way he had when he was pleased with himself.

"The theatre?" Hester sat up. "It's ages since we've been there. Couldn't we get up a play? Charades? Something? While Tom's still here?"

"It's rather damp," Sprig said.

"Nonsense, it's always been damp. How lovely!" Hester said. "Do you remember 'Midsummer Night's Dream'? Sprig was the most wonderful Puck," she laughed. "He made his entrance sliding down a tree!"

"That beautiful Cutter girl was Titania——" Aunt Jane remembered.

"The one you were so in love with?" Frances asked, looking at him over the edge of her glass, and, though it was long before she had ever been here or known Sprig, she minded the Cutter girl, the mysterious blue-eyed girl who

54

had married a Frenchman, the only girl to whom Sprig had written poems, his first love.

"Oh yes, I was madly in love with her—madly——" Sprig said, teasing.

Just then Caleb sauntered down, in a clean white shirt, though his shoelaces were half undone as usual.

"*Madly* in love, Father?" he asked ironically.

"Here, have a drink and mind your manners," Sprig answered quickly. "This conversation is not for children."

"The children are not down yet."

"Oh yes, we are, and we're not children!" Tom and Betsy ran down the stairs hand in hand, so fast it seemed almost as if they fell down, and so lightly it seemed almost as if they had flown.

Their faces were flushed from the long afternoon in the sun, and everyone turned to look at this brightness among them, so much radiant energy, one half expected to see them whirl off together in a dance.

"Sit down and be quiet," Sprig said, as if they had made a loud noise or were about to shout something, "we're exhausted."

Oh, it's so lovely when we're all together after the long day, Frances was thinking, looking from one beloved face to another as if she were drinking them in, one by one, as if each were a cordial which went straight to the heart. But it was Lucy's eyes that hers met, and then turned away. Instinctively she searched for Sprig, for some reassurance, for some certainty that whatever was in peril it was not their two selves. But he was talking with Hester now, remembering the Cutter girl no doubt, for they were suffused with laughter over something.

Frances clapped her hands. "Everyone be quiet," she commanded, "we want to hear about the sail——"

Caleb was standing at the fireplace, leaning sideways, looking down at his feet. His mother's voice had focused the attention of the whole group upon him without warning. He frowned and scratched his back with his free arm; they expected him, of course, to regale them with some tall story about danger and prowess. It had been a good sail, with a few moments of excitement when they nearly capsized, heeled over in the squall. . . .

He raised his head, shrugged his shoulders and said, "It was all right." He caught his mother's glance, imploring him as if, he thought bitterly, I were feeble-minded or something. He lived now always on the edge of rage or unforgivable rudeness and his answer, which had taken him so long to give, seemed to him a masterly avoidance of both.

But Sprig looked over at his son coldly and said, "We're a family, you know, Caleb."

"Whatever are you talking about, Sprig?" It was Hester's voice, warning.

"Caleb treats this as if it were a hotel and he hated all the fellow guests. I'm getting just a bit tired of it. Your mother asked you a question, Caleb. Perhaps you might try to answer it with a little more enthusiasm." The back of Sprig's neck had gone bright red. He stood there, glaring at his son in a huge silence. No one moved.

"Sprig, dear—" Aunt Jane said cautiously.

Frances leaped to her feet "My meat loaf!" she cried, making her escape, for surely if everyone had something to eat . . . but out in the kitchen she found her hands were shaking. It had to come, but not she begged the surrounding air, not just tonight, with Tom and Lucy here. I should never have asked him, she thought— I did it—and ran back, as she could hear the voices, the angry note still sounding harshly even through the swing door. Supper would have to wait; she appeared now with Mr. Silence hanging from one arm, as if she were coming back with an appeasing divinity to give them. But no one saw her.

"I'm pretty tired of being treated like a child," Caleb said to the floor. He hadn't moved.

"I can't understand"—Sprig's voice was icy—"why being asked about your day is being treated like a child. We have always exchanged news at this hour. It's a tradition."

"That's just it, can't you see?" Caleb stood up now, his hands clenched in his pockets, and faced them all. "It's all been done before a million times. It's all a pattern. What if you don't want a pattern?" He was shaking with the effort of tearing this inward piece of himself out, and he hated them for bringing him to it.

"Caleb is quite right, Sprig." Hester was sitting straight up now, her hands clasped, her eyes very bright.

"You don't find out anything by breaking away from things—responsibilities—even very simple ones like participating in a conversation," Sprig said.

"Don't you?" Caleb drove the question home and smiled.

"What are you talking about?"

"You're always doing it yourself, aren't you?"

"No, Caleb." Frances came forward now, dropped Mr. Silence whose tail had been wagging furiously, and slipped an arm through Sprig's. "That's not fair."

"Oh, there are rules. Father may attack son. Son mayn't attack father. I'm sorry," Caleb said. He was shaking with rage.

"No, dear," Aunt Jane's silvery voice broke in, so gentle it created a new kind of silence. "That's not what your mother means."

"What does she mean?" Caleb turned to Frances.

"Must we do this, darling?" Desperately she threw a bridge across to him. "I think everyone's tired and hungry and on edge. Why don't you and Betsy come and help me set the table."

But could the djinni of anger be forced back into his bottle now? Apparently, yes. Here there could be no violence, Tom thought, watching in amazement as Frances and her two children went out quietly, and Sprig made the rounds with the cocktail shaker one last time. Would they ever have it out? he wondered, measuring the tension under the surface. Hester was following her brother with her eyes, anxious eyes, wise eyes, and Tom wondered very much what she was thinking.

But it was not she who spoke. Lucy had gotten up from the sofa and wandered off by herself to the shadowy part of the room. There she was joined by Sprig. What they said could be heard by everyone but was spoken to each other.

"It isn't so easy, you know, to find yourself when you are surrounded from birth by quite such a definite frame, Sprig."

"There is a toleration point for rudeness," Sprig answered. "I reached it tonight. I'm sorry. Tom's one of the family now and he might as well know what monsters we are," he added with a clumsy attempt at lightness.

"Rudeness is only a symptom, Sprig," Hester added, leaning her head back on the sofa.

"So your friends the psychiatrists would say." If there was anything Sprig hated and resisted with his whole being it was the idea that human beings could be taken apart and put together to a formula like machines. He and Hester had had many an argument on this subject, but it was never closed.

"Am I still the unique subject of your interest?" Caleb asked at the door. "Supper's on the table. Perhaps I may be allowed now to join in the happy dissection."

He looked electric with life. Anger suits him, Lucy thought. Curiously enough, he seemed full of happiness suddenly. She felt she had never really seen Caleb before, that deep blue flash back of his eyes like a kingfisher's wing, his locked mouth, his long cheekbones and sullen face which only now in anger opened and showed itself. For the first time she felt his power.

And then as they went in she saw Betsy, waiting for

Tom, and the way her whole being welcomed him and turned to him slightly, as if she could hardly bear not to lean her head on his shoulder, as they stood side by side waiting for Frances and Sprig to sit down.

"So much emotion, Hannah, makes one hungry, doesn't it?" Frances said, drawing them all together, through the old dog, to whom such things might be safely said.

There was no grace spoken in this household, but, Lucy thought, the grace is that unspoken look between Sprig and Frances as they meet each other across the long table. Her eyes filled with tears. But the plates were coming down to be filled and back again, and everyone was too busy and hungry to notice. Caleb was dispatched with a tray for Gran-Quan, and it was several minutes before any conversation was possible. Besides, everyone was ravenous.

Caleb sat on the end of the brass bed in Gran-Quan's room, swinging one foot. The old man was eating his bread pudding with obvious enjoyment.

"Made your escape, eh?" he said, throwing Caleb a conspiratory look. "Too many people altogether. Better up here. I've been listening to the thrush—smoke if you want to," he said, seeing Caleb's hand go to his pocket, then hesitate.

"Thanks." Caleb took a crumpled cigarette out, smoothed it, then lit it without the frown leaving his face. He screwed up his eyes, wondered why he had come. No one understood anything, not even the old, least of all the old perhaps. He had come because he recognized in Gran-

Quan an ornery character like his own. But the old man was entirely absorbed in himself, of course.

"Anything on your mind?"

"Nope." Caleb found a piece of string in his pocket and stretched it out as taut as he could. "I just want to murder Pa," he said, and added, "at times."

"He teases you," the old man said gently, "he can't help it."

"Teases?" Caleb said with heavy irony. "He won't let me live my life, do anything I really want to do. You let him go to Japan, didn't you?" He turned his gaze fiercely on Gran-Quan.

"He had no mother," Gran-Quan said, putting the dish down on the night table. "It makes a difference. Got locked up. Had to give him a chance——" He leaned back on the pillows, his hands folded.

"I'm locked up," Caleb said.

"Hell and damnation and bloody murder, we all are. That's the human condition," the old man blazed. "Have heroes and demons in us struggling to get out, never a moment's rest——" For a few moments his attention had been held by his grandson, but now he was leaning over the familiar abysses. "You're no different from the rest of us. I hurt your aunt's feelings," he said, "unpardonable. The Old Harry."

"She seemed all right——" Caleb ventured.

"Oh, she's a saint, you know, that's what makes it so hard. Women are a great trial, Caleb. They know too much and they're too damned good." But then his mood changed.

His eyes softened and he leaned back again, "Your grand-mother," he said, "that light in her eyes. Sprig hardly re-members her, poor boy. You have to make allowances for your father," said the old man fiercely. "He's been deprived."

"I can't," Caleb answered equally fiercely. "I've got to be myself. I can't give in. Let him make allowances for me."

"Hopeless," the old man said. "Learn everything too late. Why should you listen to me, a grotesque object—self-indulgent, unworthy? But you're straight from your great-grandfather, Caleb. Did you know it? Do you feel it? You've got the power. It's come back, skipped two generations."

"How do you know?"

"You've got his hard, fierce eye. Ruthless." The old man seemed excited now. He was smiling.

"Don't," Caleb said, getting up and walking to the window. Would he never be free of it, the whole mixed-up series of relationships? If he escaped his own father there would be his great-grandfather waiting to take possession. Already they tell me this and I don't even know what I want to do, what I am. He clenched his hands in his pockets.

"Only go after something big. Something that'll burn it all, use it all." .

"What to believe in that much," Caleb murmured. "We're so naked now—my generation, I mean. No foundation. No ground under our feet."

> "Live and take comfort; thou hast great allies;
>   Thy friends are exultations, agonies,
>   And love, and man's unconquerable mind,"

Gran-Quan poured out these words to the boy like a present, and Caleb with his back turned, looking out into the dark sky, the dark trees all around, felt himself flush.

"Mr. Wordsworth, I presume?" he asked, after a moment. "Thanks, Gran-Quan," he said, before taking the dish and making for the door.

Love, he thought. What is it? So close to rage where I am concerned, something that pulls me down and makes me weak. He went to his own room and lay down on the bed, his eyes wide open. Would it ever be something you could lose yourself in and not something that found you out? Peace, he thought—wondering if Betsy and Tom had any peace. "Oh, what's it all about anyway?" he groaned.

CHAPTER SIX

WHEN the dishes were washed, Betsy pulled Tom out onto the porch, before anyone could make a plan about the evening.

"Let's escape——"

"Can we? Won't they think——" He held her hand tightly in his. It seemed hours and hours, an eternity, since they had been alone together.

"I feel like a prisoner," she whispered. "Quick, let's get away!"

She pulled him down the steps, stumbled at the bottom and nearly fell. They looked up at the house which stood there, Tom thought, like a great Ark, the windows throwing squares of light on the moss and the lawn. These they avoided, creeping like two wild animals into the soft blackness under the trees, and fell into each other's arms.

"Oh Tom," she breathed into his neck, "Tom. . . ."

"My darling." He stroked her hair; she was trembling. "Come!" He led her through the darkness until they couldn't see the house any longer. They were breathing hard as if they had been running, and Betsy felt as if her heart must be thundering through the wood like some big animal.

Tom let her go, took off his jacket and laid it down under a tree. It was cold, very black and silent. She stood there while he did this, shivering. And when it was done, she slid into his arms as if he were the force of gravity itself. It was a moment without passion, quite beyond passion and he did not kiss her, just folded her against him, her head against his shoulder.

"What is it, darling?" he whispered. "My darling, you're safe here."

"Yes—oh yes," she breathed. "Oh Tom——" But she was still trembling.

For him the transition was so abrupt from the lighted house, the strangeness of these people, the tensions of that world, to this world where he lived alone with Betsy, that he felt now as if he were on the sheer side of a cliff, just hanging on by his toes.

He was consoling her, but he did not know what he was consoling her for, nor what the need was that pinned him there.

"If they would only leave us alone—Caleb——" she whispered.

"You mustn't take it so hard."

"I feel stifled. How am I going to live through the summer without you?"

"We're here now," he whispered, bending to kiss the corner of her forehead, then one hand, "don't think."

"I can't stand it any longer," she said and he felt the tears spilling down her cheeks onto his hands, "seeing so much, not being able to do anything—not being grown-up—" and it was strange how the tears fell as if they had nothing to do with what she was saying, as if they were rain. "Mother—" she said. "Father——" And then rubbed her cheek roughly against his shoulder, drove her head against him as if to blot them all out, pulled his head toward her and kissed him on the mouth, and all the time she was crying, so Tom could feel nothing for her but compassion, but tenderness.

"My bird," he said, "rest."

"I wish I were an animal," she said, looking up through the trees, her head resting on his outstretched arm. She blew her nose. "It's so complicated to be human."

He smiled in the dark. She said such unexpected things. She was so dear. "We'll make it simple, darling." Yet, it was not. Even here, even now, safe in the dark and alone, he felt the meshing of all the conflicts in her, in him, and wondered what meeting was and why her kiss had only filled him with pity, and he sighed.

She had sensed his smile. She responded to it, by running one finger along his cheekbone, a gesture that ran through him like quicksilver, and in an instant he bent down and covered her face with kisses, held her chin in his hand and kissed her again and again, until they were breathless, and laughed.

"It's awful not to be able to see your face," she whispered, laying the palm of her hand along his cheek and pressing it as if she were to mold it in her hand.

"Tom?"

"Yes—"

"It's different—now———"

"Yes." In the first year when she had not wanted to bring him home to her family, when she had wanted to keep him secret, they had been lovers, once in a hotel in New York, once in his room at college, and they had sat in his car wrapped round each other, her dress unbuttoned, feverish, clumsy lovers who felt starved all the time. Now it was as if time had opened out for them at last, and they did not have to snatch at each other.

He leaned over her and pressed his head hard against her breast. And lying under him against the earth, looking up into the dark pine branches and to a single star floating somewhere in space a million miles away, she felt rooted, and this root, which went through her breast into the earth, hurt. It was so entirely different from anything she had ever felt, so much graver and deeper, that she couldn't speak.

After a long time she stroked his head, feeling the hair under her hand, thick and strong and life-giving as if she had never felt it before. He seemed like a stranger, a star fallen out of the sky into her arms, impersonal and great. He gave a long sigh like a groan, and she felt his legs tighten over hers and the thrust of life there, and turned her head back and forth and said in a new harsh voice, "Kiss me."

But he didn't kiss her. He took her head in his hands and she could feel his eyes searching hers in the dark.

"Betsy."

"Yes."

"I want to wait. I want to wait until we are married."

She was shivering now with the cold, with the extremity

of feeling, too, as if she had been straining to take in more than she could understand.

"You're cold, darling. We must go back."

"What's happened, Tom?" she asked, when they were standing again, his arm around her waist, and he was leading her very carefully, stooping to avoid the branches his right hand felt for as they crept along, the smell of earth and spruce strong all around them.

"I don't know."

"I think I do."

He waited a long moment for her to speak, but she could not say it in words. She clasped his hand and they walked on. I think it is that we are beginning to exchange our souls, she thought, and so every gesture is very grave. Was that it? And what a strange word to be thinking of, "soul." But everything now with Tom took her out into worlds where she had never been. She felt his warmth as a positive healing thing, felt it more here where he moved among her family in such an unexpectedly unguarded, giving way.

"The island," she whispered. "Everything has more reality here——"

Just then they saw a figure come out on the porch and peer out toward them.

"Is that you, Betsy? Tom?" Frances said in her bright anxious voice. "You'll catch cold. You didn't even take coats."

The change from what they had been saying and this totally incongruous interruption was so abrupt and violent, that Betsy tugged at Tom's arm as if to flee back into the woods, but he held her firmly, as he answered, "We were just coming in, Mrs. Wyeth."

Slowly they climbed the steps, as if they had to take time to prepare their public faces.

"Come to the fire," Frances said, "you must be frozen."

But they stood just outside the pool of light a second. Sprig was sitting under the lamp, a book open in his hands; he had evidently been reading aloud. And as they stood there, he lifted his head and saw his daughter in one of those flashes of perception, gone in an instant, hardly registered, so swift is the image as it passes—saw her as Aphrodite rising from the wave, standing as if on tiptoe, larger than life, he thought, radiant, wrapped in tenderness as in a cloak.

"Well," he said drily. "What did you see?"

Betsy stood very straight and met his glance with wide-open, gentle eyes. Then she laughed, "Nothing much—just ourselves."

"We heard an owl," Lucy said from her place on the sofa. "It sounded like a ghost."

They're magic, Frances thought, as Tom and Betsy came forward. They draw a magic circle round themselves, and everything else in the world is left out. How long does it last? she wondered, putting a hand quite unconsciously to her heart—two years, three years? Never forever. Things —children, life—break into the circle—I broke into it, just now. And she wanted to cry out to them, "Take it while it's there. Take it all. It's flowing through your hands like a river and someday it will be gone." She turned to Sprig, "Go on, Sprig. We're just coming to that wonderful part," she said, for he was reading "The Wind in the Willows." Aunt Jane, meanwhile, had gone fast asleep, and was smiling in her sleep.

*

CHAPTER SEVEN

IT was Lucy's last day. She and Frances were engaged in taming the garden, for even this cultivated patch, a semicircle cleared out with the green lawn in front of it and a ring of spruce behind it, even this man-made haven tended to go back to wilderness. The petunias spread all over the place. A new weed appeared each year and had to be rooted out; the roses had the blight, and it was touch and go whether the delphinium had survived the winter. To Mr. Silence, however, who made various bowers here, it was unchanged, and he was lying now, his paws tucked in beneath him, like a placid Rousseau tiger under a big rosebush.

Frances stood up and stretched, drinking in deep breaths of the air as if it were a restorative. Then she fumbled about in her jeans for a cigarette.

"Time for a break," she said, watching Lucy pull up another weed with angry satisfaction.

"This does me good," Lucy said. "What a wonderful outlet for frustration, for aggression——" and she turned back as if she couldn't bear to stop, her hair coming undone, her face flushed, looking, Frances thought, wonderfully untidy and happy.

"Come and have a cigarette and talk to me," Frances commanded.

71

"I don't want to talk," Lucy smiled, "I want to be left in peace to root out weeds and feel self-righteously angry. You talk," she said mischievously, "and I'll weed."

So Frances threw her pillow down and sat, looking out to sea.

"Funny how disturbing Tom and Betsy were——"

"Were?" Lucy asked.

"Well, he's gone after all—we still have the summer ahead." Again the mythical vision of the summer as an opening out into peace and family happiness took possession of her. Soon they must plan a picnic to Baker's Island, spend a day lazing around on the rocks. Everything would be as it always was. There would be bursts of irritation, people going off to brood alone on distant rocks, and a slow tide of warmth and intimacy rising as the afternoon wore on. They would be islanders, safe from intrusion. Frances sighed.

"Why were they disturbing?" Lucy asked, without turning her head. She frowned and yanked up a weed with a very long root, which dangled from her hands as she held it up in triumph. "Look at that!"

"Passion is disturbing," Frances said.

"Absolute, exclusive, and so not quite human perhaps," Lucy answered. "I'll have a cigarette after all."

"What is it really all about? And what happens when it goes?"

"Shells, seaweed, a nice flat beach. When it goes one consoles oneself by imagining that it was not very important, after all. That's what I thought until this thing happened. Now I don't know, Frances. I thought loving took

72

its place—less exclusive, less absolute, more tolerant, more human, easier to live with——" She threw up her hands in a funny awkward gesture.

"When people are shy it may be the only way to communicate love," Frances said after a moment, rubbing her hand back and forth over the grass absent-mindedly.

Lucy lifted her head and said nothing. "What with Tom, what with me, you've had rather a lot thrown at you lately, darling, haven't you?"

"It's awful to be married to someone you'll never hold, elusive as running water—that's Sprig."

"You've neither of you ever looked at anyone else. Maybe elusive loves last longer," Lucy said, in her practical voice.

"It's tiring," Frances murmured, "never to know, never to be sure. Just now you asked why Tom and Betsy were disturbing—I think I know why. They seem married already in a way I have never been. I'm jealous," and she laughed a light laugh, to cover having said so much. "Oh Lucy——"

"There's death in possession," Lucy said quietly. "That's what I'm beginning to understand."

"For them?" Frances turned intensely and looked Lucy straight in the eyes.

"Perhaps not. Betsy is so maternal. She'll translate it all into her children."

Frances, troubled, turned back to the weeding to think this over in silence.

The sun poured down on their backs and for quite

some time there was no sound at all, as the two women knelt and worked. Mr. Silence, too hot at last, yawned, stretched, and walked away. As always when she was with Lucy, Frances found all kinds of ideas and sensations opening up inside her. It was as if Lucy held a key no one else did, could open doors securely locked even against Sprig, walked quite casually in as if opening a locked door were nothing at all. There were no barriers, was that it? The exchange was everything—it was not the way into love, or the way anywhere at all. For this reason their hours together had the taste of eternity, were consoling like pure poetry, and went on haunting as a line of poetry will. When Frances spoke, the words came out of a long silence.

"Maybe possession has death in it, but I wonder whether withholding doesn't have death in it, too, the fear of being possessed or of possessing—especially of possessing because of the responsibility. You know?"

"No," Lucy said, "I don't. Whatever are you talking about?"

"Haven't you heard Sprig say over and over about a friend, 'He never feeds on you, lets you alone'—that's what he wants: to be let alone."

"We want the impossible—to be lovers, wives, friends, all in one." Lucy lay back now, a little drunk with the sun, dots and dashes of light flashing behind her closed lids.

"And why not? Of course we do. And why not?" Frances asked passionately. "I'll never settle for less."

"Poor Sprig," Lucy said mischievously.

"No," Frances' hand flew to her heart, "don't."

"Maybe you just have to accept things as they are," Lucy added, reaching over to squeeze Frances' arm fraternally.

"It sounds so depressing."

"I would accept—accept John's mistress, accept anything—you don't know what you're talking about." For just a second Lucy's blue eyes went black. She was angry. And Frances was appalled, saw suddenly the immense gulf between her perilous happiness and Lucy's being cut off altogether, stopped, allowed no way out, no compromise.

"No," she said, bowing her head, "I don't. Forgive me."

*

CHAPTER EIGHT

ALL the day of the Fourth people had gone out onto the porch to scan the sky and the sea, to frown at a low bank of clouds in the west, to tap the barometer which stayed rather maddeningly at variable. Uncle Joe, Jane's younger brother, was making his yearly visit, and then Bill Waterford, Sprig's friend, had turned up for the night, unexpectedly. So it had seemed important to have a good day. Bill was one guest they all welcomed without reservation, and especially since he had come this time without Nora, his wife. Somehow she had never quite fitted in. But Bill, a Professor of French at the University, brought a gust of life with him wherever he went, sailed with Caleb, argued religion with Gran-Quan, and made Sprig himself sparkle. On top of all this excitement, there had been various crises: the lobsters were late; Betsy dropped a box of eggs and broke four; Frances lost her temper; and when Aunt Jane murmured that she thought perhaps she would stay home this year, Gran-Quan, who considered that since he had made the enormous effort of getting up and dressing, no one had any right to renege, just glared at her and said, "I won't go if you don't." But by late afternoon the gauzy, gentle day had acted like a balm; it was, after all, to be fair; it was in fact the most perfect evening for fireworks anyone could imagine, and the only anxiety now was whether there would be enough wind in Caleb's sails. He had set out ahead with Betsy and Bill Waterford to start a fire and unpack the baskets.

The Fourth of July picnic, so eagerly planned and looked forward to, rather often turned out badly after all. It was a risk in these parts to expect the weather to conform to man's desires; a high wind could make landing on the rocky island quite a perilous affair: there was the memorable occasion when Uncle Joe, immaculate in white linen, slipped on a rock as the skiff bobbed up and down at landing; there was the year of the terrible thunderstorm when God rather ostentatiously took over the fireworks. But this year, Aunt Jane thought, when they were finally all settled in the launch—this year is just perfect. I hope I'll feel a little less queer out in the air. I hope I shan't spoil it by being ill, for indeed the boat on the glassy calm seemed to her to be swaying up and down in a most peculiar way and she saw everything through a mist.

She sat between her brother Joe and Gran-Quan who had behaved very badly getting into the boat, and now possibly felt remorse. At any rate he was silent, his eyes half closed. Frances had curled up in the stern. Sprig, as usual, sat in the bow beside the fat, black dog, stroking it absentmindedly and talking with Captain John.

They chugged slowly out into the channel, lapsing into one of those timeless moments when a family is gathered together and at peace. After all, Aunt Jane thought, I wouldn't have missed it for anything.

She sat facing the island as they followed the channel, and the scene unrolled before her like a dream: there was the swimming pool now. The farmer's children shouted and waved as the launch came into view; then it rounded the point and all they could see was deep woods coming right down to the shore. It was years since Aunt Jane had walked out here, and she turned to Joe to smile as they caught a glimpse of a high bank of rocks where they had fished when they were children. No word was needed; memory alone made the bridge.

Just at this moment Sprig turned and gave her one of his shy smiles. This is happiness, she thought, lifting her hand to wave an answer, as if he were far away and not just there in the bow. But she seemed to have lost all sense of space and time and it felt as if she were waving to Sprig down all the years and from far away. They're all right, she thought. The image floated before her of Sprig at four and Hester at six, sitting in the nursery at dusk, on one of those interminable evenings just after their mother died when it seemed as if the dark coming on flowed all around them like loneliness, and they were so strangely self-contained. Hester, she remembered, had a Teddy bear on her lap and was feeding him from a cup of milk.

"He's not hungry. He hates it." Sprig had said in his clear piping voice.

Why just this scene, just now? All around them the ocean sighed, and Aunt Jane turned her head to look away from people, to look at the long white wake behind a large motor yacht which had just passed them. They rocked on the wake, and again she felt dizzy. I mustn't, she thought. I must hold on to it all a little longer.

"I bet your Greek islands can't beat this," Sprig said, turning to Joe with one of those quick glancing movements of his head. They had come out onto the bay and all around them, scattered on the still blue surface, the other islands came into view, the dark firs, the pink and burnished rocks, and far off a horizon turning slowly rose.

"Maine at its best is pretty hard to beat," Joe conceded. "But it is not the wine-dark sea, not quite," he said, taking out a slim Manila cigar and lighting it deliberately.

"We cannot remember Greece," Aunt Jane heard herself saying, "but we remember this."

"Whatever are you talking about?" Gran-Quan roused himself. "I remember Greece perfectly though I've never been there." He shook himself like a dog and raised his head, turning toward Joe, with a mischievous smile, and recited:

> "The isles of Greece, the isles of Greece
> Where burning Sappho, loved and sung,
> Where grew the arts of war and peace
> Where Delos rose and Phoebus sprung!
> Eternal summer gilds them yet
> But all, except their sun, is set."

"Lucky man, you've kept your memory," Joe said, puffing at his cigar.

"Only for what I learned as a youth. One forgets the present."

"Well," Joe twinkled, for he always liked to prick Gran-

Quan's balloons of self-pity, "we have our memories, of course, but they can hardly be compared to the accretion of thoughts and dreams around Greece. . . . I remember, for instance, Mrs. Brooks Cabot bicycling in bloomers round Mount Desert." He chuckled. "Quite a sight in those days."

But Aunt Jane, who had come to rest against Quan's shoulder and felt the laughter and appreciation heaving in him, said nothing. She was rocked on the deep; she was beyond them all, comforted by the quiet sky. She did not even rouse herself before the impending argument or feel that she must ward it off. They are all children, she thought, *we* are all children.

Frances looked at Sprig's back, sitting there a few feet away from her, then turned to follow with her eyes the long expanding ripple of their wake. She felt wonderfully free of responsibility; for once lists did not preoccupy even the background of her thoughts. This is happiness, she thought, letting her hand trail for a moment in the icy water. Not to do, but to be; not to know, but to be. Yet at the very instant of repose she needed to find the absolute demarcation of happiness and of being, so she walked up to the bow and put her hand on Sprig's sleeve.

Of course with Captain John there beside them, he would never respond. His hand stroked the old dog's head; he looked out to sea.

"I wonder if Caleb was able to land all right," he said.

"Oh, I expect so," Captain John answered. "There's a little breeze now. Caleb is a good sailor."

"He would stay close to shore to get the wind."

"Might," said Captain John, shifting his pipe. "Might not."

They were off in the masculine world where the question of winds might be discussed between long silences for half an hour. She let her hand fall, turned back to look at the three old people sitting side by side, and was struck by Aunt Jane's pallor.

"Are you all right, dear?" she asked, kneeling down to look up into Aunt Jane's face.

"It's so peaceful," Aunt Jane murmured, laying her hand on Frances' head for a second.

"Would a drop of brandy do you good?"

"Nonsense, Jane's all right," Gran-Quan growled.

"A drop of brandy sounds rather a good idea," Joe said, giving Frances a conspiratory nod.

"I shall be quite drunk," Aunt Jane murmured, "but never mind. If Joe would like a drop, I'll take a sip of his."

She did not feel ill now, but only dissolved, as if she were about to become a mist, to follow the air and the water. She simply felt immensely weak. And the brandy, when she finally got it to her mouth, for her hand was shaking in a most idiotic way, was in the true sense of the word a cordial.

Frances, watching her anxiously, felt as if she could see life flowing back into the paper-white thin cheeks, into the fading eyes, and would have knelt there in the launch and passionately kissed the tiny birdlike hands, had she dared.

Joe coughed as he tipped his own tiny silver cup back and breathed it in with evident enjoyment. "Ah," he said, "quite a restorative," and he laid an arm affectionately along his sister's thin shoulders. They did not see each other very often; he, the youngest, was also the one of them all who was the least interested in family affairs. His house on Beacon Hill was a different world from Cambridge, was in fact "The World," as the world goes now on the Hill. He had come back from his years in the diplomatic service, to find that almost all his old friends, the nucleus of society, had scattered out to the outskirts of Milton, Beverly Farms, Bedford, Concord, but he was a club man and needed, so he often said, to be within walking distance of The Tavern Club and the Athenaeum. He stayed on, watching sardonically the encroachments as one great house after another was taken over by a World Federation of something or other, by a Divinity School or a Union for the Preservation of Birdlife. He had indulged himself without qualms in a life of aesthetic pleasures, the only one of the lot, he thought as he sat there in the launch and felt the brandy making his heart beat rather fast, the only one not to be ridden with anxiety and guilt. Yet he did feel at this moment a peculiar tenderness toward this older sister who had never approved of him, but who had cultivated tolerance as others cultivate their passions, and so had always welcomed him without a shadow of reproof in her clear blue eyes.

Now, filled like a hummingbird with just a thimbleful of brandy, she turned to him, her eyes very bright, and asked, "Isn't it queer, Joe? I feel ever so much better. Isn't it lovely to be here all together? I really hate to reach the island"—she lowered her voice, glancing in Sprig's direction—"I mean just the family, don't you know? And now, my dear, you must tell me what you've been doing. Whatever happened to that young man you told me about, the painter—was it? —or did he play the pianoforte?"

"Peter Wood? Oh, he's off to Paris to study with Nadia Boulanger, lucky boy. What I mind about growing old, Jane, is not being able to have any long dreams any more. I shall never know whether he has the real thing in him—but he's not a painter; he's a composer. You're confusing him with Percy, that was years ago—Percy was a great disappointment," and Joe retreated for a moment into the memories of various young men whom he had adopted and launched, this being his most notable extravagance, one which had caused a good deal of malicious gossip. Yet the odd thing was—as Aunt Jane always stoutly maintained—that it was just here that Joe was at his very best and had indeed given something back to the life from which he had drawn so lavishly for his own pleasures. "People believe the worst of Joe just where he's a unique individual and a real giver," she had said more than once. Besides, she was more and more convinced that nothing was more dangerous than to pigeon-hole people. Quan, for instance—she turned to observe him for a second (Was he all right?). He was feeling moody, of course. He and Joe were like fire and water, really. Quan actually was a selfish egotist of the first water, while Joe, who pretended to be interested only in himself, had done a great deal of good. "What a mystery it all is," she said aloud.

"Families? Or Joe? Or the young man who is studying

with Nadia Boulanger?" Sprig asked, twinkling at her and coming to join the group, so now Frances and he were sitting on the floor at the feet of the three old ones.

"Families," she answered briskly.

"Ill-assorted groups of people flung together by accident," Gran-Quan growled. "I have been thinking," he announced "that we, for instance, have next to nothing in common except the fact that we have shared certain things —forcibly shared them."

"For once we are in complete agreement, Quan," Joe answered, smiling.

"Well," Frances said, looking at the three men quizzically, "you have one thing in common. You all like elegance; you all of you like good clothes, the best materials. And you all suspect the *exalté*, except, of course, your own peculiar form of it. You disapprove of excess on principle and each indulge in one notable excess of your own invention. Oh, there are resemblances," she ended, the mockery in her voice not concealing the tenderness.

"Frances is being wicked," Joe said with evident satisfaction. He had always approved of Frances; she had an air. "What excesses?" he asked, egging her on. "You must be precise. You can't throw large generalities of this sort around."

"Excessive self-doubt." Aunt Jane was still excited by the brandy, her cheeks flushed.

"Yes—and that's father's doing," Quan said fiercely. "Do you realize, Joe, that he never praised us, never? Made me feel like a nincompoop from the time I was born. Brow-beat Jane. Despised you," he said gloomily.

"Sometimes it seems as if families were like tides—one generation is on a rising tide; the next on an ebbing one. People behind us loom a little larger than life," Frances said. "My parents seem like giants to me, even now."

Sprig chuckled. "I on the other hand am a pygmy to my children, some sort of peculiar little dwarf creature."

"What nonsense, Sprig!" Aunt Jane's eyes flashed.

"Look, there they are—they've landed!" Captain John announced to the company at large. The moment burst like a bubble and all eyes turned toward the island ahead, irregular pile of rocks that looked as if a giant had played at making a fort out there in the middle of the sea. The sail boat was anchored, sails safely down, and they could see the skiff bobbing along beside the one flat place where landings could safely be made. Caleb, Betsy, and Bill Waterford had climbed up to a higher rock and were waving at the launch like explorers greeting a later expedition.

Do they look on us as pygmies, Frances asked herself? Caleb stood with his legs apart like a sailor and waved with long exaggerated sweeps of his arm. As they drew nearer they could see he was smiling. Betsy stood rather stiffly and self-consciously, frowning, as if she were trying to single out their separate faces.

"Well," Sprig was saying, "we've made it."

Yes, Aunt Jane answered him, silently, as if for her at least it had been a long arduous journey, and she could not quite believe it was over. Would she be able to manage getting in and out of the skiff? There never was any real arrival, she thought. One arrived somewhere, but one always had to go on. It was never finished. The huge effort of living went on. . . .

An hour or so later they sat in small groups, watching the perfect round red sun disappear into a dark gray bank of cloud. Behind them the horizon had melted already into the night and a planet was swimming into view, almost as if it were floating on water and not on air. The litter of paper cups and plates and pieces of lettuce and lobster had all been burned or tidied up into baskets and boxes, and only Aunt Jane, her back resting against a rock, was slowly finishing her blueberry pie, drinking in the silence after all the noise and laughter. Bill Waterford and Sprig had been making mock translations of mock poems, roaring with laughter at their own jokes and enjoying each other so much that the others found themselves an audience, and the laughter a contagion. She had watched this antic Sprig, this suddenly young foolish Sprig with delight—it was Bill's doing of course. Life flowed out of him as if it cost nothing, life and a kind of lively affection which made people rise up out of apathy or self-distrust and let out buried selves like djinn out of bottles. Aunt Jane smiled. There Bill was now, sitting cross-legged, the crest of strong gray hair standing straight up on his head and his eyes crinkled up with laughter, an ebullient heavy man who walked on light feet, and talked with his hands like a Frenchman.

The circle broke up, Caleb walking over to the other side of the island to get the fireworks ready with Captain John. Betsy was sitting off on a rock by herself. Frances and the two old men stayed close to Aunt Jane. This group watched Bill Waterford and Sprig walk off to where they could talk in private, watched them as if they were magnets, more alive than anyone else, watched them a little jealously perhaps, for Sprig would never laugh with me like that, Frances was thinking, even as she smiled with pleasure at his evident happiness, felt in a queer way released by his release, and turned to look up at Aunt Jane's dear face, to catch the fleeting smile that just brushed her eyelids and the corners of her mouth, as she laid down her spoon.

"Someone should write a poem in praise of blueberry pie," she said. "That was most delicious."

"I ate too much," Gran-Quan announced lugubriously.

"I drank too much," Uncle Joe answered. "We're getting old, Quan." He had felt this like a pang, as Bill and Sprig performed—had felt too the old sore that Sprig had never been willing to confide in him. There had been one brief moment, just after this odd nephew came back from Japan, and stopped off in the Philippines where Uncle Joe was Vice-Consul. There far away from home, and keyed up by his adventures like a man in love, Sprig had seemed on the brink of really paying attention. They had gone on a long drive, Joe remembered, and Sprig had said, rather as if one were talking about going to school, "I shall get married, I suppose."

"Why do you suppose so? You don't have to. Are you

in love?" he had said testily. He had not wanted the intrusion of a woman between them at just that moment. He resented the very idea.

"I don't know," Sprig had answered, and shut up like a clam.

"You'll tie yourself down, have children, get involved in all sorts of responsibility and bother, never feel like yourself again," Joe had said. It was close to a confession.

Sprig had given him one of those quizzical, penetrating looks. "I wonder," he had answered. "Do I feel like myself now?"

Does he feel like himself now? Joe asked himself, as he observed the intimacy between the two men, the way they talked, with long lapses into silence, their heads bent, flicking cigarette ash into the water. He has never really amounted to anything like what he might have, what he was capable of. Yet he impresses people. When his name comes up at The Tavern, it is received with respect. People respect him—I wonder why. Covertly he looked at Frances, Frances with her electrical anguish and joy, Frances in whom the current of life seemed never to be turned off. A good marriage? The marriage of opposites? Maybe.

And as if she felt his eyes on her face, Frances put up a hand to her cheek, turned and gave him a rather merry, conspiratorial glance.

"A penny for your thoughts," he responded at once.

"Frances doesn't think. She feels," Quan growled. "She's a machine for registering feeling. No woman thinks," he said as if this were a personal affront, a cause of his own private suffering.

"A penny for your feelings then. I stand corrected," and Joe winked at her.

"I was thinking about Caleb and Betsy—how solemn they are. Does one have to be grown-up to play? To enjoy oneself the way Bill and Sprig do in their crazy moods?"

"They don't play in front of us, would be my guess," Joe answered, "too self-conscious."

"We talk about them as if they were some strange breed, as if we watched them across an abyss, as if we could never understand them," Frances said, taking out a cigarette. "I have a much better relationship with my future son-in-law—as a matter of fact."

"Oh well, parents and children!" Joe said, shrugging his shoulders.

Just then Caleb appeared on a rock above them, "We're about ready!" he shouted, excitement in his voice. "I can hardly wait to see that peacock tail, Uncle Joe."

Bill was on his feet at once and jumping over the rocks.

There was quite a bustle. Quan had to be helped to move, groaning, of course, all the way; Aunt Jane, too, though Sprig really lifted her in his arms, she was so light.

Before they were settled on the other side of the rocks, facing the darkness of open sea now, the Roman candles had begun to go off, making a low rushing sound, then bursting into sputtery flame, picking up impetus, and ending in a fine swishing sizzle, as they went out one by one.

The light picked up the faces like a beam that went on and off, and in a second of darkness, Sprig took Frances' hand and clasped it hard.

Betsy felt the tears pricking her eyes, as they always did at fireworks. She felt lonely for Tom, wanting to share with him everything that touched her, feeling acutely the pang of his not being here.

There was suddenly a terrific bang, hair-raising, which made everyone jump and hands go up to ears. After such a frightening noise, a couple of feeble, lighted balls shot out over the water and dribbled out.

"That was a dud all right," Caleb said.

But immediately, and before anyone had time to realize what was happening, a bright-tailed comet shot up into the dusky air, made a soft plop, and shattered into a rain of small gold and silver stars, a fountain of stars, which faded out one by one and dropped softly down into the water.

"Oh," Frances sighed, and "oh" again as the last star went out. "How beautiful!" If only, she thought, we could hold onto it for just a second, just keep it one more second —so much given and so much taken away, all in an instant.

"Do you remember them in Japan?" Uncle Joe bent down to ask Sprig, who was sitting just below beside his wife.

"Indeed, indeed I do," he said, hugging his knees.

But this pure delight was followed by a series of very noisy ones, a cannonade. Gran-Quan slipped an arm through his sister's. "I hate the noise," he said querulously. "Why do they have to be so noisy?"

There was no answer, and no response from the frail

arm. But he did not notice, for just then, another of the great comets shot out above their heads and they all looked up, turning eager faces toward the exquisite slow fall of stars.

"You haven't quoted 'brightness falls from the air,' Quan," Joe reminded him. "Surely we are not to be deprived of that."

"Too noisy," Quan managed to roar through another cannonade.

"Now, ladies and gentlemen," Caleb announced in the silence that followed, "I am about to set off the grand finale, known as the peacock's tail—imported for this occasion by Joe Wyeth, imported from Germany—how could you Uncle Joe?" he teased. "I ask perfect silence. Captain John, are you ready?"

"Ready, Admiral," Captain John said.

"Very well, sir, fire!"

For just a second there was perfect quiet, only all around them the gentle creeping sound of the waves lapping at the rocks; the ocean a great dim presence, and overhead a few stars, millions of light miles away. It was a moment of high suspense, and each person there gathered himself together and held his breath.

There was one loud bang, then a series of slithering rushes as four projectiles swam up at high speed, and burst, exploding into green and blue lights which fanned out, grew larger and burst; each of these released a dozen or so sparkling stars, which fell very very slowly and shone out over the water, a mirror that reflected the whole scene to make a shining double image.

Frances turned to see whether Aunt Jane was transported by this piece of magic as she herself was. She was startled to see the small head bent down—had she fallen asleep in all that noise and glory?

"Sprig," Frances clutched his arm hard, "Aunt Jane."

But before Sprig could turn, Uncle Joe said in a very quiet tone of voice, "Jane is dead."

"Joe, are you sure?" Sprig asked, without moving, where he stood.

"Yes, she must have just slipped away, hardly knowing——"

No one touched her. No one moved.

For a moment Frances, whose first instinct had been to protect Gran-Quan, thought he had not taken in what had happened. He just sat there, his chin leaning on his cane, his eyes very bright, wide open.

All the others had risen to their feet so there was a semi-circle round the tiny seated figure, the bent head, of her who was no longer one of them.

"I can't believe it," Joe said in a cracked voice, as if from far away, "are you quite sure? Couldn't we bring her back —some brandy . . ." He made a helpless gesture with his arm.

Bill and Captain John were kneeling now, one on each side of her, Bill feeling the wrist for the faintest possible pulse. "I think there's nothing we can do," Bill said.

"We must get her home. Help me," Sprig came forward and together the two men lifted the light bundle in their arms and carried it away from the others down to the landing rock. Captain John, who had run ahead, was already untying the rope on the skiff.

"Come, Gran-Quan," Frances said gently, "we are going home."

She could feel the heavy sobs rising in his chest, as she leaned her head for a moment against his shoulder.

"Caleb, some coffee for Gran-Quan—quick——"

She couldn't bear not to be with Aunt Jane, not to be down there with Sprig and Bill and Captain John, and it seemed an excruciating burden to have, just now, to cope with Gran-Quan. She was hardly aware of the tears streaming down her cheeks, but as they fell on his hands, he suddenly straightened up and put an arm around her where she was kneeling, and drew out of himself some unexpected reserve of real strength, of virility. "All is well with her, Frances dear. It would be wrong to grieve."

So, she thought, he must have been when he was still a minister in the church, calm and gentle and powerful. It had all flowed back into him for this supreme moment. He had lifted his head, the great tremor which she had felt in his chest, all gone, and now he spoke very distinctly and gravely, those lines which he had loved to remember on each Fourth of July,

> "Brightness falls from the air;
> Queens have died young and fair;
> Dust hath closed Helen's eye;
> I am sick, I must die,
> Lord, have mercy on us."

Caleb stood with a paper cup of coffee in his hands and waited. They all stood there, as if under a spell.

"Thank you, Quan," Joe said.

Indeed, an extraordinary peace had come over the group. No one hurried. Frances quietly planned the return home, Caleb and Betsy to sail alone, and all the others to go together with Aunt Jane. No one felt like talking. They gathered up the baskets in silence, stopping once on the way down to the skiff, as if all lifted up on the same wave of feeling, to look back at the darkening ocean behind them, and up at the immense permanently star-filled sky, that showed no trace now of the evanescent brightness of the fireworks, but had taken it all in and absorbed it. They watched Caleb's oars rise and fall as he rowed his sister out to the sailboat, watched the white sail unfurl and slowly swell and the silent boat slip away. Once Caleb turned and lifted his hand in a grave salute.

Frances sat beside Quan in the launch. In the last half hour something had happened between them, some communion, some resting within each other which had never happened before. Perhaps it was that she had come to respect him; of them all, it was his world which had broken to pieces, and yet he had been able to find comfort and to give them comfort. Dear Quan, she thought, and she thought, now Aunt Jane has gone perhaps he and all of us will have finally to grow up.

Betsy sat beside Caleb in the stern. He was absorbed at first in getting into the channel, and she took comfort in the usualness, for they always had sailed like this, preferring to be silent. In fact Caleb was furious when people, as he said, wanted to spoil a good sail with a lot of talk.

"They're off," he said, turning back once to see the launch which would soon overtake them and be there long before they would, starting up, hearing the familiar put-put-put come across the waters.

"I suppose Gran-Quan will have to come and live with us now," Betsy said suddenly.

"Christ," Caleb said, "do you suppose he will?"

"Poor Mother!"

"Tom said they had a feeble-minded aunt come and live with them for years—he thought such things didn't happen to rich people, as he calls us."

But Caleb was not in the mood to respond to tales of Tom Dorgan.

"I thought she'd live forever," he said. "I never believed she would die. Even though everyone talked about it. It's much easier to imagine the young dying than the old, somehow."

"Not Father and Mother!" Betsy protested.

"Yes. I've imagined it over and over. Haven't you? It seems to me I've lived with the idea since I was about three years old."

"I haven't. Not till this moment. Oh Caleb——" and suddenly she burst into tears.

"Listen, Betsy, please——" Caleb sounded quite angry.

She felt it was somehow an insult to his boat that she could cry in it.

"For God's sake don't cry," he said in his angry voice.

"Why not?" she answered back, just as crossly. "Nothing lasts. It's all such hell."

"Not for you; you're getting out of all this. You won't have to live with Gran-Quan. You're in love."

"That doesn't mean I have no feelings."

"Doesn't it? It seems to me you're scarcely part of the family any more. All you do is wait for the mail and write letters all day, or moon around——"

"I thought you didn't care about the family. I thought you hated the very idea of family."

It was quite true, Caleb realized, that was how he thought he felt, that was what he had said many a time to Betsy.

"I wonder how Father will take this," he said, as if there were some connection. "Sometimes they seem so innocent —vulnerable—I don't know. They've been protected from such a damn lot. They're so horribly good. Look, they're rounding the island now——"

He drew in sail a bit and the boat veered, running right in along the coast. The island looked very black and secret as they sailed beside it, lonely. . . .

"I wish I didn't feel so guilty," Caleb blurted out suddenly.

"About them?"

"Yes."

"I know," she said again. And the rest of the conversation took place without words, because they had come close to the heart of something that couldn't really be spoken about at all, too painful, too difficult—the intolerable burden.

Shall we never never feel that the debt has been paid, Caleb was thinking to himself, that we are free to go in peace?

PART TWO

Children of the Ice Age

CHAPTER ONE

"H I!" Betsy called, standing just inside the door of the
family house, looking up the long flight of stairs.
There was no answer. She walked through to the kitchen.
No one. The tea tray was set, as usual, and automatically she
went to the sink and filled the kettle, lit the gas, and set the
water to boil. There must be someone here, she thought, but
the perfect silence, the reverberating silence of the house
after her impulsive, excited walk here through the spring,
held her like a spell. She tiptoed back into the parlor and
stood there, feeling like a ghost. Then she heard a tiny
creak, followed by another, and then another. Sure enough,
Mr. Silence appeared in the doorway, stopped to lick one
paw, and then sat quite upright and gave her a long thoughtful look.

He blinked his eyes, narrowed them a little, and gave a
hopeful "Mrrrr?" as he stepped very delicately toward her.

"I know," she scratched him behind the ears and under
the chin. "You want a lap."

So, of course, she had to sit down and allow herself to
be thoroughly kneaded on the thighs while the faint purrs
rose to a throbbing roar, and then finally Mr. Silence curled
himself up in a perfect round and closed his eyes. She held

one soft paw in her hand, feeling the claws move gently in and out, prickling her palm a little, but careful (it seemed) not to hurt. And as the big gentle cat imposed his rhythm upon her, the bubble of excitement she had been carrying subsided, and she was wonderfully at peace. "Poor Mr. Silence," she said, "poor old kitten." She had never thought of him as a kitten before, but now he had become one suddenly, because she was a new person, a woman bearing a child, and this (she realized now) had shifted her whole life and every one of her relationships, even that to dear old Mr. Silence.

She heard steps, bouncing heavy steps, and Caleb, having thrown himself against the door like a projectile, gave one glance into the parlor, grunted, threw his trench coat onto the radiator and asked,

"Where is everybody?"

"I don't know," she said, incapable of movement, or even of response, she was being jerked so violently out of her round fulfilling dream into Caleb's harsh world. He stood there, half in the room and half out, blacker, more definite than ever. She admired very much, she always had, his compactness, the furious neat way he took a cigarette out and lit it.

"May I have one? I can't move——"

He threw the package and the matches half across the room, and Mr. Silence jumped down, without a parting look, and walked out.

"You brute, Caleb, you've made him go!" She got up.

"He hates cigarette smoke anyway, and besides you looked far too relaxed and cosy."

Betsy didn't answer. She went into the kitchen and stood absent-mindedly at the window, the teapot in her hands. Down at the end of the garden, she saw her mother, very far away as if in a dream, bent over the big flower bed, weeding, her quick hands moving furiously, wrenching out weeds, flinging them into the small wheelbarrow at her side. Betsy leaned forward to wrench the window open,

"Ma!" she called. "The kettle's boiling. Come and have tea!"

"Good gracious, it's Betsy—I'll be right along," her mother cried, but she could not resist one last look, one last furious attack on the weeds. It was such a little thing, nothing at all, but it struck Betsy to the heart, so vulnerable had she become since she had seen the doctor. It hurt that her mother turned back with that passion to the garden when she, Betsy, was here, was here with enormous news, was here, and nobody cared after all.

She cut bread and butter very carefully, warmed the teapot, took down the Earl Gray from the top shelf (for it was going to be the best tea today, whatever anyone said) and all the time she was frowning. She wished she had not come. She wanted to be at home with Tommy, sitting on his lap, in the only world that was really her own, where she belonged.

"Darling, how lovely to see you," said her mother's rather high excited voice. "I can't kiss you—I've got to wash."

She waved her hands at Betsy happily. "I'll be right down," and suddenly the empty shell of the house reverberated. Betsy could hear, ringing out, "Tea, Caleb—are you there?" The sound of rushing water and through it, another cry, "Betsy, beat the gong. Pa's in his office!"

Betsy opened the back door and just caught the last rays of the sun flashing deep gold on the windows of the barn where Sprig Wyeth worked. He's there, Betsy thought, leading his secret life which we have never penetrated, which we know so little about, my father, always a stranger. And she hit the gong hard, delighted to have this power in her hands, to make him pay attention and come, ambling as he now did, frowning against the light, sending Betsy, across the emerald green of the lawn, a little nonchalant wave of his hand. She ran down the back steps and into his arms.

"Well, well," he said, extricating himself. "What's all this? We haven't seen you for ages. Everything all right?"

"Fine, thank you." They walked the rest of the way side by side, leaving the golden sun behind them. "I want my tea." He was hardly listening, and looked down at Hannah who was standing at the bottom of the steps wagging her tail.

"You can do it, you know," he told her in a gentle voice. "You spoiled old thing," but of course (Betsy knew the whole rite by heart) he capitulated and went down again to lift the lazy old lady up, talked to her in the infinitely tender tones which the Wyeths reserved for animals. "But where's my darling girl?" Tom said. "Where's my black-hearted beauty? Where's my silly glory?" he said when he came home and lifted her right off her feet and kissed her and bit her little finger.

"What's so beautiful about the barn anyway?" Caleb taunted, pulling her back by the hair.

"The weathervane's all crooked," she answered coldly. "Why don't you climb up there and straighten it, Caleb?" She taunted. "Make yourself useful."

"I don't have to. I'm ornamental."

"Oh, shut up," Betsy said. "Be human for a change, can't you?"

"Here, Caleb, take the tray," their mother's clear command rang out and once more whatever was real, was felt, was covered up, pushed outside because it might be painful. "You are an angel to have fixed all that bread and butter. I'm ravenous," she said, giving Betsy a gentle pat on the shoulder blades, marshaling them back into harmony, smoothing the rough places. While Frances Wyeth poured the tea, and Caleb dutifully passed it, Betsy let her eyes rest on the portrait of her great-grandfather, the strong lean whiskered face, the piercing black eyes in his white stock and black tie, his dark purple velvet-collared jacket, one hand resting lightly on a globe.

She turned to her father at whose feet Hannah lay, snoring, her paws twitching now and then. "Did you ever really know him, Pa?"

"Know who?" Sprig answered. "What are you talking about?"

"Great-grandfather Wyeth," she answered rather solemnly.

"Caleb, light the fire, will you please?" Frances interrupted without even knowing she was interrupting, and then sipped her tea quite loudly, as she always did, then sighed and put her cup down. "One of the two worst weeds is back again," she announced to the world at large. "I dug up every root and blade last fall—I just can't understand it." She was all alight with battle; she was so full of life, Betsy thought, that they seemed to be sitting round a candle; life shone through her bones.

"Betsy asked me a question," Sprig said patiently.

"Oh dear, I interrupted," and Frances gave him a quick, bright look. What is the matter with me, Betsy thought, that I read the hurt in it, that I felt the ring of steel now in this small light exchange between my parents? She looked at them in astonishment. I don't want to see, she thought. I don't want to know. It's like Alice in Wonderland getting taller and taller and not being able to stop.

"It's not important," she said quickly, "I just wondered—"

"Well," Sprig cleared his throat, as he did when he was shy of what he was about to say. "Um—as a matter of fact I was seven years old when the old boy died, and I do remember him." Sprig set his cup down on the floor. "You've heard this a hundred times," he said, with a quick little laugh. "What do you mean by asking me if I knew him?"

"He must have been rather a good substitute for God," Caleb said, glancing up at his father from the floor, where he was sitting cross-legged.

"Don't be tiresome, Caleb," Frances warned.

"He's quite right. Grandfather Wyeth was an excellent substitute for God. He taught me the Greek alphabet."

Caleb gave a loud laugh.

"What's so funny about that?" his father shot back irritably.

"Only the non sequitur. It not being one of the functions of God to teach Greek, I would think."

"No," Sprig answered mildly, "perhaps not. His pockets were always full of round red candies rather like frozen cherries. The thing he most admired was gumption—yes," Sprig said, smiling, "gumption was one of his favorite words. I disappointed him considerably because I didn't have the gumption to run away when I was seven, or ride the ice pungs." Sprig glanced up at the portrait. "Of course his business was finished by the time I came along. But there were still pungs and you could get carried off way down to Central Square or farther on the back of one of them, clinging on behind. He gave me hot rum and milk whenever I went out to Charlestown to see him in that old house over there——"

"But what was he really like?" Betsy asked, for none of this was much help. How extraordinary it seemed that she knew so little about him, that she had always just taken him for granted all these years, hardly listened when her father brought out the old stories, and now because she was projected into the future, she was also projected into the past. She must know.

"What do you mean 'really'?" her father asked, smiling at her as if he were pleased.

107

"Did you love him?"

"There's a woman's question for you," said Caleb. The fire had caught now and begun to bubble softly after the first flare and glare of paper burning. They had something to look at besides each other, and each in his way relaxed a little. As if meeting had been a kind of collision Betsy thought, but now they could settle back, find their places.

"I don't know," Sprig was saying. "He was such a huge presence, so formidable . . ." The words faded out into the firelight.

"Did he love you?" For a second their eyes met, a bleak naked look which took place somewhere very deep down or far away, which had nothing to do with what was being said.

"Love? Love?" he was saying testily, out of the loneliness behind his eyes. "We didn't think about such things, didn't talk about them anyway."

"It would have seemed slightly indecent to be loved by your grandfather?" Caleb needled.

"Oh Caleb," Frances said and it was a sigh, which floated out into the firelight and then vanished, drawing their thoughts to it, to her, as she sat for once with her hands in her lap, her head leaning against the back of the chair, and looked, Betsy saw, very much older than she had ever looked before.

"We did not analyze. We did not dissect everything as if feelings were dead frogs," Sprig answered then, lighting a cigarette. "Of course he loved me," he went on crossly. "Whatever does it matter?"

"It *must* have mattered!" Betsy said passionately.

Just then the door was pushed open and Aunt Hester walked in.

"Am I too late for tea?" she asked, "I'm simply dying for some——" Flinging off her soft leather jacket and scarf, and giving Sprig's shoulder a pat as she went past him, she stood before Frances. Betsy felt disgruntled beyond words. Why did Aunt Hester have to come in just then? Was there never to be an uninterrupted moment?

"Darling, how good to see you," Frances was saying, pouring out tea, saying that it would be rather weak, she feared, as she had had to add water. "How are you surviving? Are you exhausted?"

"She's always exhausted," Sprig teased. "You should know better than to ask."

"Oh, it's good to be here," Hester sat down in the little Victorian corduroy chair, drinking her tea avidly, and at the same time over her cup darting pleased bright glances at them all. "Betsy—how are you, dear? How's Tom?"

And while they talked of this and that, heard that Hester had had an awful day interviewing problem parents and one child had thrown an inkpot at his teacher, while they talked, Betsy looked at her aunt from her new-found state of motherhood and saw that she was truly exhausted, and had that white look around the eyes which all teachers get in the spring, like mariners at the end of a long voyage, and that her brightness was a mask, and the warm interest she poured out was a reflex action, a trained response. She's like my father; her real self is buried very deep, Betsy thought, they are secret people with secret lives.

"Betsy's in a dream," Caleb said, "poring over Great-grandfather Wyeth as if he held the secret to all of us, children of the ice age," he said, falling into the old family joke.

Now, would she tell them? Could she?

"Give me a cigarette, Caleb."

"People who bum cigarettes have no morals. It's the beginning of general decline, the primrose path—here you are, but I shall consider it a debt. You owe me three now." But he did scramble over to light it, and doing so, caught her frown, her impatience. "What is all this anyway about the old bastard? What's on your mind?"

Trust Caleb in the end to be the one who saw.

They were waiting. For a moment they were entirely focused on her and she must say it before the kaleidoscope shifted. She must. Betsy got up and carried her cup over to the tray. "Oh Mother," she said, and it was terrible that her mother was off there behind the tray, that she could not go to her, that she must turn and face them, Aunt Hester's tired bright eyes, her father's, Caleb's. . . .

"What is it, darling?" said her mother's voice.

"It's that"—she stood among them, but she was looking straight at the old man in the portrait who had admired gumption so much—"it's that I want to call my baby William Wyeth Dorgan—if it's a boy." At last she felt her mother's arms around her, her mother at last hugging her hard, saying "Dear darling girl," closing the circle which had been so painfully open for the last hour, making it all right at last.

"My God," Aunt Hester was saying, "what a day this is."

And Caleb grinning at her over her mother's shoulder, was saying, "I'll give you the three cigarettes, cancel the debt. Whoever would have suspected our Betsy of concealing a mother?"

All this happened at once like an explosion all around and inside her, so that it was several seconds before Betsy became aware that her father was still sitting in his chair and had turned bright pink. Her father was blushing.

"Oh Pa," she said, breaking away to go over to him and lean forward to where she could kiss the side of his forehead, "are you pleased?"

"I don't know," he said, trying to smile, "it's quite a surprise, old girl. William Wyeth, eh?" But Betsy stood up then, for she had come too close; she had seen the tears glaring in his eyes. She had seen him wince.

"Sprig, this calls for a drink," Aunt Hester was saying.

But now Betsy knew that she must leave them, that she had no more time (for her watch said half past five and Tom would be home any minute). It had been her news until a moment ago, only hers, and now it had become theirs, and to them it was different news. The currents of feeling all around her were strong; she wanted to break away, to feel as she had on her way here, a natural force, a part of the spring, where past and future flowed together.

"But I have to go," she said brusquely. "Tommy will be home waiting for me. Caleb, be an angel and drive me round, will you? I'm late now," she said.

"Call Tommy up and get him to come over for supper," her mother said, "it's a casserole and I can stretch it——"

"No." She must get away, must get home to Tommy and have this time with him alone. "You see——"

"I'll drive you. Get going," Caleb said. "I've got a date," he called back from the door, "so don't expect me for supper, Ma."

When she was safely sitting in the MG, Betsy began to tremble all over. "Whew," she said, not looking at Caleb sliding in on his side. "That's over."

She was grateful to Caleb for not saying anything, as they drove, grateful, too, when the mask of irony slipped away from his face. He didn't say anything, but she felt somehow closer to him than she had since her marriage, and she was grateful.

"Thank you, Caleb," she said, at the door of the little white house on Foster Street. "That was a good deed."

"Well, you know"—he gave her a funny little smile—"parents . . ."

And then he was shifting into gear and forcing the little car forward. She stood there between her two lives for a second, watched the MG turn up into Sparks Street and disappear. Children, parents, grandparents, grandchildren—how complicated it all is.

*

CHAPTER TWO

FROM the kitchen they could hear Frances' fresh voice, singing while she set the table, muffled by the pantry, then soaring out " '. . . to ask the Lord's blessing. He chastens and hastens His will to make known,' " the voice repeated, quite unself-conscious. And there in the dying light in the parlor Hester and her brother exchanged a smile.

"I did need a drink," she said then, sipping her Old-fashioned. "Sometimes I feel like the keeper of a zoo, surrounded by wild animals, howling and pacing their cages —as I do mine, for that matter," she added. "Oh, we all take ourselves so seriously, don't we, Sprig? And why are there such tensions?"

"Because the wild animals are all in cages. They used to be allowed out," and she watched the corners of his eyes crinkle with amusement; yet, she thought, he is not really amused. He is upset. Betsy's news has upset him, but I musn't talk about that—later, perhaps, with Frances. Now we must pretend that nothing has happened.

"Were they? I wonder. . . . Gran-Quan certainly never allowed himself out, paced his cage, still does—by the way, have you been out there lately? I simply haven't been able to make the time——" Stupid of her, it was, since she did not make the time and then lay awake half the night, worrying because she hadn't gone out to McLean Hospital where Gran-Quan lay, had been lying for the last two months, rejecting life, trying to die.

"I go every week," Sprig said. "You know that. But it's only for my own sake, not his. He didn't recognize me last time—no point in your doing it, Hester. It'll only upset you," and he added, taking a long swallow of his drink, "let's talk about something more cheerful."

" 'Oh Lord make us free,' " Frances' voice carolled out suddenly and at this Hester and Sprig gave each other one look, chuckled and burst into laughter.

"Whatever is the joke?" Frances popped in, wiping her hands on her apron, her face flushed and eager.

"You, darling," Hester said, "you're the joke, only we can't explain."

"What have I done?" Frances asked with innocent anxiety and this look threw Hester and Sprig off again, "Oh, you two," she added, tossing her head, "you're drunk that's all, what with all the news," and she lingered a moment, just on the threshold, looked shyly in Sprig's direction, looked as if she wanted to come over and say something to him, touch him perhaps, then thought better of it, murmured "William Wyeth Dorgan," and gave a little laugh.

"It's preposterous," Sprig said, but if he seemed on the brink of anger, the sight of his sister wiping the tears from her eyes set him off again. "Preposterous," he repeated, but this time he was laughing, "Serves the old boy right, eh? I'm delighted," he said, rubbing his hands. "Best news in a dog's age. Come and have a drink, Frances." He was caught up now in the new mood, and marked the change by getting up and lighting the lamps, pulled the curtains close with a big free gesture, then stood with his back to the fire.

Hester wiped her eyes. She ran her fingers through her hair, thinking of Gran-Quan. "There's always too much to do. It's a hell of a life, really."

"At any rate we complain a lot," Sprig conceded with a twinkle.

"All right," Hester flashed back, "try running the school for a week."

"I'm not that crazy, thank you."

"There," Frances said, flinging her apron onto a chair, "I'm all ready and we can sit down for five minutes of peace and quiet—how blessed that the children didn't stay."

"Really, Frances," and Hester leaned over and gave her hand a squeeze. "You are the most unmaternal person I ever knew."

"I don't care," said Frances. "They were dying to get away, weren't they? I had the impression of a concerted flight. Caleb's having a hot dog now, all by himself, along the river——"

"And you don't mind?" It was amazing, really, how easily Frances took her children. It was not they who haunted and possessed her, who made her guilty and anxious, threw her into panics—no, not they, Hester thought giving her brother a long thoughtful look.

"Mind? Why should I?" said Frances, withdrawing her hand now and leaning back. "He probably was upset at the idea of being an uncle."

"Yes," Sprig said vaguely, "Caleb as an uncle is a rather curious idea."

"Well"—Frances sprang up, unable to sit still this evening for more than two seconds—"I'll dish up or everything will be dry as a cinder. How about a bottle of wine, Sprig?"

While he was down cellar, Hester went out to the kitchen with the glasses, stood by the sink watching her sister-in-law take the casserole out of the oven and peer at it, hopefully, "Do you think it's all right?" Then catching Hester's look, she went over and put her arms around her and looked into her eyes. "Are you all right?" she asked.

"All right," Hester said, "just tired—you know what the spring is at school——"

"Yes, well, you look all right, calm inside."

"You don't. You're anxious again, aren't you?"

"Depressed," Frances answered shortly, going back to the stove to take the beans off and flinging them into the colander casually. "I don't know why."

"Well, ladies . . ." Sprig came back with a bottle in his hands. "I should have warmed this by the fire," he said. "Never mind," he glanced from one to the other. "Has Hannah been fed?" Hannah's tail beat a tattoo from under the kitchen table.

"Of course Hannah's been fed. We'll give Mr. Silence something at the table. Come along," Frances said impatiently.

She was standing there, Hester thought, like some beautiful fury in disguise, before the casserole she had cooked

116

and which she was about to serve, the spoon ready in her hand—standing there and looking like a young boy, her eyes blazing, and some thirsty eagerness for life so unquenched in her that it was almost frightening—would surely frighten Sprig, but fortunately he did not see the Fury before him, and was merely impatient for his dinner.

"I'm waiting to make a toast," Frances said.

In the silence, as Sprig circled the table, filling each glass very carefully and remarking as he did so, "Those are Great-grandfather's glasses, aren't they?" it seemed to Hester that she could hear their hearts beating very fast, and beating so fast each for a different reason.

"I drink to us," Frances said, lifting her glass and looking first at Sprig and then at Hester, not tenderly at all, but as if she were measuring them, "not to our family selves, not to this web of relationships, but to our secret selves, whoever they may be."

"Well, well," Sprig said, sitting down and looking faintly embarrassed. "That's quite a toast, Fran, I must say."

"Do you do better at the Saturday Club?" she flashed back instantly.

"We're not quite so *exalté* perhaps."

"Women are really maddening," Frances said. "Oh, I do wish that I could hide under the table just once and get an idea of what the distilled essence of masculine wisdom is like—what do you talk about anyway?" she challenged him.

"Ideas," Sprig answered vaguely. "You know, the sort

of thing. Someone starts a rabbit and then we all chase after it—once in a blue moon something happens. Mostly, it's boring. We miss Whitehead, you know."

"To think of Betsy having a baby!" Hester interruped. She had not been listening. Turning the wineglass in her hand, she was remembering Betsy as a very pink angry baby who screamed her fury one whole weekend when she was left with Hester; Betsy in a red muffler and red stocking cap, being dragged along on a sled to school; Betsy, much too fat and miserable because the boys didn't want to dance with her, in her last year at Grove End. And yet it was bound to happen—it shouldn't have taken them by surprise. Hester turned the wineglass in her hand.

"Don't start remembering," Sprig said irritably.

"Why ever not?" and Hester frowned up at him. It was annoying the way he never faced a situation head-on, but always obliquely. Even Frances had deliberately pushed the occasion aside in her toast, as if to say, nothing has changed after all. We are safe. But safe from what? Other people, Hester supposed, would be excited and happy.

"Aren't you pleased, Sprig, really, *au fond*, I mean?" And quite deliberately she leveled her elder-sister-in-command look at him. "Betsy looked so grown-up and calm, so happy, too—when one thinks back even to two years ago, it seems a kind of miracle."

"Merely a natural process, Hester. Don't exaggerate," Sprig was acid. "All pregnant women look the same—so do all cows and even poor old Hannah in her day—that foolish look of astonishment and pride."

"Oh Sprig," and Hester sighed rather than answering.

"Don't give it a thought, darling." Frances who had been eating rapidly and with total concentration, now lifted her head. "You should know us by now. We never, on principle, rise to an occasion. It would be vulgar." She was badgering Sprig, of course.

"Nonsense, think of the birthday parties, Frances—and the Fourth of July and hanging up stockings at Christmas. It seems to me we rose to every occasion," Hester answered, since her brother did not.

"Except death or marriage, or anything really important, you know, anything really private. We bury the private things like a dog with a bone and snarl just as Sprig did if anyone comes anywhere near. Our marriage was so secret we scarcely believed it ourselves for nearly a year," she said, suffused with laughter.

"But why is it?" Hester would not be put off. "It's so —unnatural." There was a brief silence while each bent to his plate. "Poor Betsy," Hester said half to herself.

"Poor Betsy be damned!" Sprig exploded. "It's I who will have to teach William Wyeth Dorgan the Greek alphabet, and keep my pockets filled with candy, I suppose." He looked so glum that Hester and Frances burst into laughter. Sprig's humor was so close to desperation and his desperation so close to humor that even he could not always, it seemed, tell them apart.

"You don't have to become the image of your grandfather, Sprig—that's what the baby will have to do, obviously," Frances shouted through her laughter.

"Children should be brought up by the state," Sprig went on. "All family relationships are impossible; the analysts make huge amounts of money just trying to straighten out the harm parents and grandparents have done to their offspring—and yet you totally unrealistic women think that beginning another such cycle is a reason for drinking Burgundy!" He got up and filled the glasses.

"Tom will make a very good father," Hester was enjoying herself now. She loved to see Sprig on the rampage.

"But we shall be horrible grandparents," Frances said gloomily. "I don't want to be a grandmother," and drank down her glass of burgundy as if it were water. "I'm not ready," she said, daring Sprig across the table, but he would not catch her eye, was sitting now lost in thought apparently, and absent-mindedly passed his plate for a second helping.

"Well, we have six months or so," Sprig said, "in which to mull over this new incarnation. Shall I grow a beard?" He mocked himself. "I must brush up some simple jokes."

"I do so want to be myself," Frances went on with her chain of thought.

"But, Frances, aren't you?" Hester smiled. "No one more so. You have refused so absolutely to be anyone else."

"Have I?" Frances looked at her in amazement. "How queer. To me it seems I have been for years and years always trying to be someone else, a mother, for instance. You must admit I've hardly succeeded as *that*—or a cook. . . ." She looked thoughtful.

"The casserole is perfect," Sprig said, "although Caleb perhaps has not turned out quite so well."

Hester felt the danger now and stepped in quickly. "What is Caleb doing?"

"God knows," Sprig shrugged his shoulders. "By the way, where's that cat?" he asked, scraping some odds and ends together onto his butter plate. "Oh, there you are," for the cat now stretched a paw into the air and opened it, and could be heard to purr. He had been sitting beside Sprig's chair for some time.

"He never mews for food, isn't it amazing?" Frances came over to add a titbit to the plate and they all watched while it was put down, and watched the delicate way the cat settled to it, and began to eat only after sniffing the whole plate over twice. "Dear old thing," Frances said, gathering up the plates, and with a gesture bidding Hester sit still. "I'll do this."

"Caleb"—Sprig leaned back in his chair—"wants to spend a year abroad."

"Why not?"

"He has no money," Sprig said shortly. "Spent it on an MG."

"'I see," Hester said, but she was well aware that this was not the whole truth.

"You gave him the MG," Frances said coldly, as she brought in the desert plates and custard, plunking them down impatiently, as if she had more in mind to say, but made this gesture instead.

"Yes—well—" said Sprig, and Hester recognized the Wyeth in him, embarrassed always by any mention of money. "Anyway he'll come to Maine instead. Read philosophy or something. We don't really know," he added. "He never tells us anything."

"What was he going to do in Europe?" Hester asked. "Why wasn't he drafted?"

"Rheumatic fever, don't you remember?" Frances dished out the custard. "He's had a rotten year," she added. "The job didn't work out—he and Professor Wright didn't hit it off in the first place."

"And in the second, Caleb's lazy," Sprig broke in.

"He shouldn't have stayed here," Hester said drily. "Everyone knew that from the beginning."

"I don't see why," Sprig teased. "Boston is the hub of the universe—concerts, art, universities galore, bird-watching, what more can one ask?"

"Anything except the family——"

"He doesn't give a hoot about the family, so I can't see that we do him any harm. He hangs his hat here and raids the icebox." Sprig swallowed down his custard impatiently.

"What nonsense you do talk, Sprig." Hester glanced over at Frances and they exchanged a look which said, Sprig is impossible, as we well know.

The telephone sent its imperative peal through the house, and they all jumped. "Infernal machine! Excuse me," Sprig said, disappearing into the hall.

The two women lit cigarettes and sat on at the table. The curtains had not been drawn and from where she sat Hester looked out into a sea-green world, the sky still faintly alight and the early green of leaves foaming in the garden below, for the house itself stood high up.

"Don't be depressed, Frances. It will be all right."

"I expect so." Frances puffed at her cigarette furiously. "Anyway nothing's wrong. It's only me. I feel stifled by angers, in a perfect rage against everything, and it doesn't help to have Caleb and Sprig getting on each other's nerves." She sighed.

She got up mechanically, too restless to sit still, and carried plates out into the kitchen. But Hester sat on. She felt a little drunk with tiredness and the wine and all that had been going on, Betsy's news, the sense that here in this house, always so full of life, something was going wrong, and harmony achieved only by a great effort, and only just achieved. Yet there just outside the windows was peace, was the hazy lovely spring evening. It had been a mistake to come, perhaps, since now she wondered how she would ever pull herself together for a teachers' meeting at eight o'clock. She looked at her watch.

"That was Thorny Stiles," Sprig said. "Where's Frances?" he asked impatiently and without waiting for an answer called, "Frances, come here!"

"Here I am. What is it, Sprig? What's the matter?" She stood in the doorway. "Do you have to shout?"

"I'm sorry. But that was Thorny Stiles. It seems that Bill has cancer, can't live more then six months." Sprig stood with his hands grasping the back of a chair.

"Bill Waterford?" Hester asked. "I can't believe it."

"Does his wife know?" Frances asked.

"I don't know. I'm going over to see Thorny now."

"Oh Sprig!" Frances stood there, wiping her hands. She did not go to her husband.

"I can't seem to take it in," he said slowly. "It—it doesn't seem possible."

"He had a year off. They were going to France," Hester remembered. For years, she knew, ever since college in fact, Sprig and Thorny who was a G.P., and Bill Waterford had made a kind of triumvirate, met once a week for lunch or for long evenings of talk. In some ways, this loss would be greater for Sprig than the loss of someone in his own family. She saw all this in the few seconds. "I'll drop you on my way," she said to her brother. "You can walk back."

"I can't seem to take it in." He was standing just as he had been, his head down, clasping the back of the chair, his knuckles white. "Yes," he added. "We'd better be going."

"Darling——" Frances stood in the doorway, and her voice came out blurred. But they had left. She heard the front door closing behind them, heard Hester's car start up, die, and then start again, roar off around the corner, and then she heard the silence, and knew she was entirely alone.

*

CHAPTER THREE

"YOU wouldn't rather have a drink?" Thorny asked for the second time, bringing in a tray with a pot of China tea on it and two Chinese cups.

"Thanks," Sprig said also for the second time, "I had one before dinner."

They were sitting in Thorny's study, a small cosy room with a fireplace, a room from which medical books were banished. From where he sat Sprig's eyes rested on the familiar green backs of a set of Trollope, beside them the new biography of Freud, some anthologies of poetry, a shelf of Samuel Eliot Morison. There were three big chairs in the room, and Sprig noticed that Thorny did not sit in the wing chair, which Bill usually chose. They drank their tea in silence.

"Nothing like tea," Thorny said after a moment. "I must drink twenty cups a day." He was a tall, gentle blond man who stooped a little and seemed always in a state of extreme fatigue though actually he was inexhaustible, one of the few G.P.'s left who could be called at night, at any hour.

Sprig drank his cup down. Then lit a cigarette. The two men often sat like this without speaking, for some time.

Now they were obviously thinking the same thoughts and these were difficult to put into words—for Sprig next to impossible. He felt walled in, even here, even with Thorny; with every moment that passed, he felt he was going deeper down into some part of himself so primitive and violent that words could never express it.

"It will be at most a year," Thorny was saying.

"You told Bill that?"

"Of course not," Thorny said testily, getting up to fill their cups again, which he did awkwardly, the fat, round teapot balanced precariously in one hand. "I told him that cancer of the lung at this stage, is, as far as we know now, incurable."

"What's the difference?"

"Well, it may seem strange but there is a very great difference between a sentence that reads six months and a sentence that reads—say—two years."

"We're all sentenced to death, of course. You know, that's something I've only come to realize since your phone call. For the first time." And Sprig smiled a fleeting smile. "Only we don't believe it. Does Bill believe it?"

"I don't know. He talked of finishing that book. He put up a brave front, I must say—of course, he doesn't know either that within about six weeks he'll be feeling rather too ill to do very much."

"I think I'd shoot myself," Sprig said quietly.

"Yes, you think so," Thorny answered, "but you wouldn't. You can't believe how we all cling to life, to the very end. I've seen it. I know."

"Why do we?" and Sprig raised his head for the first time and looked at the long shambling man sitting in the chair opposite. "My father, for instance. He has gnawed himself like a fox in a trap for the last forty-five years, and now he lies there, unable even to speak, and yet he won't die. His will is like iron. He lies there, out of his mind a lot of the time, and I have to go there and see him, though it makes me sick to my stomach," Sprig said harshly.

"Yes—well, there it is, you see," Thorny said speculatively, and then he added, "I wish I had more confidence in Nora's ability to handle this."

"That flibbertygibbet. Good God," Sprig got up and walked to the window, "I had forgotten all about her." Thorny and Sprig generally avoided seeing Nora, whom they did not like or understand. "But surely he'll be in the hospital," he turned back to say, frowning. "He'll have proper care. Have you talked to her?" Sprig asked.

"I'm to see her in my office tomorrow."

"Gee whizz, I don't envy you that."

They sat there, then, for some minutes, Sprig's hands clasped between his knees, staring straight in front of him, a cigarette hanging from his lips. Now that Bill was dying, Sprig found himself considering the marriage as a marriage, hoping it had been all right for Bill in *that* way, and then shying away from the thought as if it were slightly blasphemous.

At this moment there was a tap at the window, a distinct sharp tap.

"Some kid probably," Thorny said, getting up to pull

back the curtains. But what they saw was Bill Waterford's grinning face, so much like a ghost that Sprig leaped to his feet in a kind of terror.

"Well, well," Thorny was saying at the door, "come on in. Why in hell didn't you come to the door?"

"I thought I'd scare you," Bill said, seeming at the moment so full of life that it was impossible to believe in his illness, "and I did. Old Sprig there looks quite shaken. Did you think the little people were after you?"

But Sprig could do nothing but swallow, it seemed, and stand there, his arms at his sides.

"I suppose Thorny's told you about my carcass," Bill said, and it was somehow as if he were very excited, perhaps had been drinking.

"Yes," Sprig answered, flushing to the roots of his hair. He turned away, kicked a log in the fireplace absent-mindedly. "We're drinking tea. Have some." He turned back, pain and embarrassment making him stiff as a ramrod.

"I'll make a fresh pot," Thorny said and escaped, leaving the two there to themselves.

Bill flung himself down in the wing chair and now the strain in his face did show.

"Talk about something," Bill said. "I—uh—give me a cigarette, old man, will you?"

But having been commanded to talk, Sprig felt imprisoned again by the walls of silence. He passed Bill a cigarette and stood with his back to the fire, looking out of the window, then noticing the curtains pulled back, went and closed them again. "Whatever makes Thorny take so much tea?" Bill asked. "I need a drink."

"It was the war," Sprig said, glad of a subject at last. "He started doing it in China. Liked it, I guess. Says he drinks twenty cups a day."

"Hey, none of that slop for me," Bill shouted rather too loudly as Thorny came back carrying the round pot carefully. "Give me a shot of your best Scotch."

"I offered Sprig a drink, but he said he had had one before dinner," Thorny said drily. "Change your mind?"

Bill suddenly chuckled. "A drink before dinner, eh? Whatever brought on such dissipation, Sprig? You're going to the dogs."

"Well, actually"—Sprig glanced at the two men, without smiling—"it appears that Betsy is going to have a baby. I don't believe it, but I suppose it must be true."

"Wow!" Bill said, "Sprig's going to be a grandfather!"

"I must say"—Thorny came up to stand beside Sprig after passing Bill a glass and setting the bottle down on the table by his chair—"you're extraordinarily secretive. . . . He's been here half an hour," he explained, "without a word. Well, well——"

"These things happen," said Sprig, putting a hand up to his collar as if it were too tight for him. "I can't see any reason to get so excited about it. Hester and Frances made a great to-do. We drank a bottle of my best Chateauneuf du Pape," he said with evident regret. And the expression on his face sent Bill off into a gust of laughter.

"You're incredible. You ought to be stuffed," he said,

when he could, through the laughter which literally shook him.

It was, obviously, a relief to all of them to have embarked now on a safe subject which they could ride for the next hour or so. Sprig sat down again, shaking his head.

"But you really are pleased, aren't you?" Thorny asked.

"Pleased?" Sprig said in his dry voice. "I'm shattered. When Betsy told us I felt exactly as if someone had just poured a ton of bricks on my head. Wouldn't you?" He turned to Thorny, who had four children, all of them still in school or college.

"I don't know," Thorny said, scratching his ear, "I guess I've never imagined it."

"It means the Wyeths are safe for another generation," Bill said. After all, Sprig realized and winced, there was no safe subject.

"Of course it may be a girl," he said cautiously, "but if it's a boy, she wants to name him for my grandfather, William Wyeth." He restrained the gleam which had shot up into his eyes. "Of course there will be Dorgan on the end of it."

"Wonderful," Bill roared. "William Wyeth Dorgan—that's enough to make him governor even if he turns out feeble-minded."

"How would the old man like that, I wonder?" Thorny asked gently, exchanging an amused look with Bill.

"The old man," Sprig said, flushing and sitting very straight in his chair, "was a hardheaded old pirate and no snob. Also he liked lively people and Tom's lively. I don't think," he added as if he were conjuring up his grandfather before him, "that he'd mind." For Sprig this was a long, even a fervent speech.

"Congratulations," Bill lifted his glass and drained it, then he was seized by a fit of coughing so that for a moment it looked as if he would choke. His face had turned bright red. Sprig and Thorny sat still while this happened, not looking at each other. "Damn," Bill said when he could breathe again.

"It's all moving away too fast," Sprig said. "I feel as if I were on a roller coaster." He had spoken out of his own experience of the last hours, and not for Bill.

"Yes," Bill said, very quiet. "Yes."

The moment of intimacy which they had warded off out of embarrassment, was upon them. It stayed in the air, as Bill coughed again, and poured himself another drink. Sprig lit a cigarette and snapped the match off into the fireplace. Thorny just sat with his hands clasped over one knee, and no one of the three dared raise his head.

"Damn," Bill said again. He seemed in the last few moments to have become dead sober. The superficial excitement had ebbed out of him after his coughing fit, as if he no longer had the physical strength to sustain it. He was for the first time himself, not the clown wearing a mask whom they had seen until now. "You know why I came here?" He turned to Thorny.

"I can imagine," Thorny answered from his corner.

"I don't know if you can. You're going to see Nora tomorrow, she tells me. I want you to tell her that I can get well."

"Is that quite fair?"

"Listen," Bill leaned forward. "It's the only way I can manage. I've been thinking about this for hours. Don't you see, even with you two, it's bad enough—that you know, I mean—but I can't go through all this right beside somebody watching me every minute of the day. It's a question of human dignity," his hands were clenched on his knees.

"He's right," Sprig said.

"Well, Thorny?" for Thorny had been sitting there, without moving at all, had just glanced up at Sprig an instant, as if to take in the absolute moral assurance with which he spoke, an attitude so rare in the deprecatory Sprig that it carried a good deal of weight.

"I'll do what I can."

"I'm speaking to my friend, not to my doctor, Thorny."

"I have to be a doctor first," Thorny said, getting up and standing with his back to them.

"No," Sprig said to the stooping lonely back, "you don't."

"You don't know what you're talking about, I'm afraid."

"I know that I set my friends first," said Sprig.

"Above the truth?" And Thorny turned to peer down as if from a great distance.

"This is the human truth, not the medical truth. You don't know any more about the human truth than Bill does, and in this case, I venture to suggest, a good deal less," and he gave a slight snort.

"Listen, Thorny," Bill said seriously, "Nora is over-anxious anyway, perhaps neurotically so———"

"Yes, such people sometimes can take an absolute certainty where anything indefinite throws them."

"That isn't the point." Only the extreme flatness of Sprig's tone showed that he was angry. "The point is that Bill asked you as a friend to do something you don't approve of—or not wholly—for his sake. I don't see how you can refuse."

"I thought you were a man of principle." Bill turned to Sprig, lapsing by instinct into his usual role of peacemaker.

"This *is* a principle, Bill, for God's sake. I'm talking about friendship." Sprig flushed.

"You set it higher then than the responsibility of a wife toward her husband, than the right of a wife to know the truth about her husband?" Thorny sat down, his eyes very bright. So they had argued since they were freshmen in college, earlier than that, since Thorny and Sprig had roomed together at Exeter.

"Much higher," Sprig answered without hesitation.

"A rather odd idea of marriage, perhaps," was Thorny's comment.

"Well," Bill answered thoughtfully, "it's my marriage, you know, not an idea of marriage really." It was the nearest he had ever come to saying anything about his life with Nora, and the two men received it as a confidence, instinctively edging away from the subject which they sensed to be painful.

"I'll do what I can, Bill," Thorny said. "I do realize," he added, "that Nora . . ." and left the sentence in the air.

"Just for a while," Bill repeated. "Until I can achieve some detachment," he said wryly. It was apparent that he was now very tired, and he staggered a little as he got up.

"I'll drive you home," Thorny said, "you too, if you like——" to Sprig.

"Thanks, I'll walk."

Sprig stood on the sidewalk and watched the car drive away. The smell of earth and green was very strong in the dark, and he took a deep breath, staring up into the trees lit by the street lamps, bearing their fuzz of flowers, a red maple just beside him, and a shower of dark red fluff on the macadam at his feet. All around him the houses were lit up and alive. "A rather odd idea of marriage," Thorny had said acidly and it came back to him now, getting under his skin, as he stood there. But what Thorny didn't know was that he would give almost anything at this moment to walk out of the house, leave Frances and the children (Caleb and his antagonism, Betsy and her pregnancy), and take the first plane to Japan. Bill and his human dignity in the face of the worst a man can have to bear, Thorny and his professional purity—they made him feel empty. They know what they're doing, he thought, and I'm walking in the dark, a kind of monster who has neither been a real husband nor a real father, nor perhaps even a real friend.

It seemed as if his own life had been thrown into brilliant relief by this day of emotion, so unfinished and halfbaked in every way it looked to him as he walked slowly back up the hill, making a long detour around Fayerweather Street simply to put off going home.

Japan? he thought. What I do, instead, is walk around the block. And just such ludicrously small expedients seemed the way of his life, when all the time inside him there was a buried volcano of desire for something else—for what? "A rather odd idea of marriage," Thorny's words came back to him again, as if he could not swallow them. Yes, he supposed that he had failed Frances, too. Yet when he thought of her like this, when he was alone, walking down a spring street, he loved her so much that it was like a physical pain, the worse because he knew that as soon as he got home again, he would be unable to express it, would be irritated because she was still addressing envelopes at her desk and looked absorbed, or be even more irritated because she was sewing in the empty parlor and looked lonely. She was airy and bright with him, and under the airiness she was hurt all the time, no more able to understand what had happened between them than he was. He had become excruciatingly shy of touching her, of coming close to her in any way (but here Sprig's thoughts took an instinctive turn, jumped the tracks, and he lit a cigarette and observed with interest that the Thayers were putting on a new roof, replacing the old weatherworn shingles with some newfangled fireproof stuff).

It did no good. Things he deliberately pushed aside, welled up in the spring night and he couldn't stop them.

Tom Dorgan has raped my daughter and got her with child —that was the thought he had been keeping at bay for hours, the thought that had made him blush to the roots of his hair when Betsy stood by the fireplace and looked over at the portrait of Grandfather Wyeth. Now it pounced. He threw the cigarette away half smoked and clenched his hands in his pockets. How idiotic! Tom loved Betsy and they were a happy young couple; all was well with them. It is I who am a horrible old man who will not face anything and wants to escape, escape my wife, escape my daughter's child, a prim self-contained New Englander with a volcano inside me which may at any moment erupt.

Yet people talk of us as lacking passion—that is the myth about New England. My father, for instance! And Sprig smiled to himself, walking a little faster, his head up because, although he hated his father, he also respected him, respected a man who could feel that much, irrational and terrible as an Old Testament Prophet, and because in the depths of himself where the volcano occasionally roared he was proud of being a New Englander to the marrow of his bones.

Selfish pig that I am, he thought, nearing the house now, seeing Caleb's light on and the light in the bedroom —Bill's dying. But the strangest part about this evening was that in spite of everything, even the grueling hour at Thorny's, he still did not believe it. It was not real. And he suspected that it would only be by experiencing Bill's dying, by living it through to the end, that they would be able to come to believe it.

136

He walked rapidly into the house, bearing, without any way of expressing them, his multiple selves into the house, running upstairs briskly and already feeling within him the half-open doors close and lock. So that when he stood in the bedroom and met Frances' tentative smile as she lay there, reading in bed, he was already locked back to where response was defensive, and when he came back after his shower her light was turned off and her face turned away.

CHAPTER FOUR

THEY were sitting, Lucy and Frances, in Lucy's living room drinking large cups of coffee and reviving now from the exhaustion that always overtook them when they met because everything must be poured out and examined, and after an hour of this they felt emptied out, nothing but skin drawn tight over bone, Frances thought, smoking furiously and looking around her without seeing the mess, Jack's football in the corner of one faded armchair, the flowers needing fresh water and fading on the mantelpiece, yesterday's newspaper let fall, and since, stepped on several times. Frances saw none of this. What she saw was comfort, was homeliness, was Lucy's wonderfully casual happy-go-lucky way of life which fascinated and appalled her, which she secretly envied; what she saw was Lucy herself with her clear gray eyes, the purity, the innocence of her face.

"Poor John," Frances said aloud, out of these thoughts.

"Save your pity for a worthier object," Lucy said with a funny sideways look of amusement. "I'm sure that woman is a model of order and cleanliness, and never a speck of dust touches her immaculate husband—John hated the mess. I do, too," she said unexpectedly. "I sometimes dream of throwing all the furniture out, painting the walls white, and buying a few terribly serene distant pieces of modern furniture——" And she got up and picked up the newspaper and flung it into the fireplace impatiently. "I'm turning into a sloppy old woman, Frances. It's disgraceful." Then as Frances didn't answer at once, she turned on her fiercely. "Isn't it?"

"I don't know," Frances said thoughtfully, "it all depends on how you feel inside. I mean, if it makes you miserable, then clean up the mess."

"It does make me miserable, but I'm always thinking of something I'd rather do more, like going into the Athenaeum and stacking up a lot of French poetry—or, you know —anything and everything else. You make everything sound so simple, Fran," she said earnestly, "and it isn't."

"You know," Frances said on the train of her own thoughts, "I sometimes think Sprig should go away for a year——"

"Speaking of things not being simple, I suppose——" and Lucy curled up in the big armchair again.

"Yes. John's gone—that's definite. You remake your life. You know where you are, but Sprig—it's just as if he weren't there, but he is."

"Nonsense," Lucy sat up, looking quite fierce suddenly. "You two are so aware of each other that you're like tuning forks; he's there all right."

Frances laughed, "Well, I can't hear the sound he makes. Maybe you can."

"Sprig is a subterranean person, Fran; you've always known that."

"Yes," and Frances sighed, and was silent.

"Well, then?"

"I suppose I can't accept him, never will. He's so irritating, Lucy. About money, for instance. He won't give Caleb the money for a year abroad."

"Why not?" Lucy asked, her eyes dancing.

"You don't have to look so amused. He says he can't afford it."

"And I suppose he can? Does it mean touching capital?" said Lucy, raising her eyebrows in pretended alarm.

"Heavens, no," Frances said, paying no attention to Lucy's chuckle. "But he hates even to touch the interest on the capital."

"Oh you rich people, how poor you feel," Lucy said, still chuckling. "And, of course, now he's to be a grandfather he'll get worse. You'd better be prepared for that," she added, teasing. Then she gave Frances a rather searching look. "Why don't you give Caleb the money?" she said casually.

"I don't see why I should," Frances said quickly, but she flushed. "It's not fair. And besides," she added, almost apologetically, "it would make an awful row."

"It's something I've never understood," Lucy went on, meditatively, "your whole feeling about money. It's only a means of exchange, Frances. It's not anything in itself."

"Well"—Frances responded instantly to Lucy's change of tone—"you know what I really think. We were brought up to fear money as if it were the devil. It was a positive wicked power which, if you possessed it by some stroke of

140

luck, endangered your soul and so you had to treat it with immense circumspection keep it locked up, never under any circumstances indulge yourself by means of it——" And suddenly Frances began to laugh with the pleasure of this idea brought out into the light and talked about. "I think Sprig has enormous guilt about his money. Its having been made of such a perishable substance as ice, in the first place —he's just a little ashamed. You know, he gives enormous amounts away—I'm always discovering by accident that he's endowed a bed in some hospital, or is practically the sole support of a school for Negro girls somewhere in the South. Why don't you feel this way, Lucy?" Frances asked, turning on Lucy without any humor now.

"I gather I should," and Lucy smiled. "Well, for one thing, you seem to forget that I'm poor."

"Yes, darling, but——"

"Also wasteful? Granted. My father was a miser the way other men are drunkards," she said quietly. "I couldn't bear to be like that in any way—I'd rather beg!"

"Sprig always talks about his father as if he hated him, but it isn't the truth. Oh Lucy," Frances said with sudden passion, "it's taken me all these years—forty-six—to learn that people don't mean what they say."

"They don't even mean what they do half the time," Lucy said. "Sprig doesn't. He loves you—you know that, Frances."

"No," Frances said bleakly, "I don't any more."

"My lamb, you mustn't be depressed." The heart came up into Lucy's eyes, a visible presence, and in the long look the two women exchanged across the room, their love for each other, as intense as when they were children at school, flowed out.

"Whatever would I do without you?" and Frances gave a long sigh of relief. It was as if they were suddenly out of doors, on a long stretch of beach, released to ocean and sky, free to be themselves, and all the tension gone.

"Well, I'm here," Lucy said quietly. "But I do hate middle age," she added vehemently. "It will be lovely to be old, don't you think? Through with all this——"

"All what?"

"Being neither fish, flesh, nor good red herring, I suppose. The ambiguous age."

"I wonder if I shall feel different when I'm a grandmother. . . . I've been an abominable mother, Lucy."

"I don't think so," Lucy said lightly.

"Oh yes, I have. It was Sprig for me, not the children, and they always felt that. It was Sprig *I* wanted to hug—and never could," and she laughed a little rueful laugh.

"In a way," Lucy said, after looking at Frances thoughtfully for a moment, "I suppose it's hard to have a very happy marriage just back of you. Nothing can quite come up to it."

"How do you know?" Frances was startled to realize that this was absolutely true. She did think of marriage as her parents' marriage; she did measure Sprig by her father. "How do you know?" she asked again.

"Well, it isn't really so frightfully hard to put two and two together, Frances. You're such an innocent."

"Am I?"

"We both are," Lucy said quickly. "I wonder why. After all we really belong to the Scott Fitzgerald era, gin in the bathtub, hashish in the teacup. What happened to us?"

"We lived in Cambridge," Frances said solemnly. "Do you remember how horrified we were when we heard that boys were spiking the drinks at debutante dances? But the wonderful cosiness of speak-easies in New York! Dear me," and Frances sighed. "Sprig was in Japan," she added. "He missed all that. I do wish I knew just what happened in Japan; he never talks about it, but I know nothing ever was the same afterward. His whole life has been an anticlimax to that one extraordinary experience."

"I think he was a tight little New England seed or nut and in Japan it flowered, it cracked open—the exquisiteness, the control, sensuous but always controlled—I can see how this was Sprig's thing, all right."

"All I really know is that he studied with some Zen Buddhist, studied archery of all things, and that after a year he hadn't even been allowed to shoot one arrow," and Frances giggled. "Poor Sprig."

"It's you who should go away," Lucy said.

"I? But where would I go?" And at the very idea Frances felt panic-stricken, realized that whatever the frustration here, it would be a thousand times worse without her family. The shock opened her eyes—she saw that all the things and people that seemed to prevent her from being herself, all made her herself, that without them she would be nothing, nothing at all.

143

"Well, don't look terrified; it was just a thought," Lucy said getting up now and kissing Frances on the cheek. Then patted her on the back. "We'll be all right," she said.

And all the way home, because she had seen Lucy, Frances felt as if she had been given for that brief time another dimension to live in—it was strange because, in a way, she felt too close to Lucy. It was like talking to another self, and yet this feminine world where everything became personal, where life was reduced to personal relations, in some way released her into a wider dimension, restored her faith, made her able to go on. And this, Frances realized afresh, was what Bill Waterford was to Sprig. How would Sprig's life be nourished and sustained now? Frances walked with her head bent, hardly aware of the spring all around her, and almost bumped into old Mrs. Griggs who had stopped, evidently, to admire a magnolia on Appleton Street.

"Oh, I am sorry," Frances said, "I was thinking."

"Well, well, my dear, I won't stop you. I was looking," and the dear old lady twinkled gently, and waved Frances on with her cane.

I haven't been to see her for nearly a month, Frances thought, or Miss Frost either. There is so much I haven't done, she thought with woe. There was never any escape from guilt of one sort of another, and walking up Appleton Street fast, a little out of breath, she felt as if she were pursued by the Furies.

*

CHAPTER FIVE

"DON'T be surprised," Betsy said, suddenly anxious, as she and Tom neared the house on that Sunday morning, just in time for the ritual glass of sherry before the ritual Sunday dinner, "if Pa doesn't say a word about the baby, will you?"

Tom laughed. "I don't care," he said, "if you don't." They were in a daze of happiness, had taken a long way round so as to walk arm in arm, stopping to admire other peoples' gardens (for Betsy's sake) and other peoples' houses (for Tom's, for he talked about building one day and wanted to know what was going on). Tom carried a large green paper cornet of daffodils. It had been his idea; he had thought of it as they were lying in bed after a luxurious Sunday breakfast on a tray.

"Your father must be very upset about Bill Waterford," Tom had said, "I think we should take some flowers."

"Flowers? For Pa?" Betsy sat up straight with surprise and looked back at him, her eyebrows lifted.

"Why not?"

"You're so lavish, darling. I shall never get used to it." The Wyeths sent flowers when people died or were terribly ill in the hospital. The Dorgans sent flowers whenever they felt like it, and what was wrong with that?

As they pushed open the door and Betsy called out "Here we are!" he stood with the daffodils in his hands and knew that in spite of everything he was intruding upon a strange tribe, and that he would never, never be one of them.

"Put these in water," he said stiffly to Betsy, as the family converged upon them.

"Flowers!" Frances shouted in her excitable social voice, "how lovely—I couldn't bear to pick any this morning, but the drawing room does look sad—how sweet of you, Tom. How you do spoil us!"

Frances and Betsy disappeared into the kitchen with the flowers, and Tom found himself alone with his father-in-law.

"Well, let's have a glass of sherry," Sprig led the way into the drawing room.

"We brought the flowers, Sir, because"—Tom swallowed, feeling suddenly the enormity of this simple gesture in the present context—"to express our feelings about Bill Waterford. It's hard news. I'm sorry," he said.

"Nice of you, Tom; we appreciate it," Sprig said, his face absolutely rigid.

He poured out the sherry and handed Tom his glass, then gave him a quick desperate look. "We can expect a little Dorgan, I hear." He raised his glass, but avoided Tom's eyes. And before there was time to answer, Sprig asked, "How are things at the bank?"

The hurdle, Tom thought, has been very neatly taken. In fact, now that it was done, Sprig visibly relaxed, loosened his collar a little and actually looked at Tom.

"I sometimes wonder," Tom answered "whether they teach simple arithmetic any more in the schools—we have the damnedest time straightening out these perfectly intelligent women's accounts."

"Well"—and Sprig smiled his rare amused smile—"I dare say they teach it, but you can't force a horse to water or a woman to make a simple addition."

Frances' voice called out from the dining room, "We can hear you and we protest!" She cried, "I'm very good at simple arithmetic!"

Sprig and Tom exchanged a look and dropped the subject quickly.

"We all know you are a paragon," Sprig called back, "and in no way representative."

"Stuff and nonsense!" Then they could hear the swing door creak, and there was silence, broken by the sound of an elephant apparently falling down the stairs, which turned out to be Caleb. "Hi," he said, brushing past Tom to pour himself a glass of sherry and sit down in the wing chair with a look of extreme distaste, as if he hated everyone present. He had on a clean white shirt, a black tie and a gray tweed jacket over army pants.

"That tie is dreadful," he said, glaring at his father. "You look like a Japanese juggler."

Sprig looked down at his tie, yellow silk with white spots, as if he had never seen it before, then turned up the end. "It is a Japanese tie, as a matter of fact," he said, as if he were astonished and rather pleased. "How did you know?"

Betsy came in, looking embarrassed as she always did,

Tom noted, when she was in the same room with more than one member of her family at a time. "I think it's a lovely tie, Pa, don't listen to Caleb. Where's Hester?" she asked. Caleb got up and wandered into the dining room, leaving the door open behind him.

"She said something about a meeting after church," Frances said, taking off her apron and flinging it onto the stool. "We've still got a quarter of an hour. The roast looks rather raw."

Tom poured her a glass of sherry and gave it to her.

"Thank you, dear. Come out in the garden, it's too beautiful to stay indoors. . . . We're going out, Caleb, want to come?" she called at the door.

"No thanks."

And Tom found himself alone with her. Was it simply being out of doors, melted by the gentleness of the day, the pale warm sun, the surprised look of the crocuses who all seemed to be saying a silent "Oh!" or was it being alone with Frances Wyeth? Such relief seemed slightly ridiculous. Or were the tensions inside slightly ridiculous? Never mind, he walked beside Frances to the flower beds at the end of the garden, lifting the apple branches over her head as she passed, and felt released, warmed, alive again.

"How did Sprig seem?" she asked him, as if he really were for once a member of the tribe.

"All right. A bit tense, maybe. But isn't he always? Are those tulips coming up? It looks as if you'd been working like a beaver out here——"

"It's my secret vice," she said, laughing up at him, since

she was already stooped over, her sherry glass standing in the wet earth, her quick hands busy at the weeds. "I get drunk —work so long and so hard, I feel quite ill. Yes," she added, "Sprig is tense."

She frowned, but it was hard to tell whether she was frowning at the weeds or because of Sprig. "I really must stop or I shall get filthy before lunch——" And she stood up, sniffing the air hungrily, everything about her, Tom thought, stretched taut like a race horse, trembling just under the skin. Beside her, Betsy, thank heavens, seemed as relaxed as a cow in a field.

"What are you smiling at, you wicked boy?"

"Oh at nothing—the day——"

Frances stood there, squinting a little in the sunlight, rubbing the dirt off her hands absent-mindedly, and then pounced in the sudden way she had, which always took him by surprise. "It seems awfully soon for a baby, Tom." Seeing him flush, she smiled a teasing smile, pulled him to her, laid a hand on his arm. "Of course we can't forgive you for making us into grandparents, that's the real bother——"

"You'll have to get used to it," he answered lightly, "we want a large family, so you see," he added, parrying her thrust, "we had to begin early."

"Yes"—Frances pushed a strand of hair out of her eyes and looked off into the trees—"of course," but she was thinking of something else. It was just as if a shadow fell across her face, a shadow of leaves, or a thought. She looked, Tom thought, dreadfully alone suddenly, and—old. "This business of Bill Waterford," she said, reaching into her pocket for a cigarette, "has shaken us." Tom leaned down to recover her glass which had been standing in the flower bed, forgotten. He found nothing to say, but handed it to her. "A terrible thing," he murmured, shaking his head. We are helpless, he thought; life, death, they happen *to* us. It all flows together.

"Do you miss the Church?" Suddenly, in the last few moments in which their thoughts rather than their words had merged, they had come close together, and she could ask such a question in spite of being a member of a strange tribe. "It must be such a comfort, to light candles, to pray, to be able to *do* something——"

"Of course it is," Tom said quickly, "a tremendous comfort. But I could never go back," he said quietly.

"No, I expect it's like a divorce. You can't go back."

"Some people do, though—remarry after a divorce——" And he smiled down at her, happy to be with her, happy in this intimacy which he had always wanted, which had suddenly happened between them. And they dropped the words, the conversation and left them in the garden, content to walk back together, arm in arm.

Betsy, at the kitchen door, greeted them, flushed and anxious. "Oh, Ma, for heaven's sake come and look at the roast!"

"Has Hester come?"

"Ages ago. We're waiting for you," Betsy said accusingly.

So it was when she went away for a few moments, and Frances plunged back into it all, shouting orders, scolding

Caleb, running into the living room to give Hester a kiss between dishing out the potatoes and setting the beans to drain.

It did seem always as if the last few moments before serving were a kind of extremity. Sprig had forgotten to open the wine. There was the question of butter plates, decided against because of the extra washing up, at the last minute. Was the roast done enough?

Sprig stood to carve, and carved gracefully and quickly, sending the plates down one after another to Frances at the other end of the table, to be given vegetables. Caleb, without being asked, got up to pass the gravy.

"You might open the wine, Tom," Sprig said, after a moment.

And then conversation burst out in several directions at once as Hester asked one question and Sprig at the same moment asked her what the sermon had been about, while Frances disappeared to get the jelly which had been forgotten.

"The sermon? Oh dear, you know the awful thing is I nearly fell asleep," Hester confessed. "Yet it was enormously interesting," she added, "on that passage about 'He that is not with me is against me.'"

"An attack on the lukewarm members of the congregation who come to church, but go to sleep?" Sprig asked.

"And what were you doing all morning?" she countered.

Tom watched the brother and sister, so different (Hester so much warmer and so much more expansive) and yet so alike (the shyness in the eyes, the quick speech, quick and articulate, yet always self-deprecatory, always concealing) with amusement.

"I muddled about," Sprig said cheerfully. "As a matter of fact I spent most of the morning trying to find a word for something in Greek which suggests honor and courage, not quite either, not quite both."

"And did you find it?" Frances asked, beaming upon him from her end of the table.

"No, but I enjoyed myself. And what did you do, Mr. Dorgan?" Sprig asked with a twinkle in his eye.

"Oh we just lay around," Betsy answered for him, "breakfast in bed—it's Sunday, Pa. What's Sunday for?"

"Scandalous, scandalous." Caleb spoke for the first time. "Reading Greek, going to church, even cooking," he said with a grin in his mother's direction, "are respectable Sunday occupations. Lying in bed is not, is it, Pa?"

"I work all week," Tom said, annoyed, and then annoyed with himself for taking the bait. When would he learn to underplay it all as they did?

"Oh, but in New England you are expected to be engaged in a worthy occupation every day of the week, and especially on Sunday." Caleb was obviously delighted to have nettled him.

"What did you do, then?" Betsy asked pointedly.

"I?" Caleb shrugged. "Nothing, of course. I'm the black sheep. I browsed," he added, with a quick glance at his father.

"Are you in a permanent state of frustration, Caleb, or what?" Betsy was surprisingly aggressive it seemed to Tom.

"Isn't the term 'quiet desperation' in these parts?"

Caleb flashed back. "Frustrated is too Freudian. There might be a solution to frustration—and that would be dangerous, wouldn't it, Pa?"

"I don't know what you're talking about," Sprig said blandly.

"Sprig——" Frances warned, but it was too late.

"Oh yes you do," Caleb answered, glaring at his father.

"Oh Caleb, please don't," Betsy implored, reaching under the table for Tom's hand.

"Very well," Sprig said quietly. "You should get a job," and he went on eating, as if nothing were happening, as if Caleb were not on the border of rage, looking as if he would like to throw his glass of wine in his father's face.

"Breaking stones?" Caleb asked.

"You'd get rich quick," Tom said genially, "richer than a junior banker, I've no doubt." But it was too late for banter now.

"You all make me ill," Caleb muttered to his plate.

"In that case perhaps you had better leave the table," Sprig said coldly.

"Oh dear," Frances sighed and leaned across the table to her sister-in-law. "Hester, please——"

"Sprig, why can't we talk this out?" Hester asked. "I don't understand. Caleb's upset, and maybe he has a right to be," she said, smiling over at Caleb, who kept his head down, but whose face was bright red. "Your father's not an ogre, Caleb. Are you, Sprig?" and she looked at her brother quite severely.

For a moment the whole table was suspended in the

precipitation of the moment and Tom felt that anything might happen. The suspense only lasted a second, but it was a rather frightening second. There was so much passion coursing about like lightning between them, so many currents.

Frances became the lightning conductor and brought them to safety by getting up and standing behind her son, one hand on his shoulder.

"Sprig, I want to give Caleb the money for his trip to Europe," she said. "This has been going on long enough."

Caleb lifted his head and they all saw the tears glaring in his eyes. "Oh, leave me alone," he cried out, like an animal in distress, and ran out of the room.

"Would someone like another helping of meat?" Sprig asked, as if nothing had happened.

"We'll clear away." Betsy got up quickly. No one had any more appetite, and she and Tom went back and forth with the dishes. "What is the matter with Pa?" she whispered to Tom, her face quite white.

"We can't help," Tom said, squeezing her shoulder gently. "You mustn't get upset."

"I'm going to Caleb." She ran out of the kitchen and up the stairs.

Tom stood for a moment in the kitchen, wondering if he too should make himself scarce. He could hear raised voices in the dining room, Frances, then Hester. Where to go? He busied himself rinsing plates for a while and then braced himself to go back.

"My grandfather's money is a trust," Sprig was saying

very quietly. "I cannot throw it away on a boy who can't make up his mind, won't get a job, and doesn't talk reason. That's that."

"My mother's money is a trust, too," Frances answered, as Tom took his place, after putting the dish of ice cream down in front of her. "Oh, there's chocolate sauce, Tom —in the little gray saucepan with a lid on it. Just heat it up, will you?"

They were still at it when he came back. Hester was sitting silent between them, twirling her wineglass in her hand.

"Where's Betsy?" Frances asked.

"She went up to Caleb."

"Oh."

This apparently caused some dismay. Sprig looked across at his wife with an almost pleading look, then refilled the glasses, and for a moment the three grownups sat there, like abdicating royalty, Tom thought, as if they were abandoned.

Hester stopped twirling her glass and drank some wine. "It isn't the money, Sprig, is it? It seems to me that all discussion of this in terms of money is just nonsense—there *is* money, after all, and whether it's your grandfather's or Frances' mother's seems to me quite irrelevant."

"Quite," Sprig answered, pouring a great deal of chocolate sauce on his ice cream. "I don't believe in rewarding indolence," he added.

"People grow up differently," Hester said tentatively. "Maybe Caleb has to get away to find out what he wants."

"Being able to spoil your children is no reason for doing so, Hester."

"It's hopeless," Frances said, and Tom saw that she was near to tears. "If I give him the money, Sprig will never forgive me."

"And if you don't, what about Caleb?" Hester asked into the air.

It's a funny thing that that old spinster has so much sense, Tom thought, and at this moment he caught Hester's eye.

"What are you thinking, Tom?" she asked. "You look faintly amused."

"I was agreeing with you," he said, smiling back.

"But I have only asked questions," she said, teasing him.

"Yes, I know."

"Hester's questions are only her way of exercising command," Sprig suddenly chuckled. "Damn you, Hester, you're a confounded nuisance."

For a moment of saving grace, it seemed as if the air would lighten. But just then Betsy came back, stood in the doorway, and Tom saw at once how upset she was.

"You're murderers," she said. "Caleb has a right to his own life. He's not a child."

Tom looked at her in sheer amazement. How could so much hatred exist in dear, sweet Betsy, always so loving and kind? He had never seen her like this before. It frightened him.

Sprig said, "Sit down and eat your dessert, Betsy. We've had enough drama."

Betsy obeyed, ate one spoonful of ice cream, and then laid her spoon down. Her hands, Tom could see, were clenched in her lap.

"Where are the animals?" Sprig asked. This question was so typical, so forlorn, so completely in character that it broke the tension once and for all. Frances got up, carried Mr. Silence in, and plumped him down on Sprig's lap. It took the old cat several seconds to open his eyes and wake up to the fact that he had been subjected to an indignity. But once he did he lashed his tail back and forth three times and jumped down, disappearing into the hall almost at once. Not so Hannah who came in to Frances' call and sat looking at her master with adoring eyes, thumping her tail on the floor.

"You'll have to give her some ice cream," Frances said.

And Sprig obediently bent down and let Hannah lick what was left of his ice cream off a plate.

"I suppose I am an ogre," he addressed the dog, "but at least you don't know it." Was it an admission, or mere self-pity?

"No, Pa," Betsy said quite gently, "no one thinks you're an ogre." She took a deep breath. "I'm sorry I was cross."

Sprig received this apology with a slight raising of his eyebrows, but said nothing. "But you're so afraid of spoiling Caleb," she went on, "that you're stifling him. You've always expected too much, and all through college he did what you expected, pulled down all those honors—he did it for you, Pa. Now you've just got to give him a break—"

"My dear child," Sprig looked at her gravely, "you're grown-up." The quizzical family look came back into his eyes. "Very possibly what you say is true," but it was to Frances that he turned, turned and looked with a curious faraway look, half humorous, half ironic, a look which Hester, Tom and Betsy each caught on its way. It was as if a polarity between those two that had been lost for a time, was again in play. Sprig was saying, "Shall I go up and have a talk with Caleb now, take him some ice cream?"

"Dear Sprig," Frances said a little breathlessly.

And then in the relief of it, in the warmth of it, still trembling a little from the stresses of the last half hour, they clattered the dishes together, and trooped into the kitchen to wash up.

"He's such a dear man," Frances was saying, as if she had just realized it afresh, come upon it as a revelation, "such a dear good man, Hester."

Tom stood with his arm around Betsy's shoulder, squeezing it gently. A few days ago Betsy would not have had the courage to stand up to her father, he was thinking. It had all happened overnight. It had all happened because she was becoming a parent and he felt tremendously proud of her, longing to get her away from them all and to be able to tell her so.

"And Betsy's such a dear good woman," Hester answered, flashing Tom and Betsy a smile as she stood with a towel in her hands, waiting for the dishes.

Well, Tom was thinking, you just couldn't know about the Wyeths. At the very instant when they seemed absolutely impossible, smug, self-sufficient, sure they were right, they pulled something like this. Were willing to admit they had been wrong—and he remembered his own fights with his father, that ended in his father's beating him, and because he had been beaten by physical force only, ended also in Tom's going his own way, free. That, the Wyeths would never be able to do—they were woven together like roots under the earth. They would never be free of each other. They would never be free of Great-Grandfather Wyeth and all the rest of the clan. Unless Caleb . . .

"What does Caleb think he wants to do?" Tom asked Betsy.

"Do you know, Ma?" Betsy asked quickly. "Has he told you?"

"He hasn't exactly told me," Frances said, a cigarette hanging from her mouth as she swirled soap-suds around and dumped the dishes in. "But I guess he must be writing something——" Whatever Betsy might have answered was drowned out as Frances' voice sang out over the rattle of the dishes,

" 'Speed bonnie boat like a bird on the wing . . .' " Hester took the alto and soon they were all four singing.

＊

CHAPTER SIX

CALEB heard the slow purposeful steps, heard them
pause on the landing (perhaps after all Pa was only
going to the john), then begin the second flight up. He
turned his back and stood, facing the windows, looking out
into the high branches of the maple. Pa is coming to have
"a little talk," he thought, but he felt frozen beyond emotion and concentrated on the tiny pale green parasols, the
maple flowers which must have appeared overnight. He felt
absolutely empty after the rush of words he had flung at
Betsy when she came up, the concentrated bitterness and
hatred that had been building up for the last month against
both his parents. She had listened with her big dreamy eyes,
and she had not said very much, except, "It isn't their fault,"
and this, he remembered she had said several times, as if she
were hanging onto it against him. "They can't help it," she
said.

His father was now standing in the doorway, but Caleb
didn't move, just waited, not even tense, his hands thrust
deep into his pockets.

"Betsy brought the message to Garcia," said the ironic
voice behind him. "It seems to have been a rather hard
journey. Betsy was very upset," the voice went on, getting
drier with each word.

Caleb forced himself to stand still where he was, as if this were a game of Blind Man's Buff. I won't move, he thought, clenching his teeth.

His father coughed and Caleb knew he was also loosening his collar now in that familiar nervous gesture.

There was a considerable silence, then Sprig said, "Shipshape up here." It was a tentative gesture of capitulation, as Caleb well knew. It lay on the air between them and from it flowed memories Caleb could not keep down: his father teaching him to sail; that time they got caught in a squall and nearly capsized; his father playing a neat deadly game of tennis and surprising Nat, who had expected to beat the old man without even trying; his father hacking away alone in the woods, clearing trees; always doing well everything he did. Why were they having this awful time now? What was it? But now that he had taken a stance, had not turned round, had not spoken, it was becoming harder and harder to do anything.

The creak of the bedsprings told him his father had decided to sit it out.

"Your sister made a rather telling point," he said and Caleb heard the match strike, and turned, driven now by the need for a cigarette, to fumble about on the desk for the package.

"What was that?" he asked. But he would not look at his father.

"If you sat down, Caleb, this might be a bit easier."

"I'd rather stand," he said, the anger beginning to prickle along his arms.

"Very well," and Sprig got up and wandered over to the windows. "Nice view you have. The old maple's standing up pretty well. I was afraid it might go in the last storm. But the gutters need cleaning," he added, leaning out in his absorption with this practical problem. "Come here—all choked, right down to the end of the roof."

Caleb leaned out in spite of himself, and found that he was standing quite close to his father.

"Think you could do it?" Sprig asked. "Wouldn't want you to break your neck."

"Oh, I can do it."

"Good, that's settled." It was amazing how this short exchange had cleared the air.

"What was it Betsy said?" Caleb was able to ask, as they stood there side by side looking out. It seemed astonishing that his father could be here at all, in this room that he visited not more than once a year.

"Well," Sprig said, turning over the pile of books on the desk, and stopping to read the title page of Simone Weil's "Need for Roots," then a book of Martin Buber's. "Theology, eh?" He seemed pleased.

Caleb waited while his father slowly wound himself up to the point.

"Look here, Caleb, it doesn't matter what Betsy said. One could make it a generality, I suppose, something about how fathers are terrified of what they see of their own faults in their sons. My father was a gloomy old cuss, as you know, but he did leave me frightfully free, I suppose because *his* father was such an Old Testament Yahveh."

But if we are going to have to listen to all that again
. . . Caleb thought. "I don't get your point, Pa. What are
you driving at?" he said sharply, and looked straight at his
father, the wrong thing, as he saw the look of slight shock,
of hurt, cross that closed face.

"I'm trying to tell you."

And suddenly Caleb saw that they mustn't have another fight, that they had hurt each other and been angry
with each other long enough. He was filled with loathing
of all the last months, the prison he had created for himself,
and because he felt this for the first time and saw it clearly,
he did an amazing thing, a thing he had never done in his
life. He put out a hand and touched his father's arm, without
saying a word. Then he went and sat down in the armchair,
overwhelmed by the rush of love this small gesture had released.

Sprig, too, was moved, obviously, coughed again, went
back to the bed and perched on the end of it, looking, Caleb
thought, amazingly young, tentative, his face quite pink.

"I've been so afraid of spoiling you, Caleb—that's what
Betsy said in her wisdom—but you're quite a tough speci-
men, I gather. I'm going to suggest something. I might say
first that your mother has offered to pay your expenses, but
I think Grandfather Wyeth would want his great-grandson
to—well"—and Sprig looked embarrassed—"would want
maybe to do for his great-grandson what he never did for
his son. I'll give you three thousand, Caleb, outright, if
you'll wait till after the summer." The last words came out
in a rush, and Caleb was busy for a few seconds sorting out

what all this meant. His first instinctive reaction was to pounce on the word "outright" and add "with strings attached, of course—the summer—" but something in his father's face, a look he had never seen there before, a naked wistful look, held him back.

"Very well, Pa. That's generous, I must say."

"You see"—Sprig hesitated and looked around for an ash tray, "it's your mother. I think—well, it wouldn't be the same quite without you, Caleb, maybe for one of the last summers together." And then because this was a very great deal for Sprig Wyeth to admit, he added quickly, "Besides the boat needs painting—I thought we might shingle the house."

His eyes were very bright, and Caleb seeing in them the memories of all the summers at the Point, smelling the clean smell of salt and pine and mushrooms, saw also for the first time that things would change, that his parents were growing older, and that something just now had been asked of him, the child, in just the way that he, the child had once asked passionately, "But you're not going to Europe for the whole summer, Pa?" because if it were true, he would despair.

He answered cheerfully, "I'd like to try that new rubber paint—some people say it peels off. Do you suppose we could make some experiments here?" What he knew was that in this half hour, in this making of the peace, he had in some mysterious way become his father's parent and not, any longer, his father's child. It was a major shift in the angle of vision.

164

CHAPTER SEVEN

SPRIG ran down the stairs he had mounted so slowly, ran down and out into the garden, for from the window at the landing he had seen Frances stooped over the flower beds, and he felt he must get to her now quickly before she became completely swallowed up by her passion for eradicating weeds.

"Come for a walk," he said as soon as he was within earshot. "It's Sunday afternoon, and your Puritan ancestors are turning in their graves."

"Oh Sprig," she stood there, smiling at him, a little out of breath already, looked from him to the flower beds, then wiped her hands on one of his handkerchiefs. "Darling, I'd love to."

"Must you wipe your hands on my best handkerchiefs?" he said plaintively.

"Oh dear, I'm sorry. I'll be right back. Take a look at the scillas under the pear tree—aren't they delicious?"

But Sprig stood where he was, his hands in his pockets, smiling. In those few moments alone in the garden, the warm sun flowing down from his neck into his arms and hands, it was as if time were suspended, as if he had been running for days, for weeks, running toward some unknown destination, and now he had arrived. He could stand still in the garden and breathe, look up to watch two gulls wheel, turn and float down the wind toward the river, a flash of white against the soft hazy sky, a reminder that the Atlantic Ocean was not far off, a reminder also that the weather must be changing, if the gulls had come in this far.

"What are you smiling at?" Frances said, slipping an arm through his quite casually, though this was something she had not felt able to do for months.

"Nothing," he said, still smiling. "I was watching the gulls." He turned and saw her, transformed from the gypsy he had glimpsed from the landing to Mrs. Wyeth out for a Sunday walk. She had tied a scarf round her throat and put on the jacket to her suit, even carried white gloves, he noted with amusement.

"Why all this elegance?"

"I don't know——" And, indeed, why had she run up the stairs like a young girl, stood a few seconds at the mirror choosing a scarf, trying first one then another? "We haven't been for a walk for such a long time——"

They were out on the street now, and turned back at the top of the hill, as they all did, to take a look at the house. "We must get that shutter mended, Sprig."

"Caleb will do it," he said rather smugly.

"What makes you think so?"

"Caleb and I have made our peace."

"So I gathered," she said.

All around them the green sprang out, the leaves unfurled, the scillas and snowdrops looked bluer, looked whiter, than even a day ago, for they were going for a walk together, arm in arm. And why haven't we done this before? Sprig asked himself. Whatever has been the matter with us?

Aloud, he said, "I can't get used to it, Betsy suddenly grown-up and furious, Caleb being so kind and ironic."

"Was Caleb kind and ironic?" Frances asked, with a smile. It was rather hard to imagine.

"I'm being beaten into submission by my children," Sprig said. "Soon they will begin to humor us——"

"You're not quite on the brink of the grave, darling, you know."

"Churches going up everywhere," he said as they came upon the excavations for a new church at the corner of Longfellow Park. "Gran-Quan would have a fit. Greek Armenians, Seventh Day Adventists——" He sounded quite cross, but that was not what he was really cross about, and Frances slid her arm through his again. "Caleb is reading Simone Weil, Buber, God knows what. I wouldn't be surprised if someone converted him to Catholicism."

"Well, Gran-Quan won't know," Frances said. "And Buber or Weil would, I suppose, keep him from going over the brink."

"You've read them?" and Sprig looked at her quite reproachfully, as if she had committed some secret crime, or been unfaithful. He saw the drawn look come back into her face, wished he had held his tongue, thought, How little we know about each other. She did not answer.

"Let's get to the river." That was his answer to her silence. For the river—where they had walked so many hours during their engagement, during the first years of their marriage, and not lately, was a symbol, was *their* river—became something like a word of endearment.

"Yes," she answered with a quick smile, "let's get to the river."

They hurried down Hawthorne, as if they were no longer suspended in the timeless spring, but driven forward, until they stood at the big curve of Memorial Drive, under the avenue of plane trees and their low round arches, with the blue-gold river turning away under Anderson Bridge and an old motor boat put-putting past, leaving a long V of ripples in its wake.

"Shall we sit down and smoke a cigarette?"

Smoking, sitting there side by side, they let the river possess them, let it take their thoughts for a moment, and float them into peace.

With me, Sprig thought, she is shy. She can't say what she is thinking. The realization of how he had abandoned her right there within the walls of the house, and of their life, suddenly broke over him.

But the awful thing was that knowing something did not make one able to do anything about it. The more he saw, the more he felt incapable; the silence, which had been natural at first, grew tense.

"You're thinking about Bill," she said. But he had not been thinking about Bill. He had quite forgotten Bill. He had set out with his wife into the spring day as if no one died, as if they were suspended in happiness, in relief, as if the ice had melted between them and the voice of the turtle were heard in the land. Reach over now and take her hand and tell her, the small voice spoke within him. He coughed. He loosened his collar a little.

"I was thinking—about—the river," he said. "We're floating downstream, Fran, there's no turning back."

"Who wants to turn back?" she answered sharply. "We're just beginning to be ourselves." She was always talking about being oneself these days.

"Grandparents?" he asked ironically.

"Well"—she frowned and hesitated—"maybe that's part of it. But that's not what I mean, Sprig." She threw her cigarette away and turned to him. "Sometimes I think you should go to Japan, get away from all of us, take a year for yourself."

It came as a complete surprise. That was the terrifying thing about women—they read your most secret thoughts. How did she know?

"You don't have to look like a criminal caught stealing the silver, darling!" She was laughing at him; at that moment he would have liked to bury his head on her breast, to take her in his arms, to weep away the months of their separation.

"Apparently you have second sight," he said drily, getting up.

"Why don't you, then?" she was daring him now. She had caught him, caught up with him in his inward flight, knew exactly where he was. It was disturbing.

"You know very well I can't. Besides what would you do?" he said irritably.

"I don't know," she answered, her chin lifted, her eyes

blazing but whether with anger or tears he did not know. "But it might be better than these last months, clearer"— she paused and swallowed and said quite softly—"less painful."

"What made you say we're just beginning to be ourselves then?" he asked, feeling badgered. They strode along, side by side, no thought of going arm in arm now. They walked fast, propelled by their separate emotions. Cars swooped down, rushed past—this part of the river was ruined. There used to be willows, dances at the boathouse, and Sprig thought of these things as an escape from other thoughts. "Charles Eliot would certainly be sore if he could see what they've done with this," he muttered.

"I think becoming oneself is terribly painful, I think middle age is pure hell," she said then. "A lot of the time I feel like an empty husk."

"Well then?"

"Well"—she slowed down and they stood, back to the streams of cars, facing the river, facing the calm still river where a grove of small birches opposite was reflected, "just the same we're becoming something."

"Grandparents."

"Sprig"—she turned to him with real concern—"why do you mind so much?"

"I don't know," he said, squinting his eyes at the scene before them. "I haven't an idea," he added, with an evasive smile. "Rage, panic, the sense of being betrayed—give it to the analysts," he said "they'd have a field day."

"I don't want to give it to the analysts," she answered

wearily. "What's the matter, Sprig?" she asked, driving him to the wall. "What is it?"

He had turned away at the first question; she was a little behind him, and in a moment, he bet, would tug at his sleeve. He wished he had never thought of this walk. It was only making everything worse.

"I don't know, Fran."

"Then"—her voice was cold—"I think you should go away somewhere and find out."

He was immensely relieved that she was not going to cry. He was so relieved by her anger, that he felt suddenly able to talk.

"No, Fran," he said seriously, "whatever this is, running away wouldn't help. We've got to work it out here."

"I'm at the end of my patience. I can't live like this, Sprig. I feel like a prisoner, your cook, your housekeeper." Her voice rose now and was close to breaking. "I'm a human being," she said. "You seem to have forgotten that lately." And for some reason she put on her gloves fiercely, pulling them on like a boxer's gloves, he thought, amused.

"I have always thought marriage an unnatural institution," was his reply.

"Very well, you shouldn't have taken it on, then."

They walked down Channing Street in silence, parting to let a little girl on a tricycle through.

Who was it who had talked about "the intermittences of the heart"? But it was not that; there was no intermittence in his love for Fran. The intermittence was in the power to express it, the intermittence was in being able to show it, to

171

prove it to her. He loved her, but the truth was that his greatest need for the last months had been to be alone, to listen to music, to immerse himself in a kind of emotion which ran so deep that it found no way of expressing itself at all. But none of this could he say now to the angry suffering woman at his side, and so he said nothing.

They were stopped by Mrs. Lothrop, taking a walk with her very old dachshund on a leash.

"Dear things," she cried from quite far off, "how lovely to see you. What a beautiful day!" she called, and when they came up to where she was standing, a man's felt hat pulled down over her hair, and an English Burberry in the final years of a long life flung round her shoulders, her eyes smaller and brighter than ever in the fine wrinkled face, she held out both her hands to them, so they found themselves each clasping one. "Dear things," she said again, looking from one to the other. "You look so young, so happy—how do you do it?"

"Hardness of heart," Sprig teased. "Nothing keeps one young like hardness of heart."

"Dear, delightful cynic," she murmured. And turned to Frances, "The children well, I trust?"

"Very well, thank you."

"Well"—Mrs. Lothrop yielded them up reluctantly—"I must let you go. Come and see me," she called after them.

But the incurable optimism, the blind sentimentality of Mrs. Lothrop had broken the spell, and Frances turned to Sprig pink with laughter.

"Let's stop being idiots," she said.

And so it happened that because of Mrs. Lothrop they walked up Fayerweather arm in arm again, and looked at the trees and stopped before a magnolia in full flower, and did not have to say anything more. Sprig was amazed at how much better he felt, though they had come to no solution, though he had not really said any of the things in his heart, yet somehow by the mere admission that something was wrong, by saying it to each other aloud, a fragile bridge had been set up over the abyss between them.

"I think I'll go over and see Bill," he announced suddenly.

*

CHAPTER EIGHT

S PRIG had so rarely been in Bill's new modern house, and had so little connection with Nora, that at the outer gate, he felt an impulse to turn back. He rang quickly before he could change his mind, and found himself inside the stockade, surrounded by raw red earth that would, he supposed, someday be a lawn. Nora stood in the doorway, looking anxious as always, and too thin in a white wool dress. But when she saw him, she smiled shyly.

"Oh," she said, "how nice of you to come. Now perhaps Bill will be persuaded to stop working."

"Working, eh?" Sprig walked into the big living room, and had to admit that it was an exceptionally charming one, especially just now with a big branch of dogwood standing against one wall and the fire lit.

The cheerful shelves of French paper-backed books even had an airy look; French magazines and papers were strewn about on the low table with a pot of daffodils standing among them. This is where Bill lives, he thought. How little he knew of Bill's life, or of the slender, shy woman with her peculiar ash-blonde hair—she looked rather like an Afghan hound he thought—who was offering him tea or a drink.

"It's Sprig," she called up the stairs. "Come down, darling."

"May I come in?" Sprig asked at the door of the kitchen. He watched her fill the kettle and light the gas, and caught himself wondering what she did with herself all day.

"He has suddenly taken it into his head that he has to finish that book by Christmas," she said, setting down cups and saucers. "But Dr. Stiles insisted that he must rest, at least till after the summer—I don't know what to do with him," she said, busy with getting cookies out of a tin. "Was this all an act?" Sprig asked himself. "Did she believe what she was saying?" And for a second standing there in the immaculate kitchen, he had the idea that this whole business of Bill's illness was a mad illusion. Of course he would be all right. What were they thinking of?

Then they heard the racking cough upstairs.

The Bill who came downstairs in an old sweatshirt and gray flannels, wiping the sweat off his face with the back of his hand, unshaven, was nothing like any Bill that Sprig knew. "You'll have to take us as you find us," he said, meeting Sprig's slightly surprised look. "I haven't shaved——"

"Go and sit down, you two," Nora said. "I'll bring in tea in a moment."

Bill flung himself down in a big chair and put his feet up. It was clear that he had been driving himself to exhaustion.

"Sorry if I've butted in," Sprig said cautiously. "But you do look as if it were time to stop."

"Sprig," Bill leaned forward and whispered, "I want

to finish the book. Ten years' work," he said feverishly, "I've got to finish it."

Sprig was standing just beside him; he leaned over and laid a hand on his shoulder. There seemed nothing to say.

"Randall's got my courses," Bill said, "poor guy. Nice about it, I must say. You know"—he shot Sprig a quick glance—"it's a queer thing, but I minded. Delusions of grandeur," he said. "I thought I wanted to teach those kids myself, thought no one could do it so well," and he laughed the quick harsh laugh Sprig knew.

"That's true enough," Sprig answered, glad of some one thing about which he could sound positive and affirmative. "You're a great teacher, Bill. Goodness knows," he added, smiling, "you've told me so yourself plenty of times."

"Good to see you," Bill answered. "Good you're here." But he looked anxiously toward the kitchen, "Where's that tea, Nora? And bring the rum, will you?" he called loudly and irritably.

"Coming, darling," the cool voice from the kitchen answered.

"How would you like to have a cat, Nora?" Sprig asked tentatively. He had just had an idea and hoped against hope it would work.

"Well"—she looked thoughtfully at him, the teapot in mid-air just as she was about to pour—"it depends. What sort of cat?"

"My thought is"—and Sprig leaned forward gravely —"that a cat might keep your husband quiet. God knows how many man-hours I have lost because Mr. Silence in-sisted on sitting on my lap——"

"Oh nonsense," Bill said crossly, "what would I do with a cat? Just one more interruption."

"Yes," Sprig raised his eyebrows quizzically, "exactly."

"Let's try it," said Nora, unexpectedly, and as she passed Sprig his cup, she gave him a quick little look of complicity. "I would love a cat, a marmalade cat, Bill—a big, fat, sleepy, old marmalade cat—please——"

"He'll tear up the furniture and eat us out of house and home, but—oh—very well. You're too much for me, you two——" And Bill gulped down his tea. "Ugh, those pills Thorny pours down my throat make everything taste nause-ating——"

"I'll find you one," Sprig said, "though it may not be a marmalade cat—we can't be too precise——" It was extraor-dinary how the idea of being able to do something for Bill cheered him up.

"'*Ami des amoureux fervents et des savants austères,*'" Bill smiled over his tea. It was the first time he had quoted French poetry, and Sprig knew that at last somehow and for some unknown reason Bill was in command of himself again. He even looked like a different person. It seemed as if he had taken a deep breath. "You know, Sprig," he said, "I talk about the book, but the truth is I've poured my life blood into my students. And so now"—he laid his cup down—"well, I guess I feel sort of lost——"

"They'll be there in the fall, darling," Nora said quickly.

"Yes"—Bill swallowed—"but it's that boy, Ferris. I did want to help him pull the thesis into shape. It's full of good ideas, but it needs organizing. He's got a big job ahead——"

"But surely, Randall——" Sprig interposed. "He's adequate, isn't he?"

"Of course, of course, a fine scholar, but you know how it is." He turned to Nora earnestly. "I've nursed this boy along."

"Nursed is the right word," Nora said, smiling at Sprig, "Bill must have spent weeks of time with that boy."

"Sure, he comes round and bothers me when he has no business to, but he cares. And he's got a fine mind, a truly inquiring mind. That's rare."

Bill sat there, ill, the beads of sweat standing out again on his forehead, but tremendously alive, struggling to maintain his life intact, like a swimmer pulled down by seaweed, but not for a moment giving up. This was what Grandfather Wyeth would have recognized as "gumption," Sprig thought. "What are you smiling about, you old cynic?" Bill asked, passing his cup for more tea.

"Nothing. I was envying you, I guess. You know what your life is all about, what it means."

"Do I?" Bill looked amazed. "I used to think teaching was the obstacle, always getting in the way of my book, keeping me from the Bibliothèque Nationale——" He grinned at Nora. "I used to complain a lot, didn't I? Now that I've had to stop teaching, I see that was it. That was my life. Queer, isn't it?"

For a moment there was silence. Bill had been leaning forward, now he settled back in his chair, his eyes very bright.

"Which of your lives is the real one, Sprig?" The question, so like Bill, startled Sprig out of his thoughts. He was taken aback. "What do you do, really?"

"Bill——" Nora looked as if he had been rude.

"No, sweetheart, it's Sunday afternoon and Sprig and I are old friends. I want to know."

He wants to know before he dies, Sprig thought. But he did not want to answer. Not in front of this strange woman who dressed like a girl and seemed like some strange elfin animal. And not now, when he was upset enough already. "What do I do?" he smiled his ironic smile, "attend the Board meetings of various hospitals, museums and what not——"

"My question was your real life——"

"I'm a landscape architect," Sprig said flatly.

"In your spare time?"

Sprig flushed. He had come to see a sick friend, not an inquisitor, and he had not come here for an examination of conscience. But then he looked up and saw Bill's face, the will to live so brilliant in it, and this dare to him just another way of staying alive, of refusing his illness, of saying, "I can still get you at the quick. I'm not dead yet."

"No"—in a split second, he saw it all clearly—"I had as a young man a passion for formal gardens. I came back from Japan hipped on what could be done with stones and trees. Then I traveled in France and Italy—well, when I came home full of all this, it was just before the crash. Guilt set in almost at once. After all, Bill, my profession depended absolutely on the idle rich."

"So what?"

"So—plans for zoos, plans for city parks. But all the time the terrible New England fear that this was dabbling in aesthetics. So, the hospital boards. You see, it's not quite as simple as you make it sound," Sprig said half apologetically. "This must be very boring," he turned to Nora.

"It's fascinating," she said without looking at him. But he sensed that she meant it.

"And where do the Greek plays come in?" Bill asked.

"Oh, that!" Sprig looked as self-conscious as he felt.

"There"—Bill pointed a finger at him—"there's your real life."

"*Touché*," Sprig admitted. "If I had to choose——"

"But isn't the whole point that you don't have to?" and Sprig was amazed that this question came from Nora.

"In what way? Why?"

"Because," she said earnestly, "you're an amateur. You do things for love"—and suddenly she smiled—"and then think there must be something wrong about that, so you never quite admit that you are committed to formal gardens, to Greek plays. It's the aristocratic point of view," she said, blushing suddenly.

"Well"—Bill laughed—"and we pros, we academic blokes are just hoi polloi——"

"No," she said, flustered, "I can't explain."

"Do try," Sprig said. "This is most interesting."

"You're the only completely free person I've ever known. But I suppose you're haunted by it—the freedom I mean. It must create anxiety," she said, lapsing into the jargon of the age and Sprig at once felt his hackles rise.

"Don't see why it should," he said cheerfully.

But now that Nora was launched on something she had evidently thought about, she plunged on.

"Nowhere else in this country does your kind of person exist any more—that sense of responsibility, perhaps of guilt, I don't know, the terror of not coming up to the mark——"

"But what is the mark, do you think?" Sprig inquired. Nora was turning out to be far more of a person than he had ever guessed. They had all been put off by her clothes, her little-girl air, her strangeness.

"It's not worldly," she said, feeling her way, "that's certain. I think you are all terrified of power, for instance. Is power wicked?"

Sprig laughed suddenly his surprised laugh. "It's quite true, isn't it, Bill, that we suspect people who go in for power?"

"Why?" she asked, turning her curiously blind look upon him. "Is power vulgar?"

"Corrupting," Bill said, laughing, too.

"You know," Sprig said thoughtfully, "I think the mark is character, not achievement at all. For instance, when I think of my grandfather who was a foxy old businessman if there ever was one, and who loved power as well, I forget all that and what I remember is how much he asked of himself, how far he could walk at eighty, the power of personality, his blustering forthrightness," and he added wryly, "his power to make me feel always inadequate."

"But surely," Bill said, "you were only a kid when he died."

"I was seven. You can feel very inadequate at seven."

"And later on," Nora said earnestly, "if power, success, all the things most men want, are made to seem suspect, what is there left? You have to be an amateur, because that's pure."

"But is it serious?" Sprig asked almost gaily. "We have to be terribly serious, you know."

"I don't suppose landscape architecture would have seemed quite serious to that grandfather of yours, but translating Greek plays——"

"He taught me the Greek alphabet, as a matter of fact," Sprig said and was amazed when Bill and Nora looked very much amused. "You're teasing me, Bill."

"I'll tell you one thing," Bill said quite seriously, "and that is that it's people like you who make Cambridge——"

"I should think Harvard College would come under that heading."

"Yes, but who lives on Brattle Street? College professors? Who goes to the open lectures, to the Sanders Theatre concerts?"

Sprig smiled mischievously. "It is a rather odd bunch of eccentrics."

"Rich, rich," Bill said, smiling. "Those interiors with the stuffed heads of animals, the Japanese gongs, the Canton china, the carved-oak furniture, the dusty velvet curtains, the complete sets of Dickens and Thackeray and Longfellow."

"Hey," Sprig interrupted, "you're describing my house!"

But Bill laughed too hard and started coughing again. And at a look from Nora, Sprig got up. "You'd better rest, old man," he said. "You've put in a hard day."

"Don't go," Bill said, a look of panic crossing his face, "Stay," he begged, "You've done me a world of good—Nora, too."

But Sprig saw the anxiety in her face, as she looked at her husband.

"I'll come back," he said. "Amateurs have all the time in the world," he said at the door. For a second Bill's eyes looked at him, as if he were looking out of a mask, as if he were an animal caught. "Take it easy," Sprig said.

"Come back, won't you?" Nora stood at the door and stayed there till he had clicked the fence door shut behind him.

It was curious but Sprig, standing outside now, looking back though all he could see was the top of the Japanese maple, felt exhilarated. Bill trying desperately to finish his book, Bill teasing him, moving back into life by sheer exuberance, the gust of interest and passion—the mocking gentle look in his eye. I must tell Frances he thought, walking fast. I must tell her. . . .

CHAPTER NINE

SPRIG found Frances in the garden. She had changed into dungarees and an old shirt of his, and when he first caught sight of her, flinging a handful of goose grass into the wheelbarrow, he thought for the flash of a second that she was Caleb. But then he saw Caleb raking leaves under the apple tree, and went toward them smiling. Sprig could never get accustomed to women in men's clothes; it disturbed him and fascinated him to see his wife transformed into a boy in this way, for there was actually something essentially boyish in her and when she wore her dungarees it always meant that she was feeling happy and relaxed. Now she stood up, shading her eyes against the late afternoon sun as he came toward her, smiling back at him, not saying a word, so that it seemed to Sprig as if the garden were enormous and he would never reach the end, nor come to her quickly enough with his message—but how to say it?

"It was all right, then?" she asked, eagerly, anxiously.

"I'm glad I went," he nodded, looking down, still smiling and quite unable to explain why he felt so happy.

They could hear Caleb whistling and the soft brushing of the rake among the damp leaves. They were standing in a patch of sunlight, though the rest of the garden was already in the shadow of the house, and Sprig became aware of each individual blade of grass at his feet, brilliant, fresh green, then looked up and inadvertently entered Frances' glance when she did not expect it, caught the flecks of gold in the hazel iris, was caught himself in an exchange which had in it a shade of humor, a shade of irony, as if they were saying "Well, here we are."

Then he fumbled around in his pocket for a cigarette.

"It's fearful how much there is to do," she said. All that he had thought he could tell her about Bill didn't seem important. Couldn't, perhaps, be expressed.

"I think I'll play some music," he murmured. But he turned back to her to say, "Come in and listen when you get tired——" He thought of saying something to Caleb, but was suddenly shy and instead talked to Hannah who was standing at the door of the barn wagging her tail. For a second he looked back at his wife, kneeling, bent over some small green plant as if nothing else in the world existed.

He flipped over the records thoughtfully, as if in this case the choice was an important one. Then when he had pulled out a Mozart sonata for violin and piano, he went to the window and pushed it open. For once, Frances can be Martha and Mary at the same time, he thought, setting the amplifier up loud so she would hear.

Hannah was already settled on the rug, her nose in her paws, her eyes following his every move. As he brought the needle down on the record, he shivered with anticipation, almost with fear. Always there was, for him, something sacred in this second's pause between silence and sound, when all he heard was the record revolving and then suddenly there was music. He sat down in the big armchair and put his feet up, and closed his eyes. He gave his whole being up to the two voices, the piano then the violin, first one then the other taking the lead, first one muting itself, then the other in a perfect harmony and understanding—married, he thought. The word startled him. He opened his eyes.

Frances had slipped in while he listened and was lying on her stomach on the floor, her head buried in her arms. Caleb was standing in the doorway, smoking. Startled for a moment that they could have settled themselves around him, without his even noticing it, he sat up straight, a little nervously, lost the thread of the music, then sighed, settled back and closed his eyes again. We are absolutely separate now, he was thinking, and yet we are absolutely together, part of a great circle, not (as they had been lately) rushing off on tangents. They had come back and become a family. But why this was so and how it had happened, he could not imagine, following the thread back of this day to Tom's flowers, Betsy's anger, his talk with Caleb in that immaculate room (the gutters really must be cleaned), his walk with Frances, and finally his talk with Bill and Nora. These separate events had all been painful in one way or another, had forced him to recognize things he didn't want to recognize, yet now they added up to harmony, to being alive again, as if some deep current with which he had been out of touch had come back to the surface and carried him with it. But just then the music became imperiously demanding and he stopped thinking of anything, following the design as it unfolded out of itself.

"Mozart?" Caleb asked, when it came to an end.

"Yes."

Frances sat up abruptly, "Oh Sprig, I quite forgot to tell you Uncle Joe called and wants us for dinner tomorrow night. Someone must have dropped out at the last minute—so I said we would go. Is that all right?"

"Fine. Haven't seen Uncle Joe for ages." Sprig felt a rush of affection for the exquisite old man.

"Tell him I want to see him," said Caleb unexpectedly.

"I thought you hated him." Frances hugged her knees and brooded. She was dreamy with physical fatigue and general well-being.

"I'm thinking of going to Greece in the fall——" Did Caleb guess, did he have any idea how delighted Sprig felt as he heard this? What had seemed to Sprig before his recent capitulation a crazy scheme, now seized his imagination for the first time.

"Well, Uncle Joe is your man then," Sprig said. "Of course he hasn't been there for twenty years——"

"What a wonderful idea," Frances said, as if she had taken all this time to realize what they were talking about.

"Well," Caleb said cautiously, still standing half in the big doorway and half outside, and looking up into the treetops as if he saw Greece floating there, "that's what I've been considering. A donkey," he added with a smile, and it was clear that he was now opening his heart, "to carry my luggage. I'd like to see Mount Athos."

"Rather a long walk," Sprig teased, "even with a donkey to carry your books." He looked with respect at this tall stranger who was his son. He has the right ideas, he thought, and was quite unaware that the emotion which filled him now was simply pride.

Two days ago it would have seemed impossible to Sprig that he could be talking in this way with Caleb. Then the boy seemed an utterly strange and even repulsive character, a creature of darkness who had forgotten even how to be reasonably polite. But then the image of Betsy flashed before his mind and he saw that it was his own doing—that he had been making Caleb into a child of darkness. And he felt as if they had avoided some terrible punishment just in time. It seemed to him then that the guilt of unconsciousness was the only unforgiveable sin. It had been with him in relation to Caleb's plans simply a lack of imagination, an instinctive reaction which he hadn't bothered to analyze. But the minute Caleb said "Greece," his plan became a design, became something Sprig *could* imagine. . . .

"I must go and get our suppers," Frances was saying. "Give me a hand, darling, I'm too stiff to move."

Caleb sprang forward and swung her up with one arm, as if she were a feather. They stood there, laughing, his wife who looked like a boy and his son.

"I'll come and help," he announced.

"Good gracious, Pa," Caleb teased, "are you feeling quite well?"

"Don't tease your father," Frances said, slipping an arm through Sprig's. "He can mix a cocktail."

"A cocktail?" Sprig asked suspiciously. "Whatever for?"

"Because"—and Frances hesitated, while Caleb went

on ahead, whistling again, and Sprig stopped to latch the big door. "Because you must be tired, darling. I know I am."

She leaned against him and he put his arm around her shoulders. A thrush was singing somewhere near by.

"Good gracious," Sprig said, "I locked Hannah in the barn," and turned and fled down the path.

*

CHAPTER TEN

IT had been, Frances thought, as they came out from Uncle Joe's into the spring night, a lovely party. Under the whole evening there had been a current of awareness between her and Sprig, as if they had had to see all those people in order to see each other again, as if the whole point of a dinner party was that little shy look Sprig gave her when she was flirting just a little with Hugo, that look of complicity, of amusement, of—perhaps—pride.

"Uncle Joe's in good form," he said when they were safely in the car, driving along the river.

"He doesn't understand you at all," she answered out of her own thoughts.

"Oh well," Sprig smiled across at her, "one can't expect to be understood by a work of art. That's not the point. The point is to enjoy it. You can't expect Uncle Joe to be quite human"—and he chuckled. "When I was a boy he really seemed to me a kind of djinni, a djinni who kept giving me glimpses of heaven or hell, but never forked over—there were two things I coveted and actually dreamed of stealing, and I think he knew that."

"What were they, darling?"

"One was a small jade duck and the other was a nautilus shell."

"He should have given them to you," Frances said.

"It would have been like cutting off a finger to give me that jade duck."

"I hope he leaves it to you in his will," she said and then "Oh, Sprig——"

"What?" Sprig said nervously. They had reached the bridge and he was busy turning off the Parkway and did not notice apparently that she had moved over close to him.

"Why doesn't he marry Mrs. Jeffries?" she asked. "She seems so cosy."

"He'd be involved if he married. And he wants to preserve that dear self of his."

"You do dislike him really, don't you?"

"Do I?" Sprig accelerated unconsciously and fumbled in his pocket for a cigarette. "No, I think I envy him."

"That's even worse," she felt rather cross for no reason. "But why should any human being want to be so inhuman?"

"That harmony, that composure, everything balanced——"

"And never the slightest breath of wind."

"I know, but look at Gran-Quan—he let in the wind——"

"The cold bitter wind, the wind of undoctrine which seems just a little icier than the wind of doctrine. Well, if one had to choose——" she said thoughtfully.

"Exactly."

"But you wouldn't choose to be Uncle Joe, surely—you couldn't, Sprig!" and she sat up quite straight, she felt so violently.

"Better die mad, a mad old hawk, than happy and cheerful and creating something, even something as exquisite and small as a perfect dinner party? I'm not at all sure—Uncle Joe is creating something with his own life. GranQuan, as far as I can see, created nothing but chaos and despair." Sprig's voice was harsh. "I must go and see him tomorrow," he said.

And Frances sighed. They had been at Uncle Joe's in a kind of pleasant dream, and now the blackness welled up again, the problems, the burdens they carried, and even the little thread which she had felt taut between her and Sprig during the dinner party seemed to have broken or gone slack. In a moment they would turn off from the peaceful river and the lights, and go home to bed. She was dead tired now, but too tense, she knew, to sleep.

"Don't turn off," she begged, "Let's drive around over the bridges. Let's keep this a little while."

If Sprig was surprised, he said nothing, but obediently swerved back onto the parkway.

"What is it we are keeping by doing this?" he asked with a little smile.

"I don't know—peace—suspension—why do I dread going home?" Now she had said it, she was a little afraid of the words.

The fact was, she saw suddenly, that the house had become a prison. They were locked up inside it together. Life was pouring out from it, Betsy, Caleb—and it stood there itself like a dynamo gone dead.

"Let's go to some island in the Caribbean after Caleb leaves—let's go on a trip," she said suddenly.

"Whatever for? We'll have been in Maine all summer —I'll have a couple of jobs to do, too."

"Oh, Sprig," and she sighed again. Of course, she recognized, it is not an island that I mean, it's ourselves, our own island. Shall we ever get back to it again? She was sitting stiffly away from him; they had reached the other side of the river and could see the lighted rooms in the Harvard Houses, a sight that always made her excited, thinking of all those boys and men studying, talking, drinking beer, growing up, and each square of light, a life.

For a moment she forgot what they were talking about and then, much too quickly, the time had come to swerve off, to go back into the heart of Cambridge, to go back into the prison, not dream of escape, of islands.

An hour later, Sprig was saying, "I do think I might have some buttons on my pajamas." He showed her the only one left hanging by a thread.

At this moment she hated him. She suddenly hated his closed face, even his teasing smile, his rejection of her, his making her into a sewer on of buttons. I want to be loved, she thought, damn it.

"I don't feel like sewing on buttons," she said coldly. "There are some other pajamas in the drawer, Sprig."

But the minute she had said it, she was sorry; he went off with a funny surprised expression. He is just saying to himself, "the unaccountability of women," and no doubt he was quite right. For only an hour ago she had felt wonderfully happy, she remembered. She was sitting up in bed, a soft white shawl flung round her shoulders and a novel from the Personal Bookshop open in her hands. But she realized after a few moments that she had read the first paragraph three times and had no idea what it said. She let the book fall and lay back, her hands behind her head, staring at the ceiling.

Sprig did not look at her when he came back, and she saw that he still wore the buttonless pajamas. Oh damn, she thought, here I am swearing again, and here I am about to feel guilty again. But what if I said it out loud, said quite calmly "I hate you"? What would happen then?

He was sitting on the edge of the bed, taking off his slippers with a thoughtful look.

"How would you feel if I had a love affair?" she heard herself saying. She would not look at him. She looked at the ceiling, at the perfect closed circle of light on the ceiling.

There was a silence. But she would not look at him.

Then he coughed, as he did when he was embarrassed. "Are you thinking of having one?" he asked cautiously.

She was furious. She sat up and threw the book across the room. "You fool," she said, "of course not. I should be utterly miserable. You know that perfectly well, damn you."

"Then why are you so cross?" he asked gently.

She felt the tears racing down her cheeks before she

even knew she was crying. "Damn, damn," she said, fishing around for the box of Kleenex on the night table. "What is the matter with me, Sprig? I'm sc-sc-scared," she sobbed.

"Overexcited, I expect, and tired, that's all," he said, but it did not matter what he said because he had come over and was sitting on the bed rather awkwardly holding her in his arms, and for a little while she could lean her head against him and feel his heart beating. But even while she knew the full sweetness of breaking through to this place of intimacy at last, despair welled up again and she was shaken with harsh sobs. For, she thought, it is only when I am utterly defenseless, a child wanting only to lay her head somewhere and cry, that I am no longer a threat to Sprig, and so he can take me in his arms.

She pushed him away and lay back on her pillow, blew her nose, laid an arm across her eyes as if to hide them.

"I don't understand," he said, "what have I done, Fran? What is this all about?"

She lay perfectly still now, wholly absorbed in thinking, in trying to decide whether it was the moment to explain to Sprig or whether it would be wiser to cover over this moment of abandon and weakness and go to sleep, as they had done so many times before in the last years, so many times when she had tried in one way or another to batter her way through to this man who was her husband, but for a long time now, had not been her friend even, and did not pretend to be more.

"Darling"—she said, reaching over to find his hand and

195

clasp it tight—"I don't know you any more. I don't know myself, that means. I feel l-l-lost." The tears flowed down her cheeks and onto the pillow.

He did not let her hand go, which was some comfort. "I thought somehow that things were better," he said after quite a silence. "I'm sorry I'm such a failure."

"But why? What's the matter with us, Sprig?" She sat up now, swept by passionate indignation. "Other people don't die at forty-five or fifty—marriages don't just wither away. Do they? Do they?"

She could feel him wince. "I don't know," he said, getting up and fumbling in his trouser pocket for cigarettes. "Want one?"

"Maybe it's just everything that's happening all around us—everything breaking apart, Aunt Jane, Bill—Lucy's divorce, too—as if there were nothing sure, nothing one could hold onto . . ."

"Except one's self."

"One's self is related to other people," she said coldly. "Or don't you admit that?"

He came over to light her cigarette, then walked up and down in his bare feet, the buttonless pajama jacket open, so he looked, she thought with a pang, like some miserable schoolboy being scolded.

"But you can't give yourself into another's keeping, Fran," he said quietly. "Look at my father, broken to pieces by being incapable of detachment, utterly dependent on that frail sister ten years older than he, cracks up when she dies. There has to be something in one's self," he said, bearing down hard on the last word. "Bill has it," he said half to himself, "struggling like a drowning man to finish his book."

"Maybe. But he also has Nora. And she has him." She was cold with rage. She would have liked to get up and beat her fists on Sprig's chest, batter him physically. Only it would not help. She knew enough to know that.

Sprig stopped walking up and down and gave her a single haunted haunting look. Then he went to the window, stood with his back to her, stiffly, and spoke to the night outside. She could feel the immense effort he was making, saw it in the tenseness of his shoulders, knew she must not go to him, must not move.

"Look, Fran, I love you. However limited my capacity for love may be. That's all I can say. You'll have to accept it. Maybe sometime I'll have grown a self that can meet all you have to give. Just now I'm a beggar who can't even hold out his hand——"

She measured the extremity of pity that had forced him to say so much.

"It's all right, dear," she said quietly. "If you'll take off your jacket for five minutes, I'll put on those buttons."

PART THREE

The Birth of
a Grandfather

*

CHAPTER ONE

FRANCES called that summer the summer "after the last" because it seemed to be a long decrescendo. Betsy and Tom had one of the little houses over across the long meadow for the month of Tom's vacation and were hardly ever seen. The big house without Gran-Quan and Aunt Jane seemed to Frances to stand in perpetual darkness; Sprig was always on the wing, so abstracted and knit up into Bill Waterford's struggle against time that even when he was not actually in Cambridge, he might as well have been. Without Caleb and his maps of Greece and his books about Greece, without Caleb and the eager thrust forward of his life, Frances would have been desolate indeed. She felt like a ship becalmed on a sinister quiet sea; she sat on the porch for hours, Mr. Silence on her lap, magazines and books on a table by her side. But she didn't read.

There Betsy had found her one windless gray afternoon—Frances heard slow steps coming up, the steps of a woman carrying a child.

"Hoo-ooo," Betsy called, pausing at the door.

"I'm out here, on the porch, dear. How nice to have a visit." And even as she said it, Frances realized that it was what an ill person might say, a person who depended entirely on others for whatever life she had. Hannah got up, barked, and wagged her tail till it looked as if it would fall off.

"How are things going?" she asked, as Betsy pulled over a wicker chaise lounge and lay down with a sigh. Hannah followed her over and flopped down beside her, one eye open, her head on her paws.

"Tom's out sailing with Caleb. They've become friends, you know. It's nice."

The two women looked out through the trees at the sky, at the bird feeder swinging now as a siskin flew down. They hadn't been alone together for days.

"Is there anything the matter, Mummy?" Betsy asked, after a pause. The silence, indeed, was so unusual that it was troubling. Then she saw a tear slide down her mother's cheek.

"What is it, Mummy?" she said, really alarmed. She had felt the impulse to come over this afternoon, to rouse herself out of the beautiful inertia of these days, because she had wanted to talk about her baby, about having it, with someone who knew.

"Pay no attention, darling. I think I'm just—tired."

"Oh, Mummy, you're never tired. That's not it. Please try to tell me——"

"Aunt Jane," Frances managed to say, feeling the willed smile cracking her cheek. One does not weep in front of one's children. She bit her tongue hard. "I don't know, darling—it's a strange summer." But this, meeting Betsy's clear blue gaze, so compassionate and newly aware, was not enough. "I keep wishing I could talk with Aunt Jane, as if I never did when she was here——" And Frances laughed a light embarrassed laugh.

"I miss her, too. She was like balm."

"Why?" Frances found herself asking her daughter.

Betsy looked out into the trees with the vague look Frances had found so irritating in her as a child. "She seemed to be in Heaven already."

"What an odd thing to say," Frances sat up now and lit a cigarette. She was startled out of her mood completely. "But—yes—I see what you mean. So merry and selfless— as if she had only to be, not do any more." Frances puffed at her cigarette. "Yet she was always driving herself on, physically at least, to get up early and put on the coffee. When I go down now into the kitchen, and she's not there, it's each morning like a new shock. You know," she turned to Betsy with all her usual intensity, "it's very odd when the older generation goes. You thought they were dependent on you, but actually—maybe that's what's wrong with me—you discover that you depended on them." Quite unconsciously Frances shivered, and shivering, turned to her daughter. "Are you warm enough? The wind has changed."

"Quite warm, thank you." All the relationships are shifting, Betsy was thinking. No one knows where she is. For in the last few minutes, she recognized an enormous shift, a silent earthquake taking place between her and her mother. She had come for comfort, but found herself trying to give it. And in these few seconds, it seemed as if the child in her belly and her mother were wound together, and that her mother, down whose cheek she had seen a tear fall like a shooting star, like an omen, had become her child. "It's Pa, partly, isn't it?"

"How do you know?" Frances asked, drawing in her breath sharply. The thin veil that had protected her was being torn off, and her instinct was to draw it close around her.

"He's taking Bill Waterford's dying too hard. Tom talks about it; Caleb, too. We've been anxious."

"You have?" It seemed almost incredible to Frances that someone besides herself had been anxious about Sprig, that the children should be. "Oh, darling, it is good to have you here," she said. Was she aware that almost never had she said such a thing before?

"It doesn't seem quite natural somehow," Betsy was saying, then hesitated, glanced over at her mother, "I mean, of course Bill is father's best friend, but——"

"He's thrown himself into death as if it were life, a substitute——" Frances responded instantaneously, nodding her head.

"Like going to Japan," Betsy said dreamily.

"Heavens, Betsy, you do have peculiar ideas—whatever do you mean?" It was the old, impatient tone that had closed Betsy as a child. For a second she withdrew like a sea anemone at a touch, sealed herself away.

"I don't know," she said then, shifting in her chair, for she felt too hot suddenly. The chair creaked. "Escape——" she half whispered. "I wish you could get away, Mummy,

I wish you could go off somewhere and have some fun."
But the voice was the voice of a child, a child half complaining, half insistent, and the moment of intimacy had
been broken.

"I suggested a trip after Caleb goes. Your father said
no," Frances answered in her usual definite tone of voice.

"I meant alone," Betsy faltered.

"I can't imagine it. I'd be worrying about Pa all the
time." Frances cocked her head and looked at her daughter
with amusement. "This is quite an inquisition."

"It's not only I," Betsy spoke quickly, embarrassed.
"Caleb thinks so, too."

"Oh, he does, does he? And I suppose Tom agrees,"
the irony in the grown-up voice was unmistakable.

"Don't, Mother."

"I'm sorry, darling. I know I'm impossible. Let's talk
about something else." But before they could, Frances had
got to her feet and walked over to the porch railing, looking
away. "Do you suppose Aunt Jane wanted to marry?
Wanted all sorts of things she never had?"

"She made her peace."

"Yes," and Frances gave a long sigh. "Do you suppose
I'll ever make mine?"

But this question was never answered for at just that
moment, Betsy put a hand to her belly and gave a little
jump.

"Mummy, come here, I can feel him. He gave a great
thump just then."

Frances ran over and knelt down so she could lean her head against Betsy; together they listened to the third person who had been the secret, binding element in this conversation from the beginning and who was now making himself known.

✳

CHAPTER TWO

"HE'S dying of starvation," Sprig said one evening when he and Thorny sat drinking tea in the garden, a warm September night. Cambridge seemed thick and dusty, the motionless leaves and the sky overhead like a lid closed down by the heat. "For a few days he could eat the oysters I brought, but now that's finished. Can't you do anything, Thorny?"

"Glucose. It means the hospital, but I shall have to have some X rays, anyway. Next week, possibly."

"He wants to live. He's fighting for every day of life he can manage."

"Does that surprise you?"

They were sitting in the dark. He could not see Sprig's face.

"Everything surprises me, I guess. I'm learning it all from the ground up."

"You know," Thorny said thoughtfully, "people often say in the abstract, 'Why do you keep people alive?' I can't tell you how many times I've heard that question across a dinner table when a sufficient amount of aggression has been released by the wine. Why do we?" he said, leaning back and looking up to where a few hazy stars could be half guessed, half seen, through the damp enclosing atmosphere. "It's hard on the living," he said drily, "but the fact is that the dying don't want to die, unless there is very acute pain, of course—and even then—"

"Don't laugh at me, but I have had the sensation lately that I am the dying and Bill is the living," Sprig coughed, and lit a cigarette. "You will think me quite mad, and you'll be right, I expect," he went on. "The vitality of the man, the power of enjoyment! He lies there feeling sick most of the time, but I have seen his whole face light up, seen him sit right up and blaze, just remembering a poem of Valéry's. And all the time this man is being slowly *stifled*, Thorny. How do you figure it out?"

"I can see him as the living, all right, but I don't quite see you as the dying——"

"I'm cut off from life. He's right there in the center of it, right at the quick, always has been. I'd give my life in a minute for his, if I could."

"Yes, I believe you would—except for Frances," Thorny added, perhaps deliberately.

"Frances would be better off without me." Sprig said this so softly that it was barely audible.

"How's that daughter of yours getting along?" Thorny said. He was shy of pushing whatever was on Sprig's mind any further.

"Betsy?" Sprig's voice sounded startled. "Enormous with maternal concern. I can't look at her."

"You really are rather queer, you know," Thorny said

smiling into the dark. "If I didn't know you so well, I might not even like you very much when you use that tone."

"Pregnant women make me uncomfortable."

"I saw Betsy in the Square the other day—I thought she looked radiantly beautiful. If she were my daughter, I'd feel rather proud."

"You sound damned sententious, I must say." Sprig got up and wandered off into the dark, a white shape, the light of his cigarette like a firefly in his hand.

So detached, so vulnerable, Thorny thought, pouring himself another cup of tea. That queer kind of innocence. Whatever is really going on, he wondered, this regression (for he could only call it that, lapsing into the lingo of the psychiatrist), this talk about dying, this absorption in Bill? After all Sprig would be a grandfather in another month.

"I don't understand you," Thorny said patiently, when Sprig came back and sat down again.

Sprig laughed. It was a mocking laugh and did not permit the conversation to go further.

"Have some more tea." Thorny poured out the remains of the teapot. "Rather rank, I'm afraid."

"I like it strong," Sprig said, draining the cup. "It's a nice civilized habit of your. We all drink too much— liquor, I mean." He was being polite now. And in a moment he would get up and go, leaving Thorny with the questions that hovered around their relationship, and the sense of failure. It was possible that what Sprig needed was a surgeon, some one who could go in cleanly and cut right to the heart of the trouble. But I'm not his doctor, Thorny argued with himself, and he calls me sententious when I try to be. He grunted a noncommittal assent to Sprig's last remark and waited. It had been a long day and the thought of bed and a leisurely hour with Trollope, looked inviting.

Silence enveloped them. There were times when they sat like this for half an hour, the best times they had, Thorny was thinking, when each followed his own thoughts, but followed them in a rather more lively way because of the other.

"People don't write enough about friendship," Sprig said quietly.

"Perhaps they don't know very much about it," Thorny answered. The tone now was just right. Out of the silence they were coming back to the real places again. It was a relief. "Perhaps we are self-conscious about it. It's really one of the sacred taboos. You can talk about sex in its intimate aspects in our culture, but friendship—people quiver with apprehension. Homosexuality—the fear of, *et cetera*. I suspect it runs deeper than we have words for, Sprig."

And the answer again was a long silence.

"It's a steady light, the only one I know of," Sprig said, "the only thing you can depend on. Everything else changes." He coughed his light cough, which always preceded a statement of consequence. "We grow older, but friendship stays young," but the words loomed rather too emphatically for Sprig and he chuckled. "Really, Thorny, do you think I'm in my dotage? And I called you sententious just now!" But he went on. He was on one of his talking jags, Thorny sensed, when for a little while the barriers came down. This had happened before in the last weeks and it occurred to Thorny that perhaps Sprig, who imagined himself as dying, was living rather more intensely than he had for years, or than Thorny himself ever had. When the whole of life becomes one big question—but Sprig was talking and he pulled himself back from his own thoughts to listen.

"I suppose that's why this business of Bill is so staggering." The cigarette in Sprig's hands flew off into the bushes. He leaned forward. "I expect I've lived off Bill, his excitement, his sense of life, all these years. In a way his friendship justified my existence—is that it?" he looked across at Thorny, who held still, waiting. "No, it's more that I played out my life for him, all these translations from the Greek, for instance. Bill challenged me into that one day when I was shooting my face off about the inaccurate, fancy stuff. He dared me to make a translation both beautiful and exact, that would reverberate as lots of these modern ones just don't. We can't stomach Murray. Oh, well—the point is his being there; his presence and yours were what kept me from going to seed."

"You'll never go to seed," Thorny said, chuckling.

"You mean I've hardly flowered yet, I suppose." The two men smiled and felt each other smiling in the dark. "Something holds us all back, Thorny."

"I don't feel held back a bit."

"Oh very well—something holds me back. Still, you did settle sometime ago for a comfortable rather than an arduous life, didn't you?"

"I suppose some people would call a G.P.'s life arduous at that."

"Of course. But you know what I mean. You used to

talk about research—what was that hobby of yours? Something about the blood."

"There wasn't time, the family to support. Why be on the defensive?" It was Thorny's turn now to think aloud. "I honor my profession. I don't feel wasted. I'm used to the limit—isn't that enough?"

"I'm not," Sprig said.

"You've gone into this thing with Bill rather deep. Wouldn't you say you were using yourself to the limit there?"

"Just hanging around trying to be useful when there's nothing anyone can do," he answered wryly; "I have no illusions. Bill is past needing me or anyone. I need him—that's something else again. Christ!" He swore and it was unusual to hear Sprig swear. "The man is far beyond us now. In a strange way he's ceased to care. Flowers, poems, mean more than people. I can see it, and I find it hard," he said in a harsh voice. "Unbearable. He's slipping away where we can't follow."

"He's dying," Thorny said quietly. "You have to let him go."

In the dark Thorny could see just the outline of Sprig's shoulders, tensed, the motionless tension.

"And when he's gone, I'll have to face whatever it is I won't face now. The emptiness. Of my own making. Have you ever wanted to divorce?"

The question was so unexpected that Thorny answered sharply, "Of course not. We have four children."

"That's no answer."

"I'd rather not talk about it."

"Sacred ground, eh?"

Indeed the barriers were down. It was disturbing. Thorny did not want to be disturbed. He wanted to go to bed and read Trollope in peace. "Don't be childish, Sprig."

"But I am childish—surely you know that?" The match he struck lit up the face for a moment. It was not an ironic expression. Thorny saw there, as he had half expected. Sprig was deadly serious. "What is the matter with me, Thorny?" and he held the match up to peer at Thorny's face, to demand an honest answer. No one gets drunk on tea, Thorny was thinking, yet this shy man is like a drunkard. He is pushing the limits like a child. He is asking for it.

"Is it that you've fallen in love with the impossible? With Bill now, because he's dying, because he can make no demands on you, nor wants to."

"Fallen in love?" The tone was icy cold.

"I'm looking at the evidence."

"It's time I went home," Sprig said, and Thorny felt the exhaustion back of the voice. I must say something now to help. I must try to.

"It's a transition, Sprig. Transitions are always hell," he said awkwardly. "After all, it's no small thing to wake up and find yourself a grandfather."

"God damn it," Sprig said violently.

"But you can't swear it away."

"Demands, demands——" Sprig muttered.

"What would life be without them?"

"Nirvana, the Bo-Tree," Sprig came back quickly, hotly, almost angrily. "The demands prevent one from being."

213

"Maybe, but only after one has been through it all and come out on the other side. You haven't been through it all, Sprig. Not by withholding . . ." The sentence floated on into the darkness, floated about among the thick still leaves, would not find a place to rest.

"You're the doctor," Sprig said getting up, and, most unexpectedly, yawning.

"Not by withholding . . ." Thorny said again. He was going back in his mind to Sprig's question about divorce. He suspected that there came a time in every marriage when one partner outgrew the other, or one partner needed a change, which perhaps came to the same thing. Then you compromised (a thing of which Sprig was incapable, he suspected), or you broke off. He and his wife had compromised. No one outside their marriage would ever suspect it; no one, he was sure, suspected that he had a mistress in New York, or that Phyllis for five years had been seeing in secret a famous Professor of History at Harvard. Strangely enough, from the outside at least, Sprig's marriage seemed one in which this sort of compromise would not be possible.

"By what then?" Sprig said, standing looking down at his friend.

"By letting in what you fear——"

"I guess I'd better get back," Sprig answered in a flat tone. He held out his hand. "Good night, old boy. And thank you."

And I would hug him if I could, Thorny thought, giving the outstretched hand a hard, friendly shake. But I can't.

*

CHAPTER THREE

WAS it only that after a while a mood of depression lifts like a fog, not through any radical inward change but just as fog lifts? Or was it that Frances was on her way at last to see Lucy after all these weeks of solitude and suspension? Or simply the golden September afternoon, with pale yellow elm leaves drifting down like pieces of sunlight and a smell of wood smoke in the air. Whatever it was, Cambridge seemed like heaven, and Frances strode down Brattle Street singing " 'How lovely is thy dwelling place' " *sotto voce*, and smiling all the way. She had on a new tawny shirt; the very buying of this denoted a change of mood, for on the island she had not been able to look at herself in a mirror. She felt outwardly disgraced, as if she were withering away. But when she got back, she went straight to Bonwit's and bought this shirt, far too expensive, and very becoming. She decided to have the whole downstairs of the house painted some light color, perhaps even white? And she accepted to be Deputy President of the League of Women Voters since the President, a Mrs. Buffin, had had to go into hospital for a major operation. I have been ill and I am well, she thought with astonishment. It appalled her to think that she had wasted the whole summer without knitting a sweater for the baby—in fact, she was bursting with energy and with lists of things to be done.

" 'How lovely is thy dwelling place, O Lord of Hosts,' " she sang aloud as she turned in to the ragged lawn in front of Lucy's. " 'Oh Lo——ord of Hosts.' "

"Darling, you're there," the warm voice called from upstairs and Lucy ran down. "You look beautiful—what a color! New?"

"Yes, I'm turning over a new leaf, a new blouse, a new house—everything is going to be different!"

"Well," said Lucy smiling in her quizzical way, "Tell me!" She disappeared into the kitchen. "I've made iced tea. Thought it was going to be hot."

"It is hot." Frances flopped down in one of the armchairs and drank in the familiar disorder, the familiar charm. There was a sheaf of orange-yellow roses on the mantelpiece, a pile of *New Yorkers* on the floor beside Lucy's chair; the ash trays overflowed; the sunlight poured down on the faded chintz of the sofa. "It's heaven here," she sighed as Lucy came in with a tray and two unmatched glasses beside a jug of iced tea with a sprig of mint in it, and set it down on the floor.

"My hair's falling down," Lucy said, winding a long tress round a comb and fastening it back awkwardly. "You do sound a bit manic, darling. Whatever has been happening?"

"Pour me some tea. Nothing has been happening. I died and am born again—ask God," and Frances burst into laughter—why she could not have told.

216

"Your letters sounded fearfully dreary——"

"Yes." Frances sipped her tea and looked thoughtful. "The summer was hell, Lucy, just plain hell. How are you?" She looked straight at Lucy, the deep inquiring look which one can only give a person with whom one feels perfectly free.

"I have a job."

"Where? What?"

"Teaching fourth grade for Hester—it happened quite suddenly, a crisis. Marriage, don't you know? And the young man going out to South America, or Spain or something. I'm terrified."

"Hester knows what she's doing," and Frances smiled at her friend. "The children will adore you."

"A cheerful old body," and Lucy chuckled. "A kind of old woman in a shoe, that's how I shall appear to them. It's the Greeks. I shall have to get Sprig in on this. Would he come and help direct the play?"

"Sprig is ill." Frances had never admitted this even to herself. It just jumped out.

"Not really?"

"No, but he's locked himself up in Bill to a point that seems to me a little mad. Nothing else exists. He and Nora sit and talk by the hour, when they're not sitting at the bedside; the rest of the time he spends with Thorny or in the Barn playing Haydn Masses. He hardly speaks to me."

"It's strange." Lucy sipped her tea and ate the mint absent-mindedly. "Frances, do you think if this happened to you or me we'd be like that?"

"Caleb's off to Greece in ten days; Betsy floats around like some great ship coming to port—and Sprig doesn't even know either of them exists. He's like a very young boy. He doesn't have a family." She had been thinking aloud and only now registered Lucy's question. "No, I'm sure we wouldn't. Women live multiple lives. I sometimes think men can't. They get too upset when they try."

"You've changed, Frances," Lucy said gravely.

"In what way?"

"You're more of a piece—and harder."

"Is that bad?"

"There you go making a value judgment again."

How often Lucy had teased her over the years—"you New Englanders and your 'rights' and 'wrongs'" she had said many times, but Frances could not change this inherited pattern.

"I don't know what happens when one accepts once and for all there's no hope," she said. "Maybe one does become hard."

"No hope?"

"Lucy," she was in earnest now, "I became a leper this summer. I felt so unloved I became ugly. I used to lie in my bed feeling like an elephant, wrinkled, old and disgusting."

"I know," Lucy said, getting up from the floor where she had been sitting. "I know," she said again.

"You never felt like that, did you?"

"Didn't I?" The tone was heavily ironic.

"You never said so."

"Pride," said Lucy shortly.

"I didn't have any pride," Frances said. "Except in the children. The children," she said thoughtfully, "were a great help, Lucy. And maybe that's what this queer summer has been all about. The children were pillars of strength—and kindness—Caleb especially."

"It's going to be hard to see him go."

"No," Frances said instantly. "It would have been hard. But he's grown-up now. We're friends. You know that is amazing isn't it? I used to want to shake him, he was so difficult." She laughed a rueful laugh. "I expect he wanted to shake me this summer."

They had not stopped the rapid-fire talk since Frances arrived. She felt she had just thrown things at Lucy for the last ten minutes and now Lucy was thinking them all over. For she was silent; had come back to sit down on the sofa, leaning forward, her hands clasped between her knees in the curiously masculine pose she took sometimes when she was thinking. Frances drank down the rest of her glass of tea and got the jug, to refill her glass.

"Does it all make any sense?" she asked, a little anxious now because of this long pause.

"Bill will die," Lucy said. "What then?"

Frances' hand flew to her heart. The light had gone out of her face, the light that had been there so tangibly when she first arrived. "The only way I can go on living with Sprig is to shut myself off," she said. "Not to hope. Not even to believe any longer."

"Just to love?"

"Do you think an absolutely unnourished love can

219

live, Lucy? Don't you think it finally withers away? That also was what was happening this summer. Oh, I can mother him, you know, sew on the buttons of his pajamas, get cool compresses to put on his head when he throws up —he comes back from Bill's sometimes and just throws up."

"I suppose nausea might be the logical result of so much withheld," Lucy said in her reflective voice. "Have you seen Bill yourself?" she asked after a moment.

"No. I must, of course. Only it will really be a call on Nora and I never have felt the slightest communication possible with her. Besides—is this queer?—I feel a kind of embarrassment about going. It's so much Sprig's—I was going to say, 'passion'— Really, Lucy, it is very strange, isn't it?"

"It would be enormously interesting, if it weren't so painful," Lucy said, and there was something restful in the detachment of the tone, as if for a little while they were sitting somewhere in a cloud, not participators but observers, and would come down to earth again, restored. "It does seem extraordinary for a man like Sprig to invest so much in a friendship, at his age."

"Age hasn't anything to do with it. These things are outside time," Frances said quickly. "It's not that, it's because Bill is dying—and so Sprig feels safe, don't you see?"

"He won't have to pick up the check?"

"Exactly."

"Well, it's a rather cynical point, but I expect you're right." Lucy took a long look at Frances again, as if she were trying to read what lay back of this calm, for even three months ago she would have been weeping. Now her eyes were very bright, but not with tears. "Does Sprig notice you've changed, do you think?"

"Of course not." The submerged anger flared out. "I'd have to break my neck before he noticed anything about me."

"He will," Lucy said, nodding her head. "He will."

"Too late," Frances said in her new hard voice. "I have finally detached myself, and it's been too painful a process to repeat."

"Attachment-detachment," Lucy murmured. "It seems to me we've had this conversation before," and they exchanged an amused glance. For in a way the sum of all their years of sharing each other's problems could be just this theme.

"Only each time we've become a little more detached, is that it? You don't feel the way you did last summer about John, do you?"

"No, because I can't respect him. He's going to seed, Frances—he's coasting on his reputation now. He's got a couple of assistants, bright younger men, and a big grant from Ford, and no doubt a respectable book will come out of it, but he knows he's coasting—told me so himself, the other day."

"You've seen him?"

"Oh, yes, he hangs around—comes up here about once a month and I put him off two out of three times. He comes and sits here like a ghost."

"And you don't feel anything?"

"I feel plenty," Lucy said, getting up and throwing a pillow into the sofa hard, as if to let off steam. "The waste ——" she said harshly. "It's appalling."

"Oh, Lucy," Frances said suddenly, "what is faithfulness? What is one faithful to?" As she said the words, the vision floated up behind her eyes of Aunt Jane, sitting on the porch the day Lucy arrived when the news of the divorce just broke. She had been talking about Gran-Quan. She was just going to say something about his kind of faithfulness, but she never did say it.

"Gran-Quan was only faithful to his own misery," Lucy said, as if she had been reading Frances' thoughts.

Frances laughed. "Oh you are so wonderful," she said, laughing still.

"Whatever are you laughing about?"

"Well, it's just—I see so clearly now, that that's just what I was all summer, faithful to my misery——"

"And now?"

"I don't know. But I'm myself again. And honestly, Lucy, I'd rather be hard than a leper, any day. Wouldn't you?"

But Lucy didn't answer the question, thrown out as it was on a wave of laughter and recognition.

"What will you do when Sprig comes home from his strange journey?"

"What will he do?" Frances said gravely. "That's the point, isn't it?"

"He's never left you, Frances. He's just buried you so deep he doesn't know you're there."

"He'll have to do some hard digging, that's all I can say." And there they left it, and talked of less personal matters, and of friends, and of their gardens, and of the thousand and one small links that bound them together.

The mood of exhilaration, of emancipation was still with Frances when she left. So strongly in fact that, on an impulse, she decided to stop in at Bill's house on the way home.

*

CHAPTER FOUR

B UT at the door in the high fence, that made this modern house seem like a compound, like a fortress (against whom?), Frances hesitated. She was coming empty-handed, she suddenly realized, and almost turned back to go home to see if she could find a few late summer flowers, a book, something. . . . "But this," she told herself, "is cowardice. You are here. It has to be done sooner or later." So she pushed the formidable door open and walked quickly up the path, noticing the wheelbarrow and tools by the stoop. The sprinkler was going on the small beginnings of a lawn, but the summer heat had done that frail grass no good. Perhaps I could help her in the garden, Frances thought, encouraged at once by the idea she might do something—bring a whole lot of chrysanthemums in pots, for instance, that could be bedded in against the wall.

Nora came to the door. "Frances, you're back!" she said, her narrow face actually lighting up as if she were delighted by this visit, had even been waiting for it.

"Yes."

"Come in, come in!" She was being treated as an old friend, but actually she realized, she had not been in the big white room more than two or three times in her life.

"What a nice cat!" she exclaimed, seeing Sancho curled up on a pillow on the floor.

"Sprig brought him. Thought he'd make Bill rest—you know, when he was working so hard at the book."

But she knew nothing, actually. Sprig had never mentioned the cat. "Sit down, won't you? Can I get you something, a gin and tonic?" Nora was there, was saying, was doing all the right things, but Frances had the strange sensation that she was a sleepwalker, eyes open, able to function mechanically on the surface, but altogether absent in essence.

"No, thank you," she said, "I just came for a moment."

She sat down. Nora offered her a cigarette from an enameled box and took one herself. What an open, gay, alive room it was, Frances was thinking, like the man upstairs. . . .

"How is he?" she asked, instinctively lowering her voice.

"Some days he's quite comfortable," Nora answered carefully. "It's better when Thorny has drained the lung. He can breathe a little more easily."

"You must be very tired."

"I?" Nora looked startled, as if this idea had not occurred to her. "Oh, no, I'm all right. I rest when he does." Then she added, in that odd detached childlike voice, "There's going to be a night nurse beginning tomorrow—and the District Nurse comes every morning to give him a bath."

"You are wonderful," Frances said warmly. She meant it, but not quite as people usually use the word under similar circumstances, for what she really meant was, you are strange.

"It's Sprig who's wonderful," and Nora grew pink. Even through the heavy flat make-up, the pinkness flushed through. "I don't know what we should have done without him." She looked down at her hands, lost apparently in admiration of Sprig. Frances felt so uncomfortable that she was silent.

Just then Bill called down in an amazingly strong voice. "Nora! Nora! Is someone there? Who is it?" Then he apparently reached for a bell, a handbell, and rang it, loudly.

"I must go—excuse me." Nora ran up the stairs, so quickly she seemed, like Ariel, scarcely to walk or run but to fly. Frances was left to look around her, to sit uneasily forward in her chair, for she did not feel at ease in this room. It was lovely, she had to grant. It had an air. And she liked very much one of the two paintings on the walls, a rather battered bird, walking against the wind, on a long beach— probably a Morris Graves. She got up to read the signature. Then went round to kneel down and stroke the great orange cat. . . . They had had so little time, Bill and Nora. This house was a dream they had just barely touched, but never had—for she remembered the excitement over the plans. One of the three times she had come here was before the windows were in. Sprig had said on the way home, "Maybe Nora will feel more at home now. Maybe she'll put down a root or two."

She had come to Cambridge six—or was it seven?— years ago as visibly uncomfortable as an animal in a strange world (How shabby and down-at-the-heel it must have looked to her!), tried so hard to be polite, and done all the wrong things, overdressed, over-made-up, presenting a crudely sophisticated façade which concealed what? Ariel? Some sort of sprite? A child? They had all wondered, made kind attempts to find out, and then given up. She had not seemed interested. She had in no way "taken hold," though she came dutifully to the Tuesday Afternoon Club, wearing a Paris hat, took seats for the Sanders Theatre concerts, but with no light in her eye, making no contact. And Cambridge is not famous for taking time or trouble to tame or placate the intruder, the stranger. It is not indifference, Frances thought, suddenly on the defensive, but we take people for granted, let them go their own way. It is a city of private lives. Is this what Bill and Nora had felt when they decided to build, to set up a high fence, to insulate themselves in a privacy which, after all, no one did penetrate? It was a secret marriage. What they really shared no one would ever know. What was being torn apart, day by day, hour by hour, no one would ever know. Not even Sprig, Frances suspected. Other people's relationships did not interest him very much.

"Bill would like to see you for a moment. Will you come up?" Nora said quietly from halfway down the stairs.

Frances felt panic. It was idiotic how fast her heart was beating. But there was no time to think. She was, before she knew it, standing in the doorway, looking straight at Bill who lay in the huge marital bed facing the door, a branch of yellow orchids like a flight of birds on the bed table be-

227

side him, and but for them, no sign of life, an immaculate emptiness. There were no books on the bed, not even a magazine. The man lay alone in his huge bed, staring out. He seemed to be peering at her from a long way off, frowning actually, as if he were nearsighted. And only after that first strange look, did he smile.

"Hello," Frances said, "may I sit on the end of the bed? Or?" She looked around for a chair.

"I'm not that fragile." He took a handkerchief from under the pillow and ran it over his face. "Of course, on the bed."

"I'll leave you," Nora disappeared in the instant of saying the words, and again Frances had the sensation that she was disembodied. There was no sound of feet on the stairs.

"Nora has some crazy idea that more than one person at a time is too many."

"She's probably right."

"She treats me as if I were Venetian glass," he said. There was weariness in the tone. He lay back, for he had been sitting up when she came in. He was panting.

"I won't stay but a moment."

"That's what everyone says. I want to see you," Bill said. "Stay long enough for a real visit. It's no good otherwise. I feel cheated." He smiled again, the shadow of his old brilliant smile. "Everything tires me, you see, just lying here tires me. So why not get tired for a good reason? You are looking beautiful, Frances."

Again she felt the faraway gaze focus, and penetrate, as if something in him resisted having to pay attention, while

228

something else was summoned, commanded by the will. He would not let himself go.

"Dear Bill——" she said, and could go no further.

He turned away, turned his head so that his eyes rested on the orchids. "Pretty," he said. "Sprig brought them."

"They look like birds." Oh Sprig, she was thinking, melted with pity for him, for Bill, for them all.

"That's what he said." Bill closed his eyes. For a moment Frances thought he might be going to sleep. Then she noticed the thinness of his wrists, and that one hand was clenched on the sheet.

"When this is all over"—he gave a sudden barking cough, then made a grimace—"when I'm well again——" His eyes were open now, but he still looked at the orchids, and even put one hand up as if to touch one, then let it fall. Sighed. Turned onto his back, and stared at the ceiling. "Sprig——"

"Yes, Bill, I know," she heard herself saying. "Don't worry."

He whispered, "Queer, dear man." It seemed as if that were to be all, but now after a moment's pause, Bill pushed himself up so he was looking at her hard again, his head a little on one side. "But he hasn't much time, Frances. He's got to begin pretty soon."

Begin what? Her mind faltered. She felt dizzy with his effort to say it, whatever it was, and her effort to understand. Begin what? She wanted to ask, but it was clear that Bill was formulating things he had waited a long time to say, all that long summer, and her business was to listen.

"He's got to begin it," he said again. The sweat was pouring down his face and Frances on an impulse got up, found the hankerchief and wiped him gently. "Thank you. Absurd, isn't it? That speech should become an athletic exercise."

"Lie still for a moment. I'm not going," she said. "I'll stay right here."

He closed his eyes, but he was smiling. "Thank you," he breathed. He was panting again, and Frances was torn between her promise and the obvious fact that he was making too great an effort. She wondered wildly where Nora was. Should she just slip away, after all? No, she had promised.

"Sprig's on the rampage," he went on talking though his eyes were closed. "He doesn't know it himself, but that's what it is. Another man would have a love affair," Bill smiled and opened his eyes to see how she was taking this, the old malice, such a kind malice shining out in the irony of his smile, "Sprig comes here instead." But laughter was not something Bill could afford. His face was beet red and Frances half rose to go. "Sit down," he commanded. She sat, pinned down by his will.

"So strange," he murmured when he felt assured that she would stay. "All of it. We don't know each other at all, any of us. I lie here and think. Never had so much time in my life—luxury." He turned his face away. "You can feel pretty awful but the mind ticks on. Can't stop it." He felt for the handkerchief and wiped his face. Then as he lay back, looking at her through half-closed lids, he said something. "Throw him out, Frances." That is what she thought she heard, but it sounded so unlike Bill, so strange, she could not be sure. "It's life that matters." He turned his head toward the flowers again. He smiled. "The flowers——"

And Nora was there at the door.

"Yes," Frances said, getting up and, on an impulse, lifting one of Bill's hands and clasping it in her two, trying to say in that handclasp all she could not say any other way. She stood downstairs alone while Nora no doubt arranged the pillows or gave him a sedative. She could hear faint sounds upstairs, water running. She stood there in the middle of the room, waiting. Her hands were clasped tightly together as if she were holding a bird in them, holding something elusive, wild, something that wanted to be free—love, she said to herself. But I am quite mad. I'm upset. Yet she could not unclasp her hands, though all they held was air.

"I stayed too long," she spoke quickly, nervously, as Nora finally came down, quite composed, her face showing nothing. "I couldn't help it. He kept forcing me to sit down again."

"It's all right," Nora said. "He has to live all he can" —she caught her breath—"now."

"He gives so much," Frances turned away, moving toward the door.

"You must come back."

"I will."

But when the outer door had clicked behind her and

she stood on the street, she felt as if she were waking from a dream. You cannot go back into a dream. But she would bring pots and pots of chrysanthemums. She would help Nora make the garden. She would do what she could. She was not aware that she was running, running home, running away.

*

CHAPTER FIVE

THROUGH the door into the hall Frances could see
Caleb and his father sitting by the fire. Mr. Silence lay
sprawled on the hearth, exhibiting his feathery soft tummy,
and Hannah, disturbed by the atmosphere of departure, was
under Sprig's chair where she could keep a close watch on
his feet, in case it was he whose baggage stood in the hall.
Each time Frances ran from the kitchen, where she was bast-
ing a turkey, to the front door, to look out anxiously for the
guests, she passed Caleb's rucksack, his box of books, his suit-
case with a mackintosh and pair of binoculars lying on top of
it. It was pouring outside, the tail end of a hurricane they
said, and she was a little anxious. Tom and Betsy had promised to pick Hester up on their way, should be here by now.
Uncle Joe had telephoned to say he might be late; taxis
were unobtainable.

"But I'll get there somehow, Frances. With two bottles
of champagne, so tell Sprig not to make a cocktail."

They would all be here except Gran-Quan. But Caleb
had gone out to say good-bye to him that afternoon.

"I don't know," Caleb rubbed the top of his head with
one hand, and frowned. "He seemed a bit madder than
usual; more cheerful, too. Went on at length about how

belief was the devil—as if just that were his greatest temptation."

"Yes, of course it is," Sprig said absently. He was thinking about Bill who believed in life, more than anyone he had ever known, and yet was dying.

And Caleb, sensing the withdrawal, was silent. They had become accustomed lately to sitting in silence; Caleb had been going down to the Barn when his father was playing records, to lie on the floor staring at the ceiling and then go away without a word when the music was over.

He got down on the floor and tickled Mr. Silence's tummy. "I shall miss you." One paw stretched out as far as it could, opened the claws and closed. "I imagine the cats in Greece as ravening lean beasts. No roast beef and gravy for them," he said, stroking the big cat behind the ears, and all the tenderness that could never show itself in any other way at home was visible in the gesture.

"No," Sprig said, "the cats here live grossly comfortable lives."

The doorbell gave a long insistent peal.

"Uncle Joe," Caleb said, scrambling to his feet. "His lordship." His father and he exchanged a smile.

"Well, you made it—champagne and all," Caleb said, opening the door wide. The wind blew into the house and the rugs lifted with its force.

"Yes, but close that door." Uncle Joe unwound a long cashmere scarf from his throat and revealed that he was in a black tie.

"Uncle Joe, you are disgracefully overdressed."

"Am I?" the old voice sounded plaintive. "Just old-fashioned, my boy. I could hardly drink the health of a new Theseus in my tweeds." He went in to the fire, admonishing Caleb on the way to put the wine on ice. "Where is everybody?"

"Oh, Hester's kept them waiting, no doubt. You can't pry her loose from the school these days."

"Terrible woman," Uncle Joe beamed. "How do you ever stand her goings on?"

Sprig chuckled. "My good, bountiful, loving sister?"

"She devours what she loves—I'll wager she does!"

"Whoever are you talking about?" Frances threw off her apron as she came in through the dining-room doors.

"Sprig's sister."

"That saint?"

Uncle Joe lifted his hands in a gesture of mock despair. "God preserve us from our saints."

Sprig laughed aloud. Frances felt unaccountably cross. "Men never do understand or appreciate Hester," she said. "But it's your fault, not hers," she said, giving Uncle Joe a defiant smile, before going over to shake his hand.

"She used to order me around like a general when I was a boy," Sprig said, leaning against the mantelpiece and looking into the fire.

"She is two years older," Frances came to her defense. "Naturally she did."

"Here they are," Caleb had been standing in the French windows, peering out into the storm.

"Oh, I must get the glasses," and Frances hurried out

to the kitchen while the others were greeting the late comers. Her hands were trembling with excitement, the current of arrival, of meeting and parting, of all this life pouring in suddenly after the strange, the empty weeks.

Sprig joined her to fetch the bottles.

She watched him go to the icebox. They hardly spoke to each other any more. As she pushed the swing door open with the tray, the glasses slid and jarred each other.

"Look out," Sprig called, "they're fragile!"

"Damn it," she called back, "you'll make me drop the whole tray!"

The living room seemed filled to bulging. No one was sitting down. They were all standing, talking and laughing, as if swept in by the gale, lifted up, excited. Caleb came forward to take the tray from her.

"High time those glasses were filled," Uncle Joe said. "Ah"—he lifted his hands as if he were a magician, to signal Sprig's arrival, the bottle in his hands, the cork just rising. It all happened in the flash of a second—the loud pop, and Sprig's neat deft gesture to pour while the wine fumed like a libation.

Uncle Joe lifted his glass. "We salute Caleb Wyeth, we wish him a safe voyage to the wine-dark sea. He is no merchant bearing perilous cargos of ice to the Indies, but a student with an inquiring mind and the glory he is after is no doubt intangible." Uncle Joe interrupted this formal, this evidently prepared toast to cast a look in the direction of William Wyeth's impassive face on the wall. It was a look so mocking and amused that instinctively everyone turned to follow his eyes, then turned back to catch the flitting smile on Caleb's face. He had taken a step forward and looked up himself now at the old man, slightly narrowing his eyes. "May old William's great-grandson find in Greece, his heart's desire, his golden fleece," said Uncle Joe, and they all gathered in toward Caleb, lifting their glasses to his.

"Well done, Uncle," Sprig said drily. "We shall hardly be able to maintain such heights during the rest of the evening."

Caleb stood turning the glass in his hands, his head bent, shy and silenced. They were still standing about him in a circle. "Thanks Uncle Joe. I'll make a speech when I get back, maybe."

It was such an anticlimax that everyone laughed.

"Let's sit down," Frances implored. "I want to sit down and enjoy myself, look at you."

"I miss Jane," Joe said plaintively when they were all settled.

"We all miss her," Frances answered quickly. "She's never very far away. She's always present these days."

"I don't believe in an afterlife," Joe answered testily. "She's not present, as far as I am concerned."

"You think that old boy isn't present at these family gatherings?" Caleb shot across at his uncle, his eyes twinkling.

"Not in any tangible sense."

"What's more tangible than influence?" Caleb answered.

Betsy leaned forward and found Tom's hand. They knew how much the old man was present, her hand said to his hand.

"Very well, how did Jane influence us? I miss her, but she didn't influence me." Clearly, Uncle Joe was enjoying himself, on his mettle, the old man for whom occasions were everything, who had no doubt napped all afternoon, just to be in good form, Frances was thinking.

"She didn't, eh?" Sprig raised a quizzical eyebrow.

"I found comfort in her," Uncle Joe said gravely. "She *was* family—she seemed to be the quintessence of what one might mean by the word," he went on.

"I don't agree with that." Caleb came forward. He had that look of blazing with aliveness which had used to be visible only when he was angry. "I think she's present because she was happy, and that's so rare that it's bound to radiate."

"Happiness?" Sprig picked up this idea and turned it over.

Hester smiled. "To a New Englander there's something suspect about it, of course. You'll never convince us, Caleb, that happiness is a moral virtue."

"Yes," Uncle Joe meditated aloud. "She achieved it. How did she, eh?"

It was odd that he should ask the question, Frances thought, he who had ostentatiously devoted his life to the pursuit of it and—possibly within his compass—succeeded. It was a more limited compass than Jane's though. "By giving up reforming herself or anyone else, for one thing,"

Frances said. "Oh dear," she looked at her watch, "I must go and think about dinner. I do hate to miss anything!" She turned back at the door, "Remember everything you say!"

Hester got up to help, and for a moment while the flurry of his departure subsided, there was a pause.

"She had faith," Caleb broke the pause. He said it so quietly and with such finality that one felt he was laying down a bomb on the floor.

"Well"—Uncle Joe smiled a thin smile—"if you can call that peculiar concoction she had made up out of a little bit of Emerson, a little bit of theosophy, a little bit of Christianity, a little bit of Buddhism, *faith* . . ." and he shrugged his shoulders.

"What did you mean, Caleb," his father asked, ignoring Joe, "when you said 'faith'?"

Tom Dorgan got up and slipped over to Frances' chair. They're off, he was thinking, amused, interested as always when these people started one of these discussions, stiff with concealed antagonisms, but he knew Betsy hated it, would never participate and even now was looking into the fire, absorbed in her own private world.

Caleb sat cross-legged, stroking Mr. Silence. "Well," he said thoughtfully (and even a year ago he would have utterly refused to give himself away, to answer such a question), "I find it hard to define, but maybe it's the conviction that there is some invisible force on which one can lean, some source of strength, of balance outside oneself. Once she said to me, when I was sore about something and all knotted up, 'Can't you rest on the Invisible Arms, Caleb'? I remember thinking she was a sentimental old thing, and it was nice for her to have such pretty thoughts."

"Quite," Uncle Joe smiled with approval at this suddenly articulate nephew, who was actually talking sense for a change.

"What do you think now?" Tom couldn't resist asking, for he had caught the self-directed irony Uncle Joe had obviously missed.

"It's the champagne," and Caleb darted a quick look round the room. "We're not really given to talking about this sort of thing. And maybe I don't know what I think," he turned back to the cat, scratching him under the chin. "But it does seem as if life without some belief seems pretty cheesy."

"I find it a rather rich and nourishing kind of cheese myself," and Tom smiled. He and Caleb had talked about this a lot during this summer's sails.

Uncle Joe looked from one to the other of the young men and envied them. He felt old, set outside, for he sensed that they were on a level of intimacy from which he was automatically excluded, by his age, by his temperament. Did Sprig feel this too, sitting there, so still, so silent?

He turned to his nephew. "We thought these questions were settled, that man was at last entering into an age of reason. And here the young begin all over again—Freud lets in the rational light, then Jung comes along and clouds it all over with the pale cast of soul again."

Outside the rain beat on the windows. Each in his own way went on with the conversation in silence. The smell of roast turkey floated over them, tantalizing. They were hungry. . . .

Caleb now lay full length, his chin in his hands staring at the fire. I won't be here tomorrow, he was thinking. Exultation swept over him. It was cruel to exult—he felt that it was—but after all he had wasted enough time here, enough of the young time. Now he would cut himself off and take to the open air.

"You must feel enormously proud of him," Hester was saying, while she opened a can of cranberry sauce. "In these last two years he's grown so, it's amazing."

"He's free," Frances said, stirring the gravy. "Gran-Quan was right about him. He always told me Caleb would be all right. There's something of Gran-Quan's fire and of William Wyeth's iron in him. Oh damn, I mustn't talk. I'll ruin the gravy!"

"Shall I call them now?"

Something in Hester's eyes, the unspoken understanding and compassion, made Frances stand still, the apron she had untied in her hand. Then she found herself in Hester's arms. They hugged each other hard. "What would I do without you?" she murmured. "You angel."

"I don't know what you're talking about," Hester said, flushing.

And Frances could never say it, that in Hester she found something of Sprig, a Sprig accessible, a feminine counterpart who could give tenderness, who could be hugged, and who knew everything without anything at all being said. They hardly ever met to talk, and all their brief exchanges took place like this one over the kitchen table, or when the family was gathered together. Yet, there it was. A bond so powerful that it did not need time or any living out.

"Thank God for women," Frances said, and was not surprised when Hester laughed.

They were all lifted up on a wave of release and laughter over the turkey, Frances' famous creamed baked onions and Sprig's bottle of Vouvray. Sprig was seized by one of his fits of humor; he launched into one tale after another about Thorny and himself at Exeter, and the ineptitudes he had exhibited as a young man. Frances watched him down the table, his eyes bright with laughter and, for this hour at least, apparently out of the thicket of despondency where he had hidden himself for so long. Uncle Joe laughed so much, that he had to lay down his knife and fork and wipe the tears from his eyes. And in the midst of them all Betsy smiled a quiet secret smile all her own.

What faith I know, Frances thought, I get intimations of at moments like this. It is something to do with harmony, with people lifted up together in love, and laughing. It is that we shall find our way together, if at all, she added, and just then caught Sprig's eyes upon her, for once not shy, but saying (and her heart turned over absurdly), "You're my wife."

When they went back to the living room for coffee, Sprig stayed behind to help clear away. Frances, stacking the dishes in the kitchen, wondered if she were mad to feel this bubble of happiness in her swelling with every second, when all that was happening was Sprig going in and out with piles of dishes and glasses, smiling to himself, and she herself counting tablespoons of coffee.

"Everything's going very well, Fran," he said, as he came through the swing door for the last time. He gave her shoulder a gentle squeeze, and added drily, "Even Uncle Joe approves of us, for once."

"Oh dear, I've forgotten how many spoons I put in!" She turned to him with a smile, "You wretch!"

And then because the bubble had just broken, because she was afraid if she looked at him, she would begin to weep, Frances bowed her head and leaned her forehead against his shoulder. He held her close against him, and they stood there a second, two seconds without a word. Then he was gone, the door swinging behind him, and such an ache in her chest, she felt numb. Detachment? She asked herself, bitterly. All he has to do is give me one affectionate look!

Tom did not remember ever seeing the family so relaxed and buoyant. It was a moment of departure, of parting, a real breaking up in some ways, yet the atmosphere was just the opposite. It was an atmosphere of arrival.

He got up when he saw Frances, took the tray from her, pulled up the little table to her chair, wanted to show his affection for her, and did not know quite how. "That was a wonderful dinner, Mrs. Wyeth."

"Thanks, Tom. Would you pass the cups?"

Tom passed them and so found himself standing back to the fire, a cup of coffee in his hands, the center of the room. It was his turn now to face the old man on the wall, to look up from his wife's soft open face, rosy in the fire-light to the ice-blue eyes above her.

"He's quite an antagonist," Uncle Joe, who had been observing Tom, ventured.

"No antagonist of mine," Tom said cheerfully. "Though he may be of yours."

"To what was *he* loyal?" Caleb asked. It referred back evidently to their conversation, which had been going on while Tom's thoughts were elsewhere.

"Hard work, profit, and a jealous God," Sprig shot back, then he frowned.

"I missed the beginning of all this." Tom turned to Frances. "Were you talking about loyalty?"

"Faithfulness—we began there," Hester answered. "I think it's an overrated virtue myself. We're fossilized by it —look at Gran-Quan. That's what I was saying," she ended handing the subject over to Tom, he thought, like a counter in a game, this game they played for hours.

"What does Tom think?" Frances asked. "That's what I want to know." She shot a look across at him, half smiling, half a dare. He guessed there was some tension in her on this question, that she needed backing up. It occurred to him that he was one of them at last. It was happening now at this very instant, as he stood dominating the room, their faces turned toward him.

"It's a pretty abstract subject to toss at me," he grinned back.

"People change," Hester said. "Relationships change. One changes oneself." Sadness clouded her face, so animated a moment before.

244

"Aren't you faithful to that school of yours?" Caleb smiled across at her.

"Yes, but it's changed and I've changed. Sometimes I think it would be better if I let the changes go on without me."

"You, abdicate?" Uncle Joe asked.

"Why not?" But the slight tension was there again. "Most people freeze somewhere along the way. I sometimes think I have."

"Darling, you *are* the school," Frances protested.

"Well, if that were true, it would be a pretty poor thing," Hester shot back, almost angrily.

"But you're the power, surely, Hester," Uncle Joe said.

"I was at the beginning. I suppose to live at all we have to imagine we are needed. But no one is needed absolutely."

"Yes, they are," Betsy said, flushing, "in a marriage, for instance. Or a mother with her child—at least at first." Tom walked over and sat down beside his wife.

"Love isn't an absolute," Frances said.

"Couldn't it be—if we were whole?" Betsy flushed with the effort of speech.

"If we were whole——" Joe murmured. "Yes, no doubt——"

Sprig got up nervously and began collecting cups. "You're way out of my depth," he said. It was clear that he wanted to escape, and taking out the cups to the kitchen was his way. "Where's Hannah?" he called back.

"I let her out just now. She's probably scratching at the kitchen door, poor lamb," Frances answered him; her voice, loud to reach him faraway as he was, broke the spell.

"Gran-Quan would be quoting Wordsworth now," Caleb said, getting up and walking to the windows to stare out into the night. "The rain's almost stopped," he announced.

"It's way past my bedtime," Uncle Joe got up. "All this talk—I shan't sleep a wink," and he smiled.

"If you can stand the MG I'll drive you home." Caleb turned back.

"I'd catch pneumonia, my boy. It's kind of you, but it would be even kinder to call a taxi."

"Don't go." Frances rose, too. "You make it all come to an end."

Sprig came back, in time to hear Tom saying, "Yes, Betsy must get to bed, too. It's really time we went home."

"And there's school tomorrow——" But Hester stayed where she was.

They could hear Caleb telephoning in the hall. The fire shot out a shower of sparks and everyone was busy for a moment, stamping them out.

But what shall we do tomorrow? Frances thought, looking over at her husband. We shall be left alone.

*

CHAPTER SIX

BETSY lay on a deck chair in the tiny back yard watching the leaves fall one by one from the elm over her head, listening to a starling give a long whistle, then a creaky cry as it flew off. It was five o'clock in the afternoon, and she felt she was floating on time, utterly suspended. She should get up and think about supper—Tom would be home in a few minutes—but she felt so heavy, inert and comfortable that she could not bring herself to move. She wondered lazily if she would ever run up stairs again, ever feel light again, but she didn't really care, for now in the last weeks of pregnancy she tasted to the full her earth-boundedness, liked being heavy and passive, and feeling William Wyeth stirring now and then, liked feeling that she was as fruitful as the season.

Betsy was aware that both her mother and father were not really interested. Frances came and went like a bright restless bird, came back from trips to Filene's basement in triumph with more and more baby clothes, asked quick, penetrating questions, seemed never to settle down anywhere, and closed up like a clam when Betsy, remembering their openhearted talk on the island a few weeks before, made tentative approaches. Now that Caleb was gone, Betsy wondered how the old house felt, sensed the emptiness at the heart of it, was troubled. She and Caleb had had a long talk about their parents just before he left. He brought a silver spoon for the baby and sat on the end of her bed. He was on edge that day, feeling, she suspected, more than he would admit.

"I'll certainly be glad to get away from the tension," he said, biting his lips. "It's sheer hell. If only they would have a knockdown drag-out fight, it might clear the air."

"Maybe they will—after you've gone," Betsy said.

"No, they won't. They're so terribly controlled. They imprison each other," he said morosely, "that's what I think. And this is supposed to be a happy marriage." He shrugged his shoulders. "No divorce, you know. Everything maintained as usual while a kind of strangling process goes on. I'm fed," he said shortly.

"You've been very good." Betsy lay back on her pillows.

"Of course Bill Waterford won't live forever," he went on with his own thought. "Christ, I'm glad I'll be away when that happens. Holy cats!" he said. Then laughed suddenly, for this was something they used to say when they were quite small.

"Was it always like this, or is it only that we see more?" Betsy asked. "Were they ever happy, at peace? Was it ever like Tom and me, do you think? We fight of course, but——"

"They never fight."

"We don't know, Caleb," she said, sitting up. "No one knows anything about a marriage who isn't inside it."

"We can make a good guess." The irony was biting.

"Oh Caleb," Betsy was roused now, as she had not been for a long time. "Don't go away hating them. It isn't their fault."

He had turned to stare at her then, a hard, curious stare. "They're so foolish," he said coldly.

Betsy's eyes had filled with tears. And seeing this, Caleb at once felt guilty, got up and paced up and down. "I'm sorry," he said, "I'm edgy. No point in spilling all this to you." He rubbed the top of his head with his hand, as he did when he was troubled, always had done since he was a small boy.

"You know, Caleb, you've been living too close to it, that's all. Children can't live with their parents at our age. See too much, and maybe without knowing enough." She blushed. "Do I sound awful?"

"You're right, of course. I suppose"—and he lifted his head, evoking this—"when I'm out somewhere in the middle of the Mediterranean, that I'll look back, without getting all knotted up, write them long, fond letters." He lay down on the foot of the bed, suddenly relaxed, curled up and leaned on one elbow. "Miss them, I don't doubt."

"It'll be all right, Caleb," she said, as if wishing could make it so. "People live through things—they will."

"They'll be grandparents when I get back, long before —you'll cable me, Betsy. I'll want to know whether it's a niece or a nephew——" He interrupted himself to make the demand insistently.

"Of course. . . . Can you believe it? I can't. I go in

and look at the bassinet, but I just can't imagine a living baby in it. What will he be like?"

"They'll be grandparents," he said again, as if this thought held some startling revelation in it. "That's what I can't imagine."

"Neither can they." Betsy and he exchanged a glance of understanding and amusement.

"Mother is so funny," Betsy went on. "She pounces on the idea, gets terribly excited, then lets it fall as if it didn't seem real to her. I wonder what it will be like——"

And there they had left it, for Caleb still had errands to do, remembered that he had left his camera to be fixed. "I'll see you tonight," he had said, just as it started to pour.

Now lying out in the garden, thinking of all these things, she picked them up abstractedly and with perfect detachment as if they were pebbles. Nothing touched her deeply now except the idea of the baby—and Tom, who just that moment gave his home-coming "halloo."

"I'm out in the garden!" she called. "Bring me some orange juice, will you? And make yourself a drink."

But first of all he had to come out to her, hold her face in his two hands and look at her as if he had been starving for this sight all day, as if meeting her at last, he met the lost half of himself. Are you all right, his eyes asked, and she answered, all right, in a look.

"It's all arranged. They'll let me off for a day at the bank," he said. "Mr. Middleton couldn't have been nicer about it, asked me if I had a supply of cigars," and Tom chuckled.

The Birth of a Grandfather

And later when he came to sit beside her on a canvas stool, his shirt sleeves rolled up, and sneakers on, she thought he looked absurdly young to be a father. She wanted to pull his head down and press it against her breast, now for the little while when they would still be two, quite alone.

*

CHAPTER SEVEN

IT was one of those heavy, restless, early October after-
noons when one longs for a storm or a change in the
wind, in the air, as if all were suspended. Frances and Hester
were lying under the elm in a patch of shade in two deck
chairs. Music poured out of the Barn, a chorus of some sort
—perhaps one of the Haydn Masses. The wind brought it to
them erratically. They were not listening or trying to listen,
but were each very much aware of Sprig about whom they
would perhaps have been talking had he not been so close
by. Empty iced-tea glasses lay beside them in the grass, and
a plate with cookies on it. One ant had managed to climb
up the shiny surface and was now carrying an enormous
crumb home. Frances watched this heroic effort lazily, then
looked at her watch. In a few moments Sprig would be off
down the road to the Waterfords. She was longing for him
to go.

Hester had closed her eyes. An apple fell from the apple
tree with a thud, "There goes an apple," she said, smiling
though her eyes were closed, and went on to quote a poem
of Frost's. Frances listened, observing her sister-in-law's face,
comparing it to Sprig's, wondering why even with the eyes

closed, this face looked open, not lacking in tension certainly (that taut line of the cheekbone) but—was the word, "mature" with all that word carried of richness, of a life lived to the full, not withheld? Yet Hester had not lived her life to the full in any usual sense. Never married; had no children; was the intimate and confidante of so many people, one could hardly feel that any single one represented fulfillment. She, Frances suspected, had no friend comparable to Lucy, for instance.

On an impulse she reached over and took Hester's hand where it lay on the arm of the chair. She was not prepared for the strength in it, the way in which this brown hand clasped hers, the intensity of the response. Just then the erratic wind brought them a full burst of music, some great paean of praise. Frances, Hester's hand clasped in hers, had the sensation that she was landing on the earth after whirling around in space. Tears pricked her eyes.

"Angel," she murmured and by so doing broke the spell. The moment of absolute communion had come and gone.

"I suppose," Hester said, sitting up now, as if to pull herself forcibly up out of a dream, "that we'll look back on this year sometime and understand what was really happening."

Frances did not answer; she was moved beyond the power to speak. And Hester, glancing over at her, caught this, received it, and said quietly, "We never talk, or hardly ever, yet I always feel I could say anything to you. You would not be shocked."

"Yes," Frances said, swallowing. "I'm too vulnerable. But yes," she added, "you can say anything."

There goes Sprig, she thought, watching him move off down the path, with Hannah at his heels. The two women said nothing for some seconds. But each felt the relief. Sprig's departure took the lid off. The garden was suddenly very still. A sea gull flew over.

"What is it?" Frances asked after the long pause.

"I'm trying to make up my mind to retire," Hester said.

"You're serious?" Frances asked, amazed. "I thought you just talked about it the way I talk about leaving Sprig, when I get to feeling absolutely hopeless."

"I feel the need of a private life," Hester said, leaning back and looking up through the leaves. She gave a funny little grimace. "I've been a safety valve for other people's private lives long enough. But that's not it—not really. The school has been my passion. You know that."

"It has hardly been a desert as far as personal relationships are concerned," Frances said with gentle mockery.

"No, but I have been hemmed in by responsibility. I would like to end my days as a beachcomber somewhere, irresponsible, with time to think and to be."

"You'd be miserable in a week."

"No inner resources?"

"Oh no, but surely, Hester," Frances said earnestly, "people are your life."

"It sounds pretty grim to me, that generic term. People indeed! I've been putting off my real friends, my own relationships all these years; there was always a meeting I had to attend or—worse—just exhaustion. When I had a free evening I went to bed." She gave Frances a curious musing glance, as if she was about to say something and then hesitated.

"You're too young to give up," Frances said.

"If I wait another ten years, I'll be too old."

"For what?"

"My life," she said, clasping her hands together hard, as if she held her life within them.

"But all this *is* your life, the school, the responsibilities—surely." Frances felt bewildered. She herself had talked in the same way lately, but she realized that she had not been serious. Hester perhaps was. "I don't understand."

"Neither do I." Hester did not smile. "All I know is that I get angry in a way that frightens me—over nothing. I feel full of hatred, jealousy and general ill-will."

"Darling"—Hester could not help laughing—"what nonsense!"

"Oh, I don't show it, of course." Hester smiled at her ironically. "The Wyeths are firmly encased in a straitjacket of self-control."

"I wonder if Sprig feels angry," Frances murmured to herself.

"Here I am running a school and I really feel inside about six years old on the brink of a childish tantrum—don't you see it's high time I got out?"

"But you can't imagine the school without you—I can't!"

"I see quite clearly that in some ways, I am already too

old," Hester said. The coldness of the tone was significant, and Frances registered it at once.

"You think you aren't needed?"

"I have had intimations——"

"But"——Frances spoke passionately out of a conviction she had not known was there—"no one knows about that. We don't know how or when we're needed. It's one of the mysteries. I go on the conviction, act of faith or whatever you want to call it, that Sprig does need me, though God knows he has shown no sign of it for over a year."

"You will be grandparents soon," Hester said gently.

"I don't see the relevance of that."

"Well, I think it's time I became the grandparent not the parent of the school—put it as simply as that."

"And what does that mean?" Frances asked, dismayed. For some reason she felt prickly.

"Never mind," Hester said quietly. It was not that anything had been said, but somehow without even meaning to they had reached raw places in each other. They lay back in their chairs and smoked, looking up through the leaves.

Hannah, who had followed Sprig to the gate, now came very slowly back, her tail hanging down.

"Well, old thing," Hester said, reaching out to pat her head.

How can I be a grandparent, Frances was asking herself when Sprig and I hardly know each other? How be a grandparent when one is not even married, so to speak? Desolation rose in her like a tide.

256

"We have not accepted it," she said, out of these thoughts. How could the baby be welcomed out of the war within themselves? How could they become what they were not? She threw her cigarette into the grass angrily.

"No," Hester looked over at her with a smile. "I don't suppose you have. Does anyone? It seems to me we all fight every inch of the way." She laughed suddenly and stretched out her arms. "But I'll tell you something—I don't know why it is, I have never felt life to be richer, just life itself, the apples falling—why is that?" she asked turning to her sister-in-law. "Just autumn maybe. The new beginning. Or being in such an absurd state of conflict."

"Breaking it all, remaking it," Frances murmured. "Sometimes I wonder if all that is needed is not a slight shift of the kaleidoscope, just a change in the angle of vision." She was leaning forward now, her hands clasped between her knees, her whole physical being straining. Then she relaxed, lay back. "If I could only do it—alone——"

Long after Hester had left, and while Frances was getting supper, their conversation reverberated within her, sending out long ripples to the farthest shores of her being. It was the closest she and Hester had ever come to the kind of talk she and Lucy had all the time; it was a rare occasion, and had the weight its rareness implied. Yet they had not said anything, really, nothing that either of them did not know. It was the sense of having stood for a second on the edge of an abyss, despair, whatever it was—and then drawing back together, drawing back to that quick recovery of Hester's "Life was never richer, I am sure of that." Frances found herself repeating, while she washed the lettuce, a phrase, a phrase which had no apparent relation to anything; the phrase was, curiously enough, "We are coming into our own."

＊

CHAPTER EIGHT

THAT night at a little after nine Nora called and asked Sprig to come over. Her voice sounded quite itself, cool and clear, but the fact of the call itself was so startling that Sprig dashed out of the house, just shouting "I'm going over to Bill's!"

Frances stood in the hall, wringing her hands, feeling a wild impulse to follow, to share—to be part of it, whatever it was. But she knew this was what she must not, could not do. It would be like following a lover to an assignation, she thought ironically. The house was absolutely empty. Even Mr. Silence was on one of his periodic roves and had not been seen since early that morning. Hannah was fast asleep under the stove. But the ache of loneliness she felt now was not one the animals could fill, dear and consoling as they were. Where to go? What to do? Lucy? She looked at her watch, past nine. Lucy might be in bed; she was finding the first days at school exhausting. Betsy? Betsy would be asleep. Besides, one did not batten onto one's children. No, she told herself, stopping at the threshhold of her bedroom, I must just sit and wait. That is what is asked of me. One takes one's self and breaks it down to this absence of being, this emptiness. "Is this love?" she asked herself, flinging herself down on the bed to weep. It was as if in the last few moments she had reached an extremity of tension and now the tension broke; she wept with the abandon of a child, alone in the empty house. "Is this love?" she asked herself. For the tears were healing. It was as if when Sprig left the house, entirely of his own volition, that also in some way she had been forced or forced herself to let him go—finally let him go in peace. After a time she slept.

Meanwhile Nora and Sprig sat in the white parlor, Nora curled up into a ball in one of the big chairs, holding her elbows in her hands, and all of her gathered together, it seemed, like an animal cornered.

"What is it?" Sprig asked gently. For she had greeted him with a strange look, had said nothing when he came in breathless, prepared for emergency. She had just gone to the chair and backed herself into it.

"What is it?" he asked again very gently.

He would have liked to go and put an arm around her, hold her tightly. But there had been no such intimacy between them. They kept their distance. So he waited for her to speak, feeling more than usually inadequate, coughed, and took out a cigarette automatically. The flash of the lighter focused her glance and she sighed.

"Bill wants to die," she said. "Just now, he said it. He said, 'I want to die.'" The tears slid down her cheeks but she made no sound. They were still a sleepwalker's tears.

Thoughts raced through Sprig's mind, of how they had never once admitted all these months what they knew. They had been children; now they must grow up.

"We have to let him go," he said in his driest voice.

"I can't," she said, "not yet." She fumbled for a hand-kerchief in the pocket of her skirt, and found none. "I'm not ready."

Sprig got up and handed her his large white linen one. "He's made his peace. We have to," he said. The words came to him. He did not know whether he could believe them.

"He said, 'I want to die.'" She repeated the words as if saying them over would make them less true, and this time she said them bitterly. "I couldn't answer," and the tears flowed down her cheeks. "I couldn't say anything to comfort."

He's beyond our comfort, Sprig was thinking; that's what we have to accept. That is what we have come to.

"Is he asleep now?" he asked cautiously.

"Yes—breathing in that awful way—as if it hurt——"

"The nurse?"

"She's there. I shouldn't have called you," she said in the same bitter voice she had used a few moments earlier.

"I'm glad you did."

"You can't help. I thought——" but she could not go on. She put her face in her hands, the fair hair flowing down over them so she looked more than ever like a child.

Sprig got up and walked up and down. "You thought I wouldn't give in—accept——" In the last few moments, he himself had seen and felt walls collapsing all around and within him. Quite suddenly, when Nora repeated Bill's words, the walls had gone down. For him. Not for her.

"But we have to, Nora," he stopped at the back of the chair where he had been sitting and looked straight at her.

"You were the one who believed," she said coldly. "All the others gave up long ago—even Dr. Stiles gave up. You didn't." She clenched her fists, on the arms of the chair. She was, he sensed, near to hysteria. She must be exhausted beyond the point where reason could operate. What then?

"I loved myself, not Bill." In this moment of absolutely clear vision, he saw it all. He took on the burden of guilt.

"He's my husband," she pleaded, as if this life were still in her power to hold back, to hold. "He's all I have."

Sprig winced.

"You don't understand," she said, with immense weariness, uncurling herself so that she could lean her head back against the chair.

"You can't keep him, Nora—not against his will." But the coldness of the statement, true though it was, struck him like a blow. It was his turn to put his head in his hands. There was a long silence.

When he lifted his head, she was standing with her back to the fireplace. There was no sign of tears now. She was standing quite straight, and for just a second their eyes met. "You're right," she said simply. "Thank you for coming. I think I went a little mad——"

"You must get some rest. Take a sleeping pill."

"No," she said. "I want to be—to——" but she couldn't finish the sentence.

"Would you like me to stay the night?"

"No, thank you. This may go on for weeks, Sprig. I've just got to do it alone, I guess."

He had the strange feeling as he left her, that something between them was finished forever, the intimacy of the last months and weeks, which had been woven into Bill's struggle and had come from it, as if they were together holding back an ebbing tide. Now that struggle was nearing its end, the taut thread that bound them had broken.

Outside the gate, he stood in the dark street, tempted to go down to the river and walk. But then he realized that he must be available, be reachable. The only thing he could still do was to be ready, if and when it happened. So he turned back toward home, walking slowly. A furtive cat darted across in front of him. There was a screech of brakes on Brattle Street. It was all familiar, homely, the Cambridge he had walked since he was a child. Only he felt like a stranger.

His own house greeted him with absolute silence when he opened the door and stood just inside, listening. Frances must be asleep. He went through to the kitchen, turned on the light and knelt down to pat Hannah's head. She blinked at him in a dazed way and gave a great sigh, then laid her head down again and was asleep before he turned off the light, her paws twitching in a dream.

As he went up the stairs, he knew he was more tired than he had ever been in his life. It was absurd to find merely lifting his carcass up a flight of stairs to be such an effort; he leaned on the banister halfway up and looked down into the black well of the hall. He was coming back from a long journey, the longest journey he had ever made. So once a very long time ago he had climbed the stairs of the old family house, the night he got back from Japan when everything looked strange, yet familiar, just as now. But he had come back then, unattached, a floating solitary entity.

Now—he looked upward and saw the light under the door. Frances must be awake. And, quickly, without thinking he ran up and into their bedroom. He saw Frances lying on her stomach, fully dressed; her head was turned sideways on the pillow, her mouth slightly open, one arm flung over her head. She was fast asleep. He saw this in the flash of a second, saw her as he had not seen her for months, and without a word flung himself down beside her.

She gave a little groan, turned toward him, pulled his head down on her breast and ran her fingers through his hair. But she was still fast asleep. After a while he moved to pull a quilt up over them, and again she stirred, turned over, breathed deep breaths. Once her whole body gave a nervous twitch. Then she was quite still in his arms. He could feel her heartbeat, slower than his, and little by little he came to adjust his breathing to hers, until it seemed that his heart and hers were one. It was nothing more than a sensation, yet it became some great wonder, the life they shared in the dark center of the night, where consciousness itself had almost ceased.

Caleb must be somewhere out in the black Atlantic now, tossing about in his bunk, restless, reading perhaps. Betsy. . . . For a second his mind stayed suspended at her name, and then very quietly he allowed it to rest on an image he had never admitted to himself: Betsy lying in Tom's arms, fast asleep, and the child within her, for whom there was no night or day, stirring now and then. Bill, slipping away, slipping away in the arms of death, having given himself over at last to that final embrace. Nora awake, alive, alone. And Frances, always Frances, here breathing with his breath. Through the open window came the bitter fresh smell of autumn. It was turning cold. But Sprig moved about in his life, opening door after door, seeing all freshly, and was filled with radiance, with love, so that sleep seemed the least important thing in the world and just to hold all this for a little while, tenderly, in his hands, in his thoughts, was enough, was rest.

*

CHAPTER NINE

FRANCES woke, startled to find herself fully dressed, lying under a quilt with Sprig beside her, like babes in the wood. But what had happened? She ran a finger along Sprig's cheekbone. He started up then, wide awake.

"I'm all dressed!" and he burst out laughing.

She went and stood at the window a moment, looking out. It was a brilliant morning, the sky dark blue and the maple just outside the window bright gold.

"The light has changed," she said. "It's autumn."

Nothing could or would be said of the strange, the secret night.

"Well," Sprig announced, "I'll shave."

And perhaps I'll never know from where he came home to fall down beside me and sleep, nor what happened there.

"Just let me brush my teeth, darling. And I must change—look at me!" Indeed, she looked as if she had been sleeping under a haystack.

They were sitting at the kitchen table having a second cup of coffee when Thorny came by. Nothing is as one expects. He had dreaded this call as much as he had dreaded anything in his life. But there was something reassuring in the very atmosphere of the kitchen, Mr. Silence lapping a saucer of milk by Sprig's chair, Hannah under the stove, rolling a suspicious eye toward him, then thumping her tail on the floor. What was it? Sunlight streamed down on the worn oilcloth. Frances poured him a cup of coffee.

He did not have to tell the news. It was Sprig who said, "Bill's dead."

"Yes, early this morning, without waking."

"He was ready," Sprig said. Frances stood, with the coffeepot in her hands, tears pouring down her cheeks.

"It's all right," said Sprig, after a moment.

Thorny sat down with his cup of coffee. They drank in silence.

Just for a moment, just for this moment, Frances thought, we can pause and feel before all the business of death takes us over. She thought of the way Bill had turned toward the flowers, the last thing he said that she heard was "the flowers——" But he had said also that Sprig hadn't much time. That was what he had said, that Sprig must "begin." And there Sprig sat, the sun falling on his shock of gray hair, his eyes very bright, looking off into space.

"You must go over, you two, and help Nora about the arrangements," Thorny was saying. "She's all right now. The nurse will stay on today. But she'll need your help."

"Yes, yes, of course," Sprig said, still staring off into space.

"In a moment——" Frances answered Thorny. "But just for a moment, just until we finish our coffee, let's think of Bill, himself."

Tears coursed down her cheeks and into her coffee. But

what she felt was not grief. It was more like praise. For a long time now her thoughts about Bill had been so bound up with her sense of impoverishment about herself and Sprig, their marriage, that she had not been able to think of him without pain. Now it seemed as if his dying was a final act of grace, the way he had poured out life to the end, and the dying itself a final gift.

"Don't cry," Sprig said quite gently and without his usual impatience before her tears, though he did not move from his chair. "Bill had reached it. He was there."

"I know," she said, blowing her nose. "I'm not really crying." She sat down between the two men, lifting her cup with both hands like a child. She felt as naked as a child before this moment, as if coils and coils of defenses had unwrapped themselves from her in that deep sleep beside Sprig last night, and now she was down to some defenseless human core, where grief and joy were so much alike there was no telling them apart.

Sprig turned to Thorny. "You said that the dying did not want to die. But Bill had reached it. I think he broke the last thread himself, just stopped holding on, don't you know?" He turned his coffee cup in his hands, as if his hand were thinking, not holding a cup. "When he let go that way"—he shook his head, as if what he wanted to say was taking possession of him, rather than he of it—"he let us go." But saying it broke some last defense in Sprig. He gave a retching sob.

Thorny and Frances sat perfectly still. Sprig had put his head in his hands. His shoulders were shaking. No one looked at anyone else. Sprig was set apart, sacred, that is what they felt without even thinking it. There are human moments of such intensity and largeness that it is as if the gods came down. Frances, holding her cup in both hands tightly, thought that passion had sometimes seemed such a moment, when lovers may be themselves and more than themselves; out of such passion children are born. Here what was being born? Or dying?

She was aware of the sunlight, pure and bright, dappling the table. She raised her head to find above the apple tree and over the roofs a perfectly still deep blue sky.

"Yes," she said to herself, but aloud, "it's autumn. Autumn has come."

In the few seconds that passed like an eternity, Sprig recovered himself.

"A beautiful day," he said in a somewhat stifled voice. "You're quite right, Thorny, I must get over to Nora." Then he turned to his wife. "Will you come with me, Frances?"

CHAPTER TEN

PEOPLE don't change very much, Frances was thinking, as she stood up and stretched. She had been on her knees in the garden for an hour, oblivious to time, but a glance at her wrist watch told her that Sprig would be home soon. Still, she stood for a moment smelling the damp earthy smell, stopping to pluck off a dead chrysanthemum and twirl it in her fingers. No, people don't change very much, she thought. What does happen is that sometimes we are able to change the angle of vision. Sprig had certainly not changed since that moment of acute grief the morning Bill died—a whole week ago, already—but he had, perhaps, come to see things in a new light. The autumn light, she thought, where loss itself has a bright edge like the leaves. The silences which had been so barren were once more full of meaning, of communion. Was it that she had learned to withhold and Sprig had, within the limits of his temperament, learned to give? She stood there in the garden, in the fading light, the aromatic smell of the chrysanthemum between her fingers. How little we know, she thought.

She brushed her hair back with an earthy hand, and ran quickly up the back stairs and into the kitchen.

"There you are," she greeted Sprig, who stood in the

doorway, smiling. "Dying for your tea. But I was having such a beautiful time in the garden——"

For a moment they stood like that, smiling at each other across the room.

"How was the meeting?"

"A lot of nonsense. I'm resigning. I'm not going to waste my life on all those committees any longer."

Well!" She turned to him, laughing. "A new beginning?"

"I'm going to get those translations done," he said taking the tray from her with a sudden movement of decision. "But of course," he stood in the doorway, hesitating, "the hospital. I guess I'll have to keep on with that, for another year anyway—and the museum——"

No, people don't change. Frances smiled to herself.

"I must go and see Gran-Quan tomorrow."

"Yes, dear." She poured out the tea, while Sprig lit the fire.

Then for quite a while they drank their tea in silence, watching the paper flare up and a birch log catch. Frances felt strangely quiet. She took out a knitting bag and went on with a tiny white sweater she had begun weeks before. There was no sound but Sprig turning the pages of the evening paper, giving an occasional grunt. Once she raised her eyes and looked around the room, as if to taste it again, seeing Caleb standing at the mantelpiece the night of his departure; seeing Betsy look up at the old man that afternoon so long ago when she told them about the baby; seeing Hester sitting on the low bench, laughing and teasing Sprig;

Uncle Joe. The room was alive with all that had been said and felt here.

"We really must have the curtains cleaned," she said. Then, "I wonder what this room would look like if we painted it white?"

"White?" Sprig looked up, startled. "Why? It's very nice as it is." He looked so upset, that she laughed.

"I like it too—just the way it is. I just imagine changing it the way one imagines another life one might live."

Sprig coughed and went back to reading the editorials. He heard what she had said some minutes later.

"I like things the way they are," he said, laying down the paper and looking into the fire. Then he glanced across at her, with that furtive, quizzical look she had not seen for ages. "Don't suppose I ever said that before in my life. Must be getting old." Then quite suddenly he got up with a gesture of impatience, "Do you have to knit, Frances? I do find it irritating."

"Why, I've sat here knitting for weeks——" she said.

"I wasn't paying attention. It's incongruous, impossible," he said quite violently. "When you garden you look like yourself, but when you knit"—he stopped, remembering what Uncle Joe had said about Hester—"you look like a fury in disguise."

"Darling, I'll never knit another stitch." She was blushing, as if she had just heard a declaration of love, and bundled up the sweater, stuffing it into the bag. "The baby will just have to go naked or be wrapped in an old blanket," she teased him.

"The baby?"

She looked up at him, half amused, half dismayed, and saw that it was not that he had forgotten. It was something else. He was walking up and down, his hands in his pockets as he did when he was thinking, enjoying himself. His cigarette hung from his lips. Then he turned and stood by the mantelpiece and looked up at old Captain Wyeth. "Just think," he said, "if only Bill had had children—grandchildren—it's strange, Frances. He seemed so centrally rooted in his life, so rich and leafy like some great tree. But now it seems to me that it's we who are, now in our late forties, somehow, yes, at the center of life, looking backward and forwards, as he couldn't be. It's going to be awfully queer to have that little tyke around." Then he broke off to ask Frances seriously, "I suppose Tom has had the sense to enter him at Exeter?"

"But, darling, we don't even know if he's a he yet!"

"Oh yes, quite. I forgot. It might be a girl." He looked embarrassed and coughed. "Yes, a girl——" he said again, rather ambiguously.

And there the event, which had been ripening for so long while Frances and Sprig were each too absorbed in their own transitions and problems to recognize it, finally caught up with them. Thorny called to say that Betsy was on her way to the hospital, that it looked like a quick delivery, and he advised them to hurry.

For just a second when she came back from the phone stammering this news out, a coat already in her hands, Frances stood quite still looking at her husband. Then she fell into his arms. They hugged each other hard, hastily, without a word, as if it were a necessary step, something they had to do before they could move out of the house, as if after having been suspended in the air on a long flight, they had landed.

"My God," said Sprig, fumbling around for his coat in the cupboard, "I'm not ready for this."

*

CHAPTER ELEVEN

THE next day Sprig put on a clean shirt and chose a tie with care. The odd thing was that though he had said the night before that he was not ready, he knew now that he had been ready for the advent of William Wyeth Dorgan for a long time; it was the most natural thing in the world to be on his way to the Saturday Club with the news. Frances was over at the hospital already, bearing flowers and God knows what. They had got home after one, in a state of exhilarated exhaustion, telling each other about it as if they had to make it real by repeating, "Darling Betsy, didn't she look beautiful, in spite of everything," for it had not been quite as easy as the doctors hoped. Tom had emerged from the delivery room, in his shirt sleeves, dripping wet, tears streaming down his cheeks, and sobbed like a baby in his mother's arms, saying over and over, "I didn't know."

It was only after some seconds that they were able to discover that the baby was a splendid boy, eight pounds, and the mother all right.

"I had forgotten how terribly old and wrinkled they look," Sprig had said, when at last they were shown the small red-faced irritable-looking infant.

"The perfect little hands," Frances breathed.

"He's a fine little fellow," Mrs. Dorgan said, casting a dark look at Sprig, a grandfather who could greet his first grandson in such a dispassionate way.

"A Dorgan," was Mr. Dorgan's satisfied comment, though upon what he based his opinion it would have been hard to say.

Frances caught Sprig's arm just as he stiffened, and gave it a cautionary squeeze, and Tom interposed quickly in a stage whisper, "A Dorgan *and* a Wyeth, Pop."

Then for some reason they had all gone into gales of laughter, until William Wyeth Dorgan himself sobered them down by opening his mouth in a loud miserable wail.

Sprig chuckled off and on all the way into Boston. He kept living over that scene at the hospital and now he was eager to share it with his old friends. How would he do it? Would he just say quite casually after the first glass of pale dry sherry, "Oh by the way, I'm a grandfather, you know—since last night." Or should he propose a formal toast and mystify them with the name "William Wyeth Dorgan?" Give Jack a chance to ask, "Who in hell is that?" and then have the satisfaction of answering, "My grandson." But at a red light, stopped in mid-course, this game exploded in Sprig's mind, and as he changed gears to start forward, some gear within him shifted. He was back at the Mt. Auburn Hospital twenty-four years before, his whole face aching with the effort not to weep, as he was taken in to see Frances lying there, flushed, saying "It's a boy, darling. It's Caleb." And at the same time he felt himself carried forward on the tide of life to some day or night he would never see, when William Wyeth Dorgan might be pacing up and down the corridors of a hospital, waiting for his firstborn to emerge. God knew what it was all about, but deep down inside him Sprig felt that he was at the beginning and the end of everything, of life, whatever it was. From now on, he thought gravely, I have to be something I have never been before: that is the beginning. And, indeed, as he looked along the familiar brick backs of Beacon Street and then across at the blue river dotted with sails, it looked to him entirely fresh, as if he had never seen it before. He was looking at it from within a great continuum, and he was filled with excitement. Would the boy study Greek? So few young men did nowadays. Would he be proud someday of having a grandfather who had made accurate fresh translations of the Greek plays? No, that wasn't it. What am I thinking of? The point is not what I am or may do or not do. The point is what he will be.

I must tell Frances, he thought, turning off the parkway now and once more stopped at a light on Beacon Street. But what must he tell her? Nothing that he ever could. It would take a lifetime. Then, he smiled, as if some piece of magic had just been put into his hands; it's not what I am, it's what we are—sometimes, not always, but sometimes—together. "Love, love," he murmured aloud. It meant to him a long struggling birth, which would perhaps never be finished. And that, too, seemed good. The unfinishedness. The sense of all the years ahead.

Then the light changed.